Jack watched her as they crossed the courtyard. Ariana's party continued to the Strand where a line of carriages waited. In a moment Jack would have to head home. This would be his last glimpse of her.

She turned and caught sight of him. Her face lit up and took his breath away. His gaze locked with hers, and he thought he sensed the same regret in her eyes that was gnawing at his insides.

"Goodbye," she mouthed before being assisted into a shiny, elegant barouche. Jack watched her until he could see the carriage no more. He tried to engrave her image upon his memory but could feel it fading with each moment. He needed to reach his studio. He needed paper and pencil. He needed to draw her before the image was lost to him as well.

* * *

Gallant Officer, Forbidden Lady
Harlequin® Historical #972—December 2009

Diane Gaston

GALLANT OFFICER, FORBIDDEN LADY

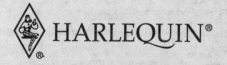

HARLEQUIN®

TORONTO • NEW YORK • LONDON
AMSTERDAM • PARIS • SYDNEY • HAMBURG
STOCKHOLM • ATHENS • TOKYO • MILAN • MADRID
PRAGUE • WARSAW • BUDAPEST • AUCKLAND

Recycling programs
for this product may
not exist in your area.

ISBN-13: 978-0-373-29572-2

GALLANT OFFICER, FORBIDDEN LADY

Copyright © 2009 by Diane Perkins.

www.eHarlequin.com

Printed in U.S.A.

Available from Harlequin® Historical and
DIANE GASTON

The Mysterious Miss M #777
The Wagering Widow #788
A Reputable Rake #800
Mistletoe Kisses #823
"A Twelfth Night Tale"
Innocence and Impropriety #840
The Vanishing Viscountess #879
Scandalizing the Ton #916
The Diamonds of Welbourne Manor #943
"Justine and the Noble Viscount"
Gallant Officer, Forbidden Lady #972

In memory of my father, Colonel Daniel J. Gaston, who showed me the honor of soldiers

Prologue

Jack Vernon dodged through the streets and alleys of Badajoz as if the very devil were at his heels. Several devils, in fact.

Drunken, marauding British soldiers poured out of doorways and set buildings afire, the flames illuminating their gargoyle-like faces. Bodies of their victims littered the pavement, French soldiers and ordinary citizens, men, women and children, their bright-hued Spanish clothing stained red with blood. Jack's ears rang with the roar of the fires, screams of women, wails of babies, but no sound was as terrible as the laughter of madmen with a lust to rape, plunder and pillage.

Jack gripped his pistol in his hand while several redcoated marauders chased him, hoping for the few coins in his pockets. These were the same men at whose sides he'd scaled the walls of Badajoz earlier that day while French musket fire rained down on them. Now they would impale him with their bayonets for the sheer sport of it.

The men were consumed with bloodlust, a result of the desperately hard fighting they'd been through that left almost half their number dead. A rumour spread through the

ranks that Wellington had issued permission for three hours
of plunder. It had been like a spark to tinder. The rumour
was untrue, but once they had begun there was no stopping
them.

The real nightmare had begun.

After the French retreated to San Crisobal and the looting
started, Jack's major ordered Jack and a few others to accompany him on a patrol of the streets. 'We shall stop the looting,'
his commanding officer had said.

The plunderers almost immediately turned on Jack's patrol,
who ran for their lives. Separated from the others, all Jack
wanted now was a safe place to hide until the carnage was over.

He ran through the maze of streets, turning so often he no
longer knew where he was or how to get out. Finally the
pounding of feet behind him ceased, and he slowed, daring
to look back and to catch his breath. He proceeded slowly, flattening himself against the ancient walls, and hoping the sound
of his laboured breathing did not give him away. All he needed
to find was an open door or a nook in an alley.

Shouts and screams still echoed and dark figures ran past
him like phantoms in the night. The odour of burning wood,
of spirits, blood and gunpowder, assaulted his nostrils.

Jack sidled along the wall until he turned into a small
courtyard. From the light of a burning building he could see
a British soldier holding down a struggling woman. A boy
tried to pry the man's hands off her, but another soldier
plucked the boy off and tossed him on a nearby body. The man
laughed as if he were merely playing a game of skittles.

A third soldier picked the boy up and raised a knife, as if
to slash the boy's throat. Jack charged into the courtyard,
roaring like an ancient Celt. He fired his pistol. The soldier
dropped the knife and the boy and ran, his companion with
him. The man attacking the woman seemed to give Jack's
attack no heed.

.Fumbling to undo his trousers, he laughed. 'Come join the fun. Plenty for you, as well.'

Jack suddenly could see this man wore the red sash of an officer. The man turned and revealed his face.

Jack knew him.

He was Lieutenant Edwin Tranville, aide-de-camp to Brigadier-General Lionel Tranville, his father. Jack grew up knowing them both. Before Jack's father had been dead a year, General Tranville had made Jack's mother his mistress. Jack had only been eleven years old.

He stepped back into the shadows before Edwin could recognise him. He'd always known Edwin to be a bully and a coward, but he never suspected this level of depravity.

'Leave the woman alone,' Jack ordered.

'Won't do it.' Edwin's words were slurred. He was obviously very intoxicated. 'Want her too much. Deserve her.' A demonic expression came over his weak-chinned face and his pale blond hair fell into his eyes. He brushed it away with his hand and pointed a finger at the woman, 'Don't fight me or I'll have to kill you.'

Jack stuck his pistol in his belt and drew his sword, but the woman managed to knock Edwin off balance and now stood between Jack and her attacker. She pushed at Edwin's chest, driving him away while the boy vaulted on to his back. Edwin cried out in surprise and thrashed about, trying to pull the child off. He knocked the woman to the ground and finally managed to seize the boy by his throat.

Jack gripped the handle of his sword, but before he could take a step forwards, the woman sprang to her feet, the runaway soldier's knife in her hand.

'*Non!*' she cried.

She slashed at Edwin like a wildcat defending her cub. Edwin backed away, but the drink seemed to have affected his judgement.

'Stop it!' he cried, the smile still on his face. 'Or I'll break his neck.' He laughed as if he'd made a huge jest. 'I can kill him with my hands.'

'*Non!*' the woman cried again and she lunged towards him.

Edwin stumbled and the boy squirmed out of his grasp. The woman sliced into Edwin's cheek with the knife, cutting a long gash from ear to mouth.

Edwin wailed and dropped to his knees, pressing his hand against his bleeding face. 'I'll kill you for that!'

The woman shook her head and lifted her arms to sink the knife deep into Edwin's exposed back.

She was suddenly grabbed from behind by another British officer.

'Oh, no, you don't, *señora*.' He disarmed her with ease.

A second officer joined him. They were a captain and a lieutenant wearing the uniforms of the Royal Scots, a regiment Tranville had once commanded.

Edwin pointed to the woman. 'She tried to kill me!' He made an effort to stand, but swayed and collapsed in a heap on the cobblestones, passed out from drink and pain.

The captain held on to the woman. 'You'll have to come with us, *señora*.'

'Captain—' the lieutenant protested.

Jack sheathed his sword and showed himself. 'Wait.'

Both men whirled around, and the lieutenant aimed his pistol at Jack's chest.

Jack held up both hands. 'I am Ensign Vernon of the East Essex. He was trying to kill the boy and rape the woman. I saw it. He and two others. The others ran.'

'What boy?' the captain asked.

A figure sprang from the shadows. The lieutenant turned the pistol on him.

Jack put his hand on the lieutenant's arm. 'Do not shoot. It is the boy.'

The captain held the woman's arm while he walked over to Edwin, rolling him on to his back with his foot. He looked up at the lieutenant. 'Good God, Landon, do you see who this is?'

'General Tranville's son,' Jack answered.

'You jest. What the devil is he doing here?' the lieutenant asked.

Jack pointed to Edwin. 'He tried to choke the boy and she defended him with the knife.'

Blood still oozed from Edwin's cheek, but he remained unconscious.

'He is drunk,' Jack added.

The boy ran to the body of the French soldier. '*Papa!*'

'*Non, non, non, Claude,*' the woman cried, pulling away from the captain.

'Deuce, they are French.' The captain knelt down next to the body and placed his fingers on the man's throat. 'He's dead.'

The woman said, '*Mon mari.*' Her husband.

The captain rose and strode back to Edwin. He swung his leg as if to kick him, but stopped himself. Edwin rolled over again and curled into a ball, whimpering.

The boy tugged at his father's coat. '*Papa! Papa! Réveillez!*'

'*Il est mort, Claude.*' The woman gently coaxed the boy away.

The captain looked at Jack. 'Did Tranville kill him?'

Jack shook his head. 'I did not see.'

'Deuce. What will happen to her now?' The captain gazed back at the woman.

Shouts sounded nearby, and the captain straightened. 'We must get them out of here.' He gestured to the lieutenant. 'Landon, take Tranville back to camp. Ensign, I'll need your help.'

Lieutenant Landon looked aghast. 'You do not intend to turn her in?'

'Of course not,' said the captain sharply. 'I'm going to find her a safe place to stay. Maybe a church. Or somewhere.' He glared at both his lieutenant and at Jack. 'We say nothing of this. Agreed?'

'He ought to hang for this,' the lieutenant protested.

'He's the general's son,' the captain shot back. 'If we report his crime, the general will have our necks, not his son's.' He tilted his head towards the woman. 'He may even come after her and the boy.' The captain looked down at Edwin, now quiet. 'This bastard is so drunk he may not even know what he did.'

'Drink is no excuse.' After several seconds, the lieutenant nodded his head. 'Very well. We say nothing.'

The captain turned to Jack. 'Do I have your word, Ensign?'

'You do, sir.' Jack did not much relish either father or son knowing he'd been here.

Glass shattered nearby and the roof of a burning building collapsed, sending sparks high into the air.

'We must hurry,' the captain said, although he paused to extend his hand to Jack. 'I am Captain Deane. That is Lieutenant Landon.'

Jack shook his hand. 'Sir.'

Captain Deane turned to the woman and her son. 'Is there a church nearby?' His hand flew to his forehead. 'Deuce. What is the French word?' He tapped his brow. '*Église?*'

'*Non,* no *église, capitaine,*' the woman replied. 'My…my *maison*—my house. Come.'

'You speak English, *madame*?'

'*Oui, un peu*—a little.'

The lieutenant threw Edwin over his shoulder.

'Take care,' the captain said to him.

The lieutenant gave a curt nod, glanced around and trudged off in the same direction they had come.

The captain turned to Jack. 'I want you to come with me.' He looked over at the Frenchman's body. 'We will have to leave him here.'

'Yes, sir.'

'Come.' The woman, with a despairing last glance towards her husband, put her arm around her son's shoulder and gestured for them to follow her.

They made their way through the alley to a doorway facing a narrow street not far from where they had been.

'My house,' she whispered.

The door was ajar. The captain signalled them to stay while he entered. A few moments later he returned. 'No one is here.'

Jack stepped inside. The place had been ransacked. Furniture was shattered, dishes broken, papers scattered everywhere. The house consisted only of a front room, a kitchen and a bedroom. He kicked debris aside to make room for them to walk. Captain Deane pulled what remained of a bed's mattress into the front room, clearing a space for it in the corner. The woman came from the kitchen with cups of water for them. The boy stayed at her side, looking numb.

Jack drank thirstily.

'Can you keep watch?' the captain asked after drinking his fill. 'I'll sleep for an hour or so, then relieve you.'

'Yes, sir,' Jack replied. He might as well stand watch. He certainly could not sleep. Indeed, he wondered if he would ever sleep again.

They barricaded the door with some of the broken furniture, and Jack salvaged a chair whose seat and legs were still intact. He placed it at the window and sat.

The captain gestured for the woman and her son to sleep on the mattress. He sat on the floor, his back leaning against the wall.

Outside the sounds of carnage continued, but no one approached. Jack stared out on to a street that looked deceptively innocent and peaceful.

Perhaps by morning the carnage would be over, and Jack would be able to return to his camp. Perhaps his major and the others in their patrol would still be alive. Perhaps someone, before this war was over, would put a sword through Edwin Tranville's heart for his part in this horror.

Jack reloaded his pistol and kept it at the ready. In the stillness, images flooded into his mind, over and over, flashing like torture, forcing him to relive the horror of this day.

His fingers itched to make the images stop, to capture them, imprison them, store them away so they would leave him alone.

The sky lightened as dawn arrived, but Jack still heard the drunken shouts, the musket shots, the screams. They were real. Even though it was day, the plundering continued.

Captain Deane woke and walked over to Jack, standing for a moment to listen.

'By God, they are still at it.' The captain rubbed his face. 'Get some sleep, Ensign. We'll wait. Maybe things will quieten down soon.'

Jack gave the captain his seat. He glanced at the corner of the room where the woman and boy lay. The boy was curled up in a ball and looked very young and vulnerable. The woman was awake.

Jack surveyed the room and started picking up the sheets of paper scattered about the floor. He examined them. Some sides were blank.

'Do you need these?' he asked the woman, holding up a fist full of paper.

'*Non.*' She turned away.

Some of the sheets appeared to contain correspondence, perhaps from loved ones at home. Jack felt mildly guilty for taking them, but his notebook was stored safely in his kit back at his regiment's encampment and he'd not realised how badly he would need paper.

He found a wide piece of board and carried it to a spot of light from another window. Sitting cross-legged on the floor, he placed the board on his lap and fished in his pockets for his wooden graphite pencil. Jack placed one of the sheets of paper on the board, and heaved a heavy breath.

He started to draw.

The images trapped in his brain flowed from his fingers to the tip of his pencil on to the paper. He could not get them out fast enough. He filled one, two, three sheets and still he was not done. He needed to draw them all.

Only then, after he'd captured every image, would he be free of them. Only then could he dare to rest. Only then could he sleep.

Chapter One

⟨∿∿∿⟩

London—June 1814

It was like walking in a dream.

All around him, history paintings, landscapes, allegories, portraits hung one next to the other like puzzle pieces until every space, floor to ceiling, was covered.

Jack wandered through the exhibition room of the Royal Academy of Art, gazing at the incredible variety, the skill, the *beauty* of the works. He could not believe he was here.

His regiment had been called back to England a year ago. Napoleon had abdicated, and the army had no immediate need for his services. Jack, like most of the young officers who'd lived through the war, had risen in rank. He'd been promoted to lieutenant, which gave him a bit more money when he went on half-pay. This gave him the opportunity to do what he yearned to do, *needed* to do. To draw. To paint. To create beauty and forget death and destruction.

Jack had gone directly to Bath, to the home of his mother and sister, the town where his mentor, Sir Cecil Harper, also lived. Sir Cecil had fostered Jack's need to draw ever since he'd been a boy and he became Jack's tutor again. Somehow the war had not robbed Jack of the ability to paint. At Sir Cecil's insistence, he submitted his paintings to the Royal Academy for its summer exhibition. Miraculously the Royal Academy accepted two of them.

They now hung here on the walls of Somerset House, home of the Royal Academy, next to the likes of Lawrence and Fuseli and Turner, in a room crowded with spectators who had not yet left the city for the summer.

Crowds disquieted Jack. The rumble of voices sounded in his ears like distant cannonade and set off memories that threatened to propel him back into the nightmare of war.

A gentleman brushed against him, and Jack almost swung at him. Luckily the man took no notice. Jack unclenched his fist, but the rumble grew louder and the sensation of cannons, more vivid. His heart beat faster and it seemed as if the room grew darker. This had happened before, a harbinger of a vision. Soon he would be back in battle again, complete with sounds and smells and fears.

Jack closed his eyes and held very still, hoping no one could tell the battle that waged inside. When he opened his eyes again, he gazed up at his sister's portrait, hung high and difficult to see, as befitted his status as a nobody. The painting grounded him. He was in London, at Somerset House, amid beauty. He smiled gratefully at her image.

'Which painting pleases you so?' a low and musical voice asked.

At Jack's elbow stood a young woman, breathtakingly lovely, looking precisely as if she had emerged from one of the canvases. For a brief moment he wondered if she too was a trick his mind was playing on him. Her skin was like silk of the palest rose, beautifully contrasted by her rich auburn hair. Her lips, deep and dusky pink, shimmered as if she'd that moment moistened them with her tongue. Large, sparkling eyes, the green of lush meadows and fringed with long mink-brown lashes, met his gaze with a fleeting expression of sympathy.

'Do say it is the one of the young lady.' She pointed to his sister's portrait.

Tearing his eyes away from her for a moment, he glanced back at the painting of his sister. 'Do you like that one?' he managed to respond.

'I do, indeed.' Her eyes narrowed in consideration. 'She is so fresh and lovely. The rendering is most life-like, but that is not the whole of it, I think—' she paused, moistening her lips, and more than Jack's artistic sensibilities came alive with the gesture '—it is most lovingly painted.'

'Lovingly painted?' Jack glanced back again at the canvas, but just for a second, because he could not bear to wrest his eyes from her.

'Yes.' She spoke as if conversing with a man to whom she had not been introduced was the most natural thing in the world, as if she were the calm in this room where Jack had just battled old demons. 'The young lady's expression. Her posture. It all bespeaks to emotion, her eagerness to see what the future holds for her and the fondness the artist has for her. It makes her even more beautiful. The painting is quite re-markable indeed.'

Jack could not help but flush with pride.

He'd painted Nancy's portrait primarily to lure commis-sions from prospective clients, but it had also given him the opportunity to become reacquainted with the sister who'd been a child when he'd kissed her goodbye before departing for the Peninsula. Nancy was eighteen now and had blos-somed into a beauty as fresh and lovely as her portrait had been described. The painting's exquisite admirer looked to be no more than one or two years older than Nancy. If Jack painted her, however, he'd show a woman who knew pre-cisely what she desired in life.

She laughed. 'I ought not to expect a gentleman to understand emotion.' She gazed back at the painting. 'Except the artist. He captures it perfectly.'

He smiled inwardly. If she only knew how often emotion was his enemy, skirmishing with him even in this room.

Again her green eyes sought his. 'Did you know the artist has another painting here?' She took his arm. 'Come. I will show you. You will be surprised.'

She led him to another corner of the room where, among all the great artists, she had discovered his other work.

'See?' She pointed to the painting of a British soldier raising the flag at Badajoz. 'The one above the landscape. Of the soldier. Look at the emotions of relief and victory and fatigue on the soldier's face.' She opened her catalogue and scanned the pages. '*Victory at Badajoz*, it is called, and the artist is Jack Vernon.' Her gaze returned to the painting. 'What is so fascinating to me is that Vernon also hints at the amount of suffering the man must have endured to reach this place. Is that not marvellous?

'You like this one, too, then?' Jack could not have felt more gratified had the President of the Academy, Benjamin West himself, made the comment.

'I do.' She nodded emphatically.

He'd painted *Victory at Badajoz* to show that fleeting moment when it felt as if the siege of Badajoz had been worth what it cost. She had seen precisely what he'd wanted to convey.

Jack turned to her. 'Do you know so much of soldiering?'

She laughed again. 'Nothing at all, I assure you. But this is exactly how I would imagine such a moment to feel.' She took his arm again. 'Let me show you another.'

She led him to a painting the catalogue listed as *The Surrender of Pamplona*. Wellington, who only this month had become Duke of Wellington, was shown in Roman garb and on horseback accepting the surrender of the Spanish city of Pamplona, depicted in the painting as a female figure. The painting was stunningly composed and evocative of classical Roman friezes. Its technique was flawless.

'You like this one, as well?' he asked her. 'It is well done. Very well done.'

She gave it a dismissive gesture. 'It is ridiculous, Wellington in Roman robes!'

He smiled in amusement. 'It is allegorical.'

She sent him a withering look. 'I know it is allegorical, but do you not think it ridiculous to depict such an event as if it occurred in ancient Rome?' Her gaze swung back to the painting. 'Look at it. I do not dispute that it is well done, but it pales in comparison to the other painting of victory, does it not? Where is the emotion in this one?'

He examined the painting again, as she had demanded, but could not resist continuing the debate. 'Is it not unfair to compare the two when the aim of each is so different? One is an allegory and the other a history painting.'

She made a frustrated sound and shook her head in dismay. 'You do not understand me. I am saying that this artist takes all the meaning, all the emotion, away by making this painting an allegory. A victory in war must be an emotional event, can you not agree? The painting of Badajoz shows that. I much prefer to see how it really was.'

How it really was? If only she knew to what extent he had idealised that moment in Badajoz. He'd not shown the stone of the fortress slick with blood, nor the mutilated bodies, nor the agony of the dying.

He glanced back at his painting. He'd not deliberately set about depicting the emotion of victory in the painting of it. He'd meant only to show he could do more than paint portraits. With the war over, he supposed there might be some interest in military art. If someone wished him to paint a scene from a battle, he would do it, even if he must hide how it really was.

Jack glanced back at his painting and again at the allegory.

Some emotion, indeed, had crept into his painting, emotion absent from the other.

He turned his gaze upon the woman. 'I do see your point.'

She grinned in triumph. 'Excellent.'

'I cede to your expertise on the subject of art.' He bowed.

'Expertise? Nonsense. I know even less of art than of soldiering.' Her eyes sparkled with mischief. 'But that does not prevent me from expressing my opinion, does it?'

Jack was suddenly eager to identify himself to her, to let her know he was the artist she so admired. 'Allow me to make myself known to you—'

'Ariana!' At that moment an older woman, also quite beautiful, rushed up to her. 'I have been searching the rooms for you. There is someone you must meet.'

The young woman gave Jack an apologetic look as her companion pulled on her arm. 'We must hurry.'

Jack bowed and the young woman made a hurried curtsy before being pulled away.

Ariana. Jack repeated the name in his mind, a name as lovely and unusual as its bearer.

Ariana.

Ariana Blane glanced back at the tall gentleman with whom she had so boldly spoken. She left him with regret, certain she would prefer his company to whomever her mother was so determined she should meet.

She doubted she would ever forget him, so tall, well formed and muscular. He wore his clothes so very well one could forget his coat and trousers were not the most fashionable. His face was strong, chiselled, solid, the face of a man one could depend upon to do what needed to be done. His dark hair was slightly tousled and in need of a trim, and the shadow of a beard was already evident in mid-afternoon. It gave him a rakish air that was quite irresistible.

But it was that fleeting moment of emotion she'd seen in him that had made her so brazenly decide to speak to him. She doubted anyone else would have noticed, but something had shaken him and he'd fought to overcome it. All in an instant.

When she approached him his eyes held her captive. As light a brown as matured brandy, they were unlike any she had seen before. They gave the impression that he had seen more of the world than he found bearable.

And that he could see more of her than she might wish to show.

She sighed. Such an intriguing man.

He had almost introduced himself when her mother interrupted. Ariana wished she'd discovered who he was. She was not in the habit of showing an interest in a man, but he had piqued her curiosity. Now she might never see him again.

Unless she managed to appear on stage, as she was determined to do. Perhaps he would see her perform and seek her out in the Green Room afterwards.

Her mother brought her over to a dignified-looking gentleman of compact build and suppressed energy. Her brows rose. He did not appear to be one of the ageing men of wealth to whom her mother persisted in introducing her. You would think her mother wished her to place herself under a gentleman's protection rather than seek a career on the London stage.

Of course, her mother had been successful doing both and very likely had the same future in mind for her daughter.

'Allow me to make you known to my daughter, Mr Arnold.' Her mother gave her a tight smile full of warning that this introduction was important. 'My daughter, Miss Ariana Blane.'

She needn't have worried. Ariana recognised the name. She bestowed on Mr Arnold her most glittery smile and made a graceful curtsy. 'Sir.'

'Why, she is lovely, Daphne.' Mr Arnold beamed. 'Very lovely indeed.'

Her mother pursed her lips, not quite as pleased with Mr Arnold's enthusiastic assessment as Ariana was. 'Mr Arnold manages the Drury Lane Theatre, dear.'

'An explanation is unnecessary, Mama.' Ariana took a step forwards. 'Everyone in the theatre knows who Mr Arnold is. I am greatly honoured to meet you, sir.' She extended her hand to him.

He clasped her fingers. 'And I, you, Miss Blane.'

Ariana inclined her head towards him. 'I believe you have breathed new life into the theatre with your remarkable Edmund Kean.'

Edmund Kean's performance of Shylock in *The Merchant of Venice* had been a sensation, critically acclaimed far and wide.

The man smiled. 'Did you see Kean's performance?'

'I did and was most impressed,' Ariana responded.

'You saw the performance?' Her mother looked astonished. 'I did not know you had been in London.'

Ariana turned to her. 'A few of us came just to see Kean. There was no time to contact you. We returned almost immediately lest we miss our own performance.'

Arnold continued without heeding the interruption. 'Your mother has informed me that you are an actress.'

Ariana smiled. 'Of course I am! What else should the daughter of the famous Daphne Blane be but an actress? It is in my blood, sir. It is my passion.'

He nodded with approval. 'You have been with a company?'

'The Fisher Company.'

'A very minor company,' her mother said.

'I am acquainted with Mr Fisher.' Mr Arnold appeared impressed.

Four years ago, when Ariana had just turned eighteen, she'd accepted a position teaching poetry at the boarding school in Bury St Edmunds she'd attended since age nine. She'd thought she had no other means of making a life for herself. At the time her mother had a new gentleman under her roof, and would not have welcomed Ariana's return. Fate intervened when the Fisher Company came to the town to perform *Blood Will Have Blood* at the Theatre Royal, and Ariana attended the performance.

The play could not have been more exciting, complete with storm, shipwreck, horses and battle. The next day Ariana packed up her belongings, left the school, and sought out Mr Fisher, begging for a chance to join the company. She knew he hired her only because she was the famous Daphne Blane's daughter, but she did not care. Ariana had found the life she wanted to live.

'What have you performed?' Mr Arnold asked her.

'My heavens, too many to count. I was with the company for four years.'

With the Fisher Company she'd performed in a series of hired barns and small theatres in places like Wells-next-the-Sea and Lowestoft, but she had won better parts as her experience grew.

She considered her answer. '*Love's Frailties, She Stoops to Conquer, The Rivals.*' She made certain to mention *The Rivals*, knowing its author, Richard Brinsley Sheridan, still owned the Drury Lane Theatre.

Her mother added, 'Mere comedies of manners, and some of her roles were minor ones.'

'Oh, but I played Lucy in *The Rivals.*' Ariana glanced at her mother. Why had she insisted upon her meeting Mr Arnold only to thwart every attempt Ariana made to impress the man?

'Tell me,' Mr Arnold went on, paying heed to Ariana and ignoring the famous Daphne Blane, 'have you played Shakespeare?'

'The company did not perform much Shakespeare,' Ariana admitted. 'I did play Hippolyta in *A Midsummer Night's Dream*. Why do you ask, sir?'

Mr Arnold leaned towards her in a conspiratorial manner.

'I am considering a production of *Romeo and Juliet*, to capitalise on the success of Kean. If I am able to find the financing for it, that is.'

Ariana's mother placed her hand on Arnold's arm. 'Will Kean perform?'

He patted her hand. 'He will be asked, I assure you, but even if he cannot, a play featuring Daphne Blane and her daughter should be equally as popular.'

Her mother beamed at the compliment. 'That is an exciting prospect.'

Arnold nodded. 'Come to the theatre tomorrow, both of you, and we will discuss it.'

'We will be there,' her mother assured him.

He bowed and excused himself.

Ariana watched him walk away, her heart racing in excitement. She might perform at the Drury Lane Theatre on the same stage as Edmund Kean, the same stage as her mother.

Hoping for another glance at Ariana, Jack wandered around the room now, only pretending to look at the paintings.

Could he approach her? What would he say? *I am the artist whose work you admired.* He did want her to know.

The war's demons niggled at him again as he meandered through the crowd. He forced himself to listen to snippets of conversations about the paintings, but it was not enough. He needed to see her again.

On his third walk around the room, he found her. She and the woman who'd snatched her from his side now conversed with an intense-looking gentleman. Jack's Ariana seemed quite animated in her responses to the man, quite pleased to be speaking to him. Even from this distance he could feel the power of her smile, see the sparkle in her eyes.

When the man took leave of them, the older woman walked Ariana over to two aristocratic-looking gentlemen. Ariana

did not seem as pleased to be conversing with these gentlemen as she had with the intense-looking fellow, but it was
clear to Jack he could devise no further encounter with her.

He backed away and returned to examining the paintings,
this time assessing them for the presence or absence of emotion.

Someone clapped him on the shoulder. 'Well, my boy. How
does it feel to have your work hanging in Somerset House?'

It was his mentor, Sir Cecil.

'It is a pleasure unlike any I have ever before experienced,
my good friend, and I have you to thank for it.' Jack shook
the man's hand. 'I did not expect you in London. I am glad
to see you.'

Sir Cecil strolled with him back to the spot in the room
where Nancy's portrait hung. 'Had to come, my boy. Had to
come.' He gazed up at the portrait. 'This is fine work. Its
place here is well deserved. Unfortunate your sister cannot see
her portrait hanging in such honour.'

'She has seen it,' Jack responded. 'She is here. She and my
mother. They are this moment repairing a tear in my mother's
gown. They should return soon.'

'I am astonished.' Sir Cecil blinked. 'It is unlike your
mother to come to London, is it not?'

His mother had not been in London since his father died,
so many years ago. 'She wished to be here for this, I think.'

That was only part of the reason. The truth was, his mother
had come to London because Tranville, the man who'd made
her his mistress, had also come to town.

When Jack's father, the nephew of an earl, had been an
officer in the Life Guards, the whole family lived in London.
John and Mary Vernon were accepted everywhere, and Jack
could remember them dressed in finery, ready for one ball or
another. All that changed with his father's death. Suddenly
there were too many debts to pay and not enough money to
pay them. Jack's mother moved them to Bath where Tranville

took notice of the pretty young widow and put her under his protection.

Jack's mother always insisted Tranville had been the family's salvation, but as Jack got older, he realised she could have appealed to his father's uncle. The earl would not have allowed them to starve. Once his mother chose Tranville and abandoned all respectability, his great-uncle washed his hands of them.

Sir Cecil patted Jack on the arm. 'It is good your mother and sister have come. How long do they stay?'

Jack shrugged. 'It depends.'

Depends upon how long Tranville remained in London, Jack suspected. Jack's mother was a foolish woman. Tranville had been no more faithful to her than he'd been to his own wife. He did return to her from time to time, between other conquests.

Matters were different now. Tranville had unexpectedly inherited a barony and become even more wealthy than before. Shortly thereafter, his wife died. Since suddenly becoming a rich, titled and eligible widower, he'd not called upon Jack's mother at all. There was no reason to expect him to do so while she was in London.

Jack cleared his throat. 'My mother and sister have taken rooms on Adam Street, a few doors from my studio.'

'You have established a studio?' Sir Cecil beamed with approval. 'Excellent, my boy.'

Tranville's money paid for his mother's rooms. Practically every penny she possessed came from him. He had thus far kept his promise to support her for life. His money had kept her and her children in great comfort. It had paid for Jack's education and his commission in the army. Jack swore he would pay that money back some day.

'The studio is not much,' Jack admitted to Sir Cecil. 'Little more than a room to paint and a room to sleep, but the light is good.'

'And the address is acceptable,' added the older man, thoughtfully.

The address was not prestigious, but it was an area of town near both Covent Garden and the Adelphi Buildings, which attracted respectable residents.

'I should like to see it,' Sir Cecil said. 'And to call upon your mother. I am in London for a few weeks. My son, you know, is studying architecture here at the Academy.'

'I hope to see you both, then.' Jack spied his mother and sister searching through the crowd. 'One moment, sir. My mother and Nancy approach.'

Nancy caught sight of him and waved. She led their mother to where Jack stood. Sir Cecil greeted them warmly.

'Jack.' Nancy's eyes sparkled with excitement. 'I cannot tell you how many people have asked me if I am the young lady in your portrait. I told them all the direction of your studio.'

His mother lifted her eyebrows. 'I would say some of those enquiries were from very impertinent gentlemen.'

Jack straightened and glanced around the room.

'Do not get in a huff, Brother.' Nancy laughed. 'I came to no harm. It was mere idle curiosity on their part, I am certain.'

Jack was not so certain. He worried about Nancy in London. With her dark hair, fair complexion and bright blue eyes, she was indeed as fresh and lovely as the incomparable Ariana had said. Jack worried about Nancy's future even more. What chance did she have to meet eligible gentlemen? What sort of man would marry the dowerless daughter of a kept woman?

He frowned.

His mother touched his arm. 'I confess to being fatigued, my son. How much longer do you wish to stay?'

He glanced around the room. The crowd was suddenly thinning. The afternoon had grown late and many of those in attendance would be heading to their townhouses in Mayfair. Some of them, perhaps, would take their carriages for a turn in Hyde Park before returning home. It was the fashionable hour to ride through the park.

Jack, his mother, and sister would walk to Adam Street.

'We may leave now, if you like.' Jack glanced around the room again, hoping for one more glimpse of Ariana.

Luck was with him when he and Sir Cecil escorted his mother and sister to the door. Ariana appeared a few steps ahead, but there was no question of approaching her. She and her companion walked with two wealthy-looking and attentive gentlemen.

Jack pushed aside his flash of envy. Instead, he focused on the way she carried herself, the graceful nature of her walk. He watched how her pale pink gown swirled about her legs with each step, how the blue shawl draped around her shoulders moved with each sway of her hips.

Jack watched her as they reached the outside and crossed the courtyard. No more than five feet behind her, he might as well have been a mile. Her party continued to the Strand where a line of carriages waited. In a moment Jack would have to head towards home. This would be his last glimpse of her.

She turned and caught sight of him. Her face lit up and took his breath away. His gaze locked with hers, and he thought he sensed the same regret in her eyes that was gnawing at his insides.

One of the gentlemen accompanying her took her arm. 'The carriage, my dear,' he said in a proprietary tone, apparently unaware of Jack staring at her.

She turned back one more time and found him again. 'Goodbye,' she mouthed before being assisted into a shiny, elegant barouche.

Jack watched her until he could see the barouche no more. He tried to engrave her image upon his memory but could feel it fading with each moment. He needed to reach his studio. He needed paper and pencil. He needed to draw her before the image was lost to him as well.

Chapter Two

London—*January 1815*

This chilly January night, Jack escorted his mother and sister to the theatre. His latest commission, a wealthy banker, offered Jack the use of his box to see Edmund Kean in *Romeo and Juliet*.

Jack had acquired some good commissions because of the exhibition, until the oppressive heat of August drove most of the wealthy from London. The banker, Mr Slayton, was his final one. Jack's mother and sister also returned to Bath, but they came back to London with the new year. Jack had placed an advertisement seeking some fresh commissions in the *Morning Post*, but, thus far, no one had answered it.

Jack tried to set his financial worries aside as he assisted his mother to her seat in the theatre box. Sir Cecil's son, Michael, was also in their company attending Jack's sister. Michael, as kind-faced as his father, but tall, dark-haired and slim, continued with his architectural studies and had again become a frequent addition to Jack's mother's dinner table now that she and Nancy were back in London.

As Nancy took her seat, it was clear she was already enjoying herself. 'It is so beautiful from up here.'

They'd attended the theatre once the previous summer, but sat on the orchestra floor with the general admission. From the theatre box the rich reds and gleaming golds of the décor were displayed in all their splendour.

Nancy turned to Jack. 'Thank you so much for bringing us.'

He was glad she was pleased. 'You should thank Mr Slayton for giving me the tickets.'

'Oh, I do.' She turned to their mother. 'Perhaps we should write him a note of gratitude.'

'We shall do precisely that,' her mother agreed.

'Well, I am grateful, as well.' Michael stood gazing out at the house. 'This is a fine building.'

Nancy left her chair to stand beside him. 'You will probably gaze all evening at the arches and ceiling and miss the play entirely.'

He grinned. 'I confess they will distract me.'

She gave an exaggerated sigh. 'But the play is *Romeo and Juliet*. How can you think of a building when you shall see quite possibly the most romantic play ever written?'

He laughed. 'Miss Vernon, I could try to convince you that beautiful arches and elegant columns are romantic, but I suspect you will never agree with me.'

'I am certain I will not.' She nodded.

'I remember coming here in my first Season.' Jack's mother spoke in a wistful tone. 'Of course, that was the old theatre. There were not so many boxes in that auditorium.'

That Drury Lane Theatre burned down in 1809.

Nancy surveyed the crowd. 'There are many grand people here.'

The play was quite well attended, even though most of the *beau monde* would not come to London for another month or so. Perhaps Jack's commissions would increase then. Of course, with the peace, many people had chosen to travel to Paris or Vienna and would not be in London at all. Still, the theatre had an impressive crowd. Edmund Kean had been drawing audiences all year in a series of Shakespearean plays.

Nancy leaned even further over the parapet. 'Mama, I see Lord Tranville.'

'Do you?' Jack's mother's voice rose an octave.

'There.' Nancy stepped aside so her mother could see. 'The third balcony. Near the stage.'

'I believe you are correct.' Her voice was breathless.

Tranville stood with another gentleman in a box close to the stage, the two men in conversation while surveying the theatre. If Tranville spied his former mistress in the crowd, he made no show of it.

The curtain rose and Nancy and Michael sat in their chairs. Nancy's gaze was riveted to the stage, but their mother's drifted to the nearby box where Tranville sat.

Jack's jaw flexed.

Edmund Kean walked on.

'He is old!' Nancy whispered.

Shakespeare had written Romeo as a young man who falls in love as only a young man could. Kean's youth was definitely behind him. Still, Kean made an impressive figure in the costume of old Verona, moving about the stage in a dramatic manner. It would be a challenge to capture that movement in oils, Jack thought.

Artists such as Hogarth and Reynolds painted the famous actors and actresses, Kemble and Garrick, Sarah Siddons and Daphne Blane. The portraits were engraved and printed in magazines and on posters in order to entice people to the theatre. Jack straightened. Perhaps the theatre could provide him with a clientele. He might not get commissions for the principal actors, but maybe the lesser known ones, or maybe he could depict whole scenes as they occurred on the stage.

If he could paint the action of battle, he could easily paint the action of a London stage.

The idea took firm root in Jack's mind. His studio was quite near to Covent Garden, so it would be convenient for the actors. Or he could easily come to the theatre. He began to imagine the scene onstage as he might paint it. He was ready to assess every scene for its artistic potential.

Romeo spoke the lines about planning to attend the Capulets' supper. He left the stage, and Lady Capulet and the nurse entered, looking for Juliet.

Jack's fingers itched for a pencil, wishing to sketch Lady Capulet and the nurse with their heads together.

'See,' Nancy whispered to her mother. 'Lady Capulet is Daphne Blane. Her natural daughter is playing Juliet.'

Jack had the notion he'd seen Daphne Blane before. Of course, she was a notorious beauty whose conquests were as legendary as her performances on stage so he might have seen her image somewhere. The birth of her natural daughter had been the scandal of its day with much speculation on who the father might be. Many artists had painted Daphne Blane's portrait. Why not Jack?

Juliet made her entrance. 'How now? Who calls?'

'Your mother,' the nurse replied.

Juliet faced the audience. 'Madam, I am here…'

Jack nearly rose from his chair.

Ariana.

Juliet was Ariana. From this distance, her features were not clear, but she moved like Ariana, sounded like her. He'd found her. He'd despaired of ever doing so.

His eyes never left her while she was on stage. His fingers moved on the arm of the chair as if he were drawing the graceful arch of her neck, the sinuous curves of her body.

The intermission was almost torture, because he could not record her on paper and he had to act as if his world had not suddenly tumbled on its ear. As the curtain closed on the actors' final bows, Jack remained in his seat, staring at the curtain.

Michael gave his hand to Jack's mother to help her rise, and Jack noticed his mother glancing in the direction of Tranville's box.

Nancy sprang to her feet, her hands pressed together. 'Was it not splendid? I mean, it was so sad, but so lovely, did you not think?'

Jack smiled at her, still partially abstracted. 'You enjoyed it, then?'

Her blue eyes shone with pleasure. 'I adored it.' Michael helped her on with her cloak. 'Well, perhaps not Romeo. Mr Kean was not my idea of Romeo, I assure you.'

Michael grinned. 'Was he not romantic enough?'

'He was *old*.' Nancy made a face.

Jack's mother glanced over her shoulder once more as they all made their way to the door. Once they were out in the noisy, crowded hallway, Jack would lose his chance to talk to them.

He placed a hand on his mother's arm. 'I should like your permission to part from you here.'

His mother shook her head. 'Forgive me, Jack. What did you say?'

'I would bid you goodnight here.' He turned to Michael. 'Would you escort the ladies home?'

'I would be honoured and delighted,' Michael replied. 'But this is a surprise. Why do you leave us?'

Jack's primary reason was to go in search of Ariana, but he had no wish to tell them that. He'd give them a partial truth. 'I had the notion that I might paint the actors performing their roles. I want to seek out the manager and give him my card.'

'You would paint the actors?' Nancy exclaimed. 'Why, that would be splendid! The print shops are always full of prints of actors. How perfect since you are so close to the theatre.'

'My thoughts precisely,' he responded, knowing this was

not true. It was far less complicated than explaining about Ariana, however. 'I should be able to offer a reasonable price.'

Nancy nodded. 'Very sensible, Jack.'

'Proceed, my son,' his mother said. 'We will manage without you.'

His mother rarely complained, not even when Tranville failed to call upon her. It had been a year since he had bothered.

'Then I bid you all goodnight.' He leaned over and kissed his mother's cheek.

Nancy smiled. 'Thank you for bringing us, Jack.'

Michael made as if fighting with a sword. 'Do not fret. I shall scare off any foes who dare to cross our path.'

Nancy giggled. 'What nonsense. We shall take a hackney coach.'

Michael put his arm around her. 'Yes, we shall, and I shall pay for it.'

Out in the hallway, they made for the theatre door and Jack for the stage. He did not know the location of the Green Room, where the actors and actresses gathered after the performance and where wealthy gentlemen went to arrange assignations with the loveliest of the women, but he suspected that would be where he would find Ariana.

Backstage he followed a group of wealthy-looking gentlemen, some carrying bouquets of flowers. Jack walked behind them, but suddenly stopped.

Tranville stood to the side of the door.

He still retained his military bearing, even though he was attired in the black coat, white breeches and stockings that made up the formal dress of a gentleman. His figure remained trim and only his shock of white hair gave a clue that he was a man who had passed his fiftieth year.

Tranville, unfortunately, also saw Jack.

'Jack!' He stepped in the younger man's path. 'What are you doing here? Why are you not in Bath?'

Jack bristled. He'd never been able to disguise his dislike of this man, although when a child he doubted Tranville had even noticed. A few adolescent altercations with Tranville's son Edwin had made the animosity clear and mutual. Jack never initiated the fisticuffs, but he always won and that rankled Tranville greatly.

Jack straightened and looked down on the older man. 'I have business with the theatre manager.'

'You?' Tranville eyed him with surprise. 'What business could you have with Mr Arnold?'

Jack felt an inward triumph. He now knew the manager's name. 'Business to be discussed with Mr Arnold.'

Tranville's jaw flexed. 'If it is theatre business, you may tell me. I am a member of the committee.'

'The committee.' This meant nothing to Jack.

Tranville averted his gaze for a moment. 'The subcommittee for developing the theatre as a centre for national culture.'

Jack remembered it. Control of the theatre had been wrested from the debt-ridden owner, Richard Brinsley Sheridan, and given to a manager and a board of directors. A subcommittee of notables had been appointed, but Jack doubted they had access to the purse strings. Nevertheless, if Jack had encountered any other member of the subcommittee he would have spoken of how his art work could further the committee's goals. This was Tranville blocking his way, however.

Jack maintained a steady gaze. 'My business will not concern you.'

Jack would wager Tranville's theatrical interests were in fostering liaisons with the actresses, not fostering national culture. Actresses and dancers encouraged the attentions of wealthy lords who wanted to indulge them with jewels and gowns and carriages.

He frowned. He had nothing to offer Ariana.

He told himself he merely wanted to renew their brief acquaintance. He wanted her to know *he* had been the artist whose work she so admired.

Two gentleman approached the door and Tranville was forced to step aside for them. Jack took the opportunity to follow them.

Tranville grabbed his arm. 'You cannot go in there, Jack. You do not have entrée.'

Jack shot him a menacing look. 'Entrée?

Tranville did not flinch. 'Not everyone is welcome. Do not force me to have you removed from the building.' He glanced towards two muscular stagehands standing nearby.

Had Tranville forgotten Jack had also been on the Peninsula? His was the regiment that captured the Imperial Eagle at Salamanca. Jack would like to see how many men it would take to eject him from the theatre.

More *gentlemen* approached, however, and Jack chose not to make a scene. It would not serve his purpose.

Tranville smiled, thinking his intimidation had succeeded. He dropped his hand. 'Now, if you wish me to speak to Mr Arnold on your behalf, you will have to tell me what it is about.'

The other gentlemen were in earshot, the only reason Jack spoke. He made certain his voice carried. 'A proposition for Mr Arnold. To paint his actors and actresses.'

'Paint them?' Tranville's brow furrowed.

'I am an artist, sir.' Jack wanted the other gentlemen, now looking mildly interested, to hear him.

With luck one of them might mention to Mr Arnold that an artist wanted to see him. That might help gain him an interview with the manager when Jack called the next afternoon.

Convincing Mr Arnold to hire him to publicise his plays would serve both Jack's ambitions: to earn new commissions and to see Ariana again.

Tranville made an impatient gesture. 'Well, give me your card and I will speak to Arnold.'

Jack took a card from his pocket. 'Tell him Jack Vernon has a business proposition for him. Tell him my work was included in last summer's exhibition.'

The most curious of the onlookers appeared satisfied. They had heard Jack's name, at any rate.

Jack nodded to the men. He was resigned. These men would see Ariana tonight. He would not.

And all because of Tranville's interference. Jack's hand curled into a fist.

Tranville snatched the card from Jack's other hand and stuck it in his pocket without even looking at it. Jack turned to leave.

Tranville stopped him. 'Tell me, Jack—how is your mother?'

The question surprised him. 'In good health.' He added, 'She was at the performance. Did you not see her?'

Jack meant it as a jibe, to show his mother doing well without Tranville's company, but instead the man cocked his head in interest. 'Was she?' He spoke more to himself than to Jack. 'So Mary is in London.'

Another man walked past and opened the door to the Green Room. Tranville emerged from his brief reverie. 'I must go.'

Jack was more than ready to be rid of him.

Still, he would have tolerated even Tranville's presence if it meant seeing Ariana again. Instead Tranville had prevented him.

Another reason to despise the man.

The next day, Jack, wearing only an old shirt and trousers, both spattered with paint, put the finishing touches on Mr Slayton's portrait. There was a rap on the door.

Before he could put down his palette and don a coat, the door opened and Tranville strode in.

'Jack—' Like many military men, Tranville apparently had not lost the military habit of rising early.

'What is the meaning of this?' Jack stepped out from behind his easel. 'You cannot just walk in here without a by your leave.'

Tranville, looking perfectly at ease, removed his hat and gloves and placed them on a table by the door. 'You work in this place?' He glanced around with disdain.

White sheets covered the furniture, wooden boxes and rolls of canvas littered the floor, but Jack had no intention of apologising to Tranville for the clutter. He tidied the place when he had sittings scheduled.

'Tell me why you intrude or leave.' Jack crossed his arms over his chest.

Tranville wandered over to the easel and examined Mr Slayton's portrait. He shrugged and turned back to Jack. 'You do seem to have some skill. More than one fellow told me so after I left you last night.'

He'd been discussed? Remembered from the exhibition, perhaps? Jack hid his pleasure. He hoped these admirers mentioned him to Mr Arnold as well. 'You have not told me why you are here.'

Tranville's lips curled. 'I want to hire you for a commission.'

Jack did not miss a beat. 'No.'

Tranville's brows shot up. 'You've heard nothing about it.'

'I do not need to hear. I am not interested in painting you. The reasons should be obvious.' He headed to the door.

Tranville, remaining where he stood, laughed. 'If I were to commission a portrait of myself, I'd hire Lawrence or someone of his calibre. No, this portrait would be of someone else. A woman.'

Jack's eyes narrowed. He ought to have guessed. 'Most emphatically no.'

It sickened Jack that Tranville would ask him to paint a woman. Who else could it be but Tranville's latest conquest? Not if he were down to his last shilling, would Jack do such a thing.

He opened the door, but Tranville ignored the demand to leave. 'I checked with my man of business this morning—'

Rousing the poor man from his bed, no doubt.

'He gave me your mother's direction. A few doors up from here, eh?' Tranville's tone was pleasant, but Jack did not miss the hint of menace beneath it.

He gripped the door knob. 'Speak plain, sir.'

Tranville smiled, and Jack recoiled in disgust. 'Why, I thought I would call upon her. That is all.'

Jack's nostrils flared.

Tranville's smile fled. 'Surely you have no objection.'

Jack had a barrelful of objections, but none he could voice. As much as he despised the idea, his mother would desire the visit. 'It is my mother's decision.'

Tranville sauntered towards the door, retrieving his hat and gloves. As he passed Jack, he paused and leaned close. 'I always get my way, Jack.'

The rumble of imaginary cannon fire sounded in Jack's ear. A battle loomed, Jack would wager, this time in his London rooms and not on the battlefield.

It took Jack an hour before he could again focus on Mr Slayton's portrait, attending to its finishing touches. Better to concentrate on the tiniest brush stroke than to dwell upon Tranville visiting his mother.

He peered at the painting before him. He'd posed Mr Slayton at a desk with a pen in his hand. It would have been faster to merely paint the banker's head on a dark background, but Jack preferred some context to his painting, some sense of movement. Whether it had emotion, he could not tell. The emotion Ariana had seen in his two paintings at Somerset House had been unconsciously done.

He picked up a small brush and stared at the painting, but saw Ariana instead. Thoughts of her were the best antidote to the encounter with Tranville. He might see her today. He planned to visit the theatre this afternoon.

Another knock sounded at the door. Jack braced himself

for a further intrusion by Tranville, but the person knocking apparently did not feel entitled to burst in as Tranville had done. The knock came again. Jack put down his palette, wiped his brush and crossed the room to open the door.

'Jack!' Nancy entered. 'Mama wishes to see you.'

'What has happened?' What has Tranville done? he meant.

She pinched his arm. 'Nothing terrible.' She smiled. 'Lord Tranville called upon her.'

He frowned. 'Did he upset her?'

Nancy looked puzzled. 'Of course not. She was in raptures. You know how Mama feels about him.'

Yes, but he could not fathom it. 'Then why does she wish to see me?'

'I am not certain.' Nancy removed her cloak and hung it on one of the pegs by the door. 'I did not remain with them above a few minutes. Lord Tranville said very pretty things to me. And to Mama. It was quite a pleasure to see him.'

'Is he still there?' If so, Jack preferred to avoid him.

She shook her head. 'He left, and then Mama asked me to fetch you.'

Jack walked over to his easel to clean his brushes. He covered his palette with a cloth so that the paint would not dry and wiped his hands. 'Give me a moment to change my clothes.'

A few minutes later he and Nancy walked the short distance to his mother's set of rooms on Adam Street. Jack liked having his family near after the long separation of war, and Tranville's money could well pay for rooms in both London and Bath, but his mother would have been far wiser to save that money for Nancy's future.

Nancy paused mid-step. 'Do you think Lord Tranville has asked Mama to marry him? Perhaps that is why she wants to see you?'

He gave a dry laugh. 'That is a ridiculous notion, Nancy.'

She pursed her lips. 'Why is it ridiculous? He is an eligible man now.'

He shook his head. 'He has not seen fit to call upon her for over a year. That is hardly prelude to a proposal.'

Nancy gaped at him as if he'd lost his wits. 'Surely Lord Tranville was concerned as to how it would appear to see Mama so soon after his wife died. He was being protective of her reputation.'

Jack resumed walking. 'He was never so protective of her reputation before his wife died.'

She hurried to catch up. 'You do not understand it at all. Now that he is an eligible man of rank, it becomes more important to protect her from talk.'

Jack bit his tongue. He'd always tried to shield Nancy from the sordid reality of Tranville's relationship with their mother. He wasn't about to change now.

'I do not understand why you dislike Tranville so.' Nancy looked wounded.

Jack never intended for Nancy to think well of Tranville, merely to prevent her from thinking ill of their mother. 'I suppose I dislike him because he is not our father.' And because he so quickly replaced their father in their mother's bed.

She squeezed his arm. 'I cannot remember our father like you do. I only remember that Tranville helped our mother when we were so poor.'

They had never been so poor that their mother would not have had a chance for a respectable second marriage. Tranville ruined that for her.

They arrived at his mother's door, but Nancy held him back. 'Can you not perceive the situation between Mama and Lord Tranville as romantic?'

'Romantic?' He could not lie. 'No, I cannot.'

'Well, I can.' Her tone was definite. 'They have loved each other for so many years, but because Lord Tranville was married, they could not be together. Even so, he loved her with such a passion he could never stay away completely.'

He gave her a disapproving look. 'A passion?'

She lifted her chin. 'I am not a child any more. I know what happens between a man and a woman.'

Jack put his hand on the doorknob. 'What happens between a man and a woman is not necessarily romantic, my dear sister.'

Nancy stood her ground. 'He *must* love her. He pays for everything for her. Our food. Our house. Everything.'

'He has done so.' It was the only thing to Tranville's credit and it had always puzzled Jack. A man of Tranville's character would cut funds the minute he tired of a woman.

'Why would he spend that money on her if he did not love her?' Nancy asked.

'I confess, I do not know,' Jack responded honestly, turning the knob and ending the discussion.

When they entered the rented rooms, their mother's manservant, Wilson, appeared in the hall to take Nancy's cloak and Jack's hat and gloves. 'Your mother awaits you in the parlour.'

Jack opened the parlour door for Nancy and followed her in.

His mother stood by the fireplace and turned at their entrance. 'Jack, I am pleased you could come right away.'

He crossed the room and kissed her on the cheek. 'Mother.'

Slanting him a somewhat determined look, she gestured for them to sit. Jack waited for her to lower herself in a chair.

Her hands nervously smoothed the fabric of her skirt. 'I am certain Nancy has told you Lionel—Lord Tranville—called upon me.' Her eyes flickered with a momentary pleasure.

'He informed me of his intention to call.' Jack tried to keep his voice even.

'We had a lovely time,' his mother went on.

'Indeed.' Jack fought sarcasm.

His mother took a breath. 'Well, I suppose I should just say that Lionel told me he offered you a commission.'

'He did.'

'He did?' Nancy sat forward in surprise. 'You never said. How exciting.'

Jack turned to her. 'I did not accept it, Nancy.'

His mother broke in. 'The thing is, Jack, I want you to accept it.'

'I will not.' She must be mad.

'Ja-ack.' Nancy drew out his name, sounding disappointed.

Jack stared at his mother. 'A woman, Mother.'

She shot a glance to Nancy and back to Jack with an almost imperceptible shake of her head. Very well. He would not delve into why he presumed Tranville wished him to paint a woman, even though his mother was not deluded about it.

His mother answered calmly, 'He is financing a production of Shakespeare's *Antony and Cleopatra* and wishes the portrait to be used in advertisements. It is precisely what you said you wanted last night.'

'I did not say I would work for Tranville.'

'But, Jack—' Nancy inserted.

'Do not be foolish, my son,' his mother went on. 'He offers you a good price—better, I dare say, than you have earned on your other paintings.' She named the price Tranville had offered. It was a staggering amount.

Jack gritted his teeth. 'I do not want his charity.'

Lines formed between her brows. 'This animosity does you no credit.'

He shrugged.

He'd tried to explain before, telling her of Tranville's harsh treatment of his men during the war while toadying to his superiors, of how Tranville turned a blind eye to his son avoiding combat, but sent better men to their deaths.

'You know what sort of man he is.'

'Say no more.' She lifted both hands to halt further discussion. 'I accepted the commission for you.'

He stood. 'You did not!'

She regarded him with a steely glance. 'You will paint this portrait for *me*, Jack, because I wish it. I ask little of you, but I ask this.'

He remained standing, looking down at her. She'd aged since he'd left for war. Her brown hair was streaked with grey and tiny lines had formed at the corners of her eyes and her mouth. Still, he thought her as beautiful as when he'd been a boy and she'd been young and carefree. He wished he could paint that memory.

She continued, 'And I insist you do not cross him. Treat Lord Tranville with civility for my sake, because it is important to me.' Her eyes pleaded. 'It is important to me that you have this work, the money it will pay, and it is important to me that Lionel succeed in gaining his desires. He wishes to make this play a success and, therefore, I wish it for him.'

Tranville wished to make a conquest of this actress, if he was not bedding her already. Who was it? An actress as sought after by men as Daphne Blane? Jack would not put it past Tranville to try to buy his way into her bed by financing a play. He'd bought his way into his mother's bed, after all, and now his mother wanted her son to paint this woman? It was absurd.

Jack narrowed his eyes. 'Did he threaten you? Threaten to withhold your funds or some such thing?'

She looked surprised. 'Threaten? Of course he did not. Lionel has always paid my quarterly allowance. I ask merely out of my gratitude for all he has done for us.'

Jack averted his gaze and stared into the carpet whose pile had worn thin in places.

'Say you will do this for me, my son,' his mother murmured.

He wanted to refuse, but his mother so rarely asked for anything, certainly nothing from him. Jack slowly nodded.

'For you, Mother, I will do as you ask.' He raised his chin. 'But only for you.'

Only for his mother would he would paint her lover's new conquest.

Chapter Three

Ariana descended the stairs at the boarding house on Henrietta Street where she and other actresses and actors lived. The rooms were comfortably furnished and the company, excellent. The landlady of the establishment was an accommodating woman, a stickler for propriety, if one desired, or equally willing to ignore propriety completely.

Today Ariana chose propriety. Betsy, the maid, had announced that Lord Tranville had called. Had he not been funding Drury Lane's production of *Antony and Cleopatra*, selecting her to play Cleopatra, she would have refused to see him. She kept him waiting in the drawing room a full ten minutes to discourage any notion he might have about how far her gratitude might reach.

She had no doubt her mother had told him where she resided. Her mother believed in patronage above all things.

Ariana wrinkled her nose.

What was her mother thinking? The gentleman was old enough to be her father, at least fifty years old, ten years older than her mother, even.

She swept into the drawing room. 'Lord Tranville. What a surprise.' She extended her hand, thinking he would shake it.

Instead he grasped it and brought it to his lips, actually placing a wet kiss upon it. 'My dear Miss Blane.'

She grimaced and pulled her hand away as soon as she could. Gone was any hope his interest was confined to her acting ability. She sighed. It would require skill to remain in his good graces while discouraging his advances. She'd managed it with other gentlemen; she could do it with him.

She made no effort to look at him directly. 'I am astonished you are here. Have you come on theatre business?'

He smiled wide enough to show all his white teeth. At least he had teeth, one point in his favour. 'I hoped my desire to gaze upon your loveliness would be reason enough to call upon you.'

With effort she kept her expression bland, staring blankly at him, as if waiting for him to stop spouting nonsense.

He fiddled with his watch fob. 'My—my visit does involve the theatre. In a manner of speaking.'

'Oh?' Only then did she gesture for him to sit. He chose one of the sofas. She lowered herself on to a chair, making a show of brushing off an invisible piece of lint from her sleeve.

Finally she looked at him again. 'Do tell me why you have called.'

He leaned towards her. 'I have a notion to advertise your role in *Antony and Cleopatra.*'

She lifted a brow.

He went on. 'If you are agreeable, an artist will paint you as Cleopatra. We shall have engravings made that can be printed for advertising. In magazines. On handbills. It will increase your success, I am certain.'

She looked at him with a wary eye. 'Who will pay for all this?' Surely not the theatre.

Mr Sheridan had run Drury Lane Theatre into terrible debt. Kean's performances, so very popular, helped to ease the burden, but that did not mean the theatre would expend money on behalf of a new actress whose popularity had not yet been established. Her performance had been barely mentioned when the critics gave *Romeo and Juliet* a very unfavourable review, greatly criticising Kean's performance.

'I will pay for everything,' Tranville said. 'And, if it pleases you, I will make the portrait my gift to you.'

She wanted no gifts from him, but she did need this play to be a success.

He tilted his head in a manner he probably thought charming. 'If it is convenient, the artist can see you this afternoon to discuss the painting. I will be honoured to escort you.'

She had no plans for the afternoon. 'Where is this artist?'

'On the corner of Adam Street and Adelphi.'

'Near the Adelphi Terraces?' It was only a few streets away.

'Yes.'

A good enough address and nearby. 'Who is the artist?'

He leaned even closer to her. 'His name is Jack Vernon.'

Ariana gaped at him, 'Jack Vernon!'

Tranville looked apologetic. 'I realise he is not as fashionable as Lawrence or Westall, but he did have some paintings in the Royal Exhibition, I've heard tell.'

How well she remembered. She'd used her admiration of Vernon's paintings to brazenly approach the tall, handsome, solitary young gentleman whose inner struggle of some sort had fascinated her. Sadly, she had never learned who he was.

She resisted another sigh. What good was it to dwell on what was gone? Here was an opportunity to meet the artist and be painted by him.

'I will do it, my lord,' she told Tranville. 'But there is no need for you to escort me such a short distance. Merely give me the exact direction and tell me the time I am expected.'

His lower lip jutted out. 'I would be delighted to escort you.'

Her hand fluttered. 'Do not trouble yourself.'

'But—'

She gave him a level look. 'I prefer going alone. It is daylight. The streets are full of people. No harm will come to me.'

'I insist.' He persisted.

Her brows rose. 'Is your escort a condition of this agreement? I will not do it if there are conditions to which I must comply.' Ariana knew better than to make herself beholden to any man.

'No, no conditions—' he blustered.

'Good.' She rearranged her skirt. 'Tell me when I am expected.'

An hour later Ariana stood at Mr Vernon's door, her heart thumping with anticipation. She looked down at herself, brushing off her cloak, pulling up her gloves, straightening her hat. She took a quick breath and knocked.

Almost immediately the door opened.

Framed in the doorway was the handsome gentleman she'd met in Somerset House, the one she'd thought she would never see again.

'You!' She gasped. 'I—I have an appointment with Mr Vernon.'

He looked equally surprised. It took him several seconds before he stepped aside.

As she brushed by him she felt a flurry of excitement. She'd found him, the man who'd so intrigued her at the Summer Exhibition. He was taller than she remembered, and his sheer physical presence seemed more powerful than it had been in the crowded exhibition hall. In the light pouring through the windows, his brown eyes were even more enthralling and every bit as beset with private demons.

'Is Mr Vernon here?' she asked.

He slowly closed the door behind her. 'I am Vernon.'

'You are Vernon?' The breath left her lungs.

His frown deepened. 'I—I did not know you would be coming.'

He did not seem happy to see her. In fact, his displeasure wounded her. 'Forgive me. Tranville said I was expected at this hour.'

He stiffened. 'Tranville.'

She began to unfasten her cloak, but stopped. Perhaps she would not be staying. 'Did you desire him to accompany me?'

His eyes were singed with anger. 'Not at all.'

He confused her with his vague answers. She straightened her spine and put her hands on her hips. 'Mr Vernon, if you do not wish me to be here, I will leave, but I beg you will simply tell me what you want.'

He ran a hand through his thick brown hair and his lovely lips formed a rueful smile. 'Tranville told me to expect an actress. I did not know it would be you.'

His smile encouraged her. 'Then we are both of us surprised.'

His shoulders seemed to relax a little.

He stepped forwards to take her cloak, and as he came so close she inhaled the scent of him, bergamot soap and linseed oil, turpentine and pure male.

He seemed unaware of her reaction and completely immune to her, which somehow made her want to weep. Only once before had she wanted to weep over a man. He took her cloak and hung it upon a peg by the door, moving with the same masculine elegance that had drawn her to him when she first caught sight of him. He had been the first man to ignite her senses in years, a fact that surprised and intoxicated her even now.

He faced her again, and she hid her interest in a quick glance around the studio, all bright and neat, except for where an easel stood by the windows, a paint-smeared shirt hanging from it. She removed her hat and gloves and placed them on a nearby chair.

He did not move.

So she must. She walked to him. 'Let us start over.' She extended her hand. 'I am Ariana Blane.'

He shook it, his grasp firm, but still holding something back.

Her brows knit. 'Why did you not tell me, that day, that you were the artist? That you were Jack Vernon?'

He averted his gaze. 'I intended to, but the moment passed.'

'Come, now.' She tried smiling and shaking her finger at him. 'You allowed me to rattle on for quite a long time without telling me.'

He turned his intense brown eyes upon her. 'I wanted your true opinion of my paintings. You would not have given it, had you known I had painted them.'

She laughed. 'Oh, yes, I would. I am never hesitant to say what I think.'

Indeed, she had half a mind to ask him why he scowled when looking at her. He made her senses sing with pleasure. She longed to feel the touch of his hand against her skin, but he seemed completely ill at ease with her.

There had been no unease between them in that first, fleeting, hopeful encounter.

She cleared her throat but disguised her thoughts. 'What happens now, Mr Vernon? This is my first time having my portrait painted.'

He walked over to a pretty brocade upholstered chair and held its back. 'Please be seated, Miss Blane. I will bring tea.'

She sat down, very aware of his hands so near to the sensitive skin of her neck. When he released her chair, she swivelled around to see him disappear behind a curtained doorway to a small galley in the back. A moment later he returned, tray in hand.

He placed the tray on a small table in front of her chair.

She touched his arm and his gaze flew to her face. 'Allow me to pour,' she murmured, as affected by the touch as he appeared to be. 'How do you like your tea? Milk and sugar?'

He lowered himself in the chair on the other side of the table. 'I grew accustomed to going without both on the Peninsula.'

'You were in the war?' she asked as she poured his tea and handed him the cup.

His gaze held. 'In the infantry.'

Her voice turned low. 'Now I comprehend why your history painting had such authenticity.'

He looked away.

Ariana poured her own tea, adding both milk and sugar. She gazed at him when she lifted the cup to her lips. A barrier had risen between them, one that had not existed when they had met at the exhibition. That conversation had been exhilarating; this one dampened her spirits.

She placed her teacup on the table. 'So, how do we proceed with this portrait?'

A crease formed between his brows. 'I need to know what you would like it to be.'

She waved a hand. 'I have no notion. I first heard of this idea an hour ago.'

He glanced away and his brooding expression intensified. 'I first heard this morning.'

'Lord Tranville has been busy,' she murmured, taking a sip of tea.

He made a sound of disgust, pausing before looking back at her with shrouded eyes. 'I did not expect you to come alone. If you desire it, I shall ask my sister to be present. She is but a few doors away.'

What maggot had taken up lodging in his brain? 'Why did you think that?' Actresses did not require chaperons.

He continued to stare at her. 'Tranville is not with you. Perhaps you would like another woman to be present.'

'Tranville?' Why did he persist in bringing up Tranville? He wasn't her father. Who else would care if she were chaperoned?

Suddenly her brows rose. He thought Tranville was her lover.

Jack Vernon would be surprised to know she'd had only one lover, a long time ago. Yes, she'd been deceived once, even though she ought to have learned of men's fickle natures at her mother's knee. Never again. In fact, she'd not even been tempted—until meeting the mysterious stranger at the Summer Exhibition.

In spite of his present behaviour, he still tempted her with his sorrowful eyes holding wounds of the past.

She gave herself a mental shake and made an effort to retrieve their conversation. 'I require no chaperon, Mr Vernon. No one expects propriety from actresses. There is some freedom in that.'

He merely sipped his tea.

She took a breath and tried again. 'Shall we discuss the portrait?'

'You and I must decide how you are to appear as Cleopatra.' He spoke as if all emotion had been leached out of him.

Except from his eyes.

'I am not at all certain how to do that,' she murmured.

He shrugged. 'We try different poses. I sketch you, and we select the best image.'

This struck her as insufficient, like trying to prepare for a play by guessing one's lines.

'Have you read the play?' She rubbed one finger on the arm of the chair. 'It might provide you with some ideas.'

'Not since school days.'

He glanced at her hand, and she curled her fingers into her palm. 'I have my copy in my rooms. Let us get it so you can read it.'

He blinked. 'There is no need. Bring it tomorrow.'

'Then we will be delayed another day. My residence is nearby. It will take no time at all.'

He stared at her and the moment stretched on. 'Very well,' he finally said.

He went into another room to get his top coat, and a minute later they were outside in the cool, breezy air.

She took his arm and glanced at the street ahead. 'Which of the "few doors away" is your sister?'

'Not far.' As they passed, he pointed to it. 'This one.'

'And is there a wife behind those doors, as well?' Please say no, she thought.

He shook his head. 'I am in no position to marry. My sister lives with my mother in those rooms.'

Her heart skipped a beat.

'You have seen my sister,' he said to her as they walked on.

She glanced at him in surprise. 'I have?'

'Hers was the painting you admired at the exhibition.'

She stopped. 'Of course it was. Now I understand.'

'Understand what?'

She met his eyes. 'Why it was such a loving portrait.'

His colour heightened and she sensed him withdrawing from her again.

And they'd almost returned to the comfort between them at the exhibition.

Ariana asked more questions about his sister, hoping she'd not lost him again. She asked his sister's age, her interests, how she'd been educated, anything she could think of that seemed safe. The short walk, a mere few hundred yards to her residence on Henrietta Street, was by far the most pleasant she'd had in an age.

When they entered the house, he turned towards the open drawing-room door.

She pulled him back. 'Come up to my room.'

His brows rose. 'To your room?'

She waved a hand. 'No one will mind, I promise.'

She chattered to him about how she came to live at this place, about the other boarders who lived there as well, anything to put him at ease, to put her at ease, as well.

When they entered the room, Ariana pointedly ignored the bed, the most prominent piece of furniture and the one that turned her thoughts to what it might be like to share it with him. It unsettled her that he could so quickly arouse such dormant urges in her. If she'd learned anything from her former lover, it had been that her senses were not always the best judge of a man's character.

She took off her cloak and flung it over a chair. He removed his hat and gloves, but not his top coat.

He glanced about the room. 'Where is your copy of the play?'

'On the table.' She pulled off her gloves and gestured to a small table by the window.

He picked up the small, leather-bound volume. 'I will have it read by tomorrow.'

He opened the book and flicked idly through the pages. Quickly snapping it closed, he slipped the book into a pocket of his top coat.

Which passage had caused that reaction? she wondered. Antony's line, perhaps?

There's not a minute of our lives should stretch; Without some pleasure now.

He seemed to gain no pleasure from her company. 'I should return to my studio.'

She had not moved from the doorway. 'When should I come and sit for you tomorrow?'

'At the same time, if it is convenient.' His manner was stiff.

'Tomorrow, then.' She nodded.

He strode towards her. As he passed, she caught his hand. 'I would greatly desire our time together to be pleasant. We started as friends. May we not continue that way?'

Again that mysterious distress flashed through his eyes. What bothered him so?

He stared into her eyes. ''Til tomorrow, Miss Blane.'

She released his hand and he hurried out of the door. From the hallway she watched him descend the stairs and walk through the front door, not even pausing to put on his hat and gloves.

When Jack reached Adam Street he was still reeling with the unexpected pleasure of being in Ariana's company again, as well as the crushing knowledge that she was Tranville's actress.

Jack walked with his head down against the chilly wind from the river. It was even more appalling that Tranville had chosen an actress young enough to be his daughter.

Instead of going back to the studio, Jack called upon his mother. He found her alone in her sitting room doing needle-work by the light of the window.

She looked up as he entered. 'Jack, you are back again.'

He glanced around the room. 'Where is Nancy?'

'She and our maid went to the market.' His mother's smile was tight. 'I fear Nancy finds these four walls tedious. She takes every opportunity to venture out of them.'

He did not respond, but stared blankly at the carpet.

'Sit, Jack.' She indicated a chair. 'Tell me why you are here.'

He wandered over to the mantel, absently moving one of the matched pair of figurines flanking a porcelain clock.

Finally he looked at her. 'Did Tranville tell you that his actress is almost as young as Nancy?'

She stabbed her needle through the cloth. 'That is no concern of mine, and ought to be no concern of yours, Jack.'

'No concern!' He swung away, then turned back to face her. 'Does it not trouble you? How can it not? How are you able to insist I paint this portrait?'

Her eyes creased in pain. 'It is what he wishes.'

He felt his face flush with anger. 'You do not have to do what he wishes, Mother. He treats you abominably.'

Her expression was stern. 'That is your opinion. In my opinion he has enabled me to live in comfort, to rear my children in comfort, to give them an education, a future.'

He gave a dry laugh. 'I could debate what sort of future he's provided Nancy with, but, that aside, have you not more than paid him for what he has done for you?'

She merely pulled her needle through the cloth.

Jack paced before walking to her chair and crouching down so that he was at eye level with her. 'Mother, I will make a living as an artist. I will earn more commissions. If we economise I will have enough to care for you and Nancy. You do not need to accept another shilling from Tranville. You can tell him to go to the devil.'

She gazed directly into his eyes. 'I will not do that.'

He blinked. 'Why not? I promise I can take care of you.'

She went back to her sewing. 'I am certain you will be very successful, my son, but I still will not spurn Lionel.'

Jack stood. 'He has spurned you. In the most insulting way.'

She gazed up at him again. 'I do not need to explain myself to you and I have no intention of doing so. I will not change my arrangement with Lionel.'

It was no use. Where Tranville was concerned his mother was blind and deaf.

'Do you stay for dinner?' she asked, breaking the silence. 'It is not for a few hours yet, but you are welcome to stay. If you are hungry now, I'll send for tea and biscuits.'

He shook his head. To sit down at dinner and pretend this day had not happened would be impossible. 'Do not expect me for dinner. I have much to do tonight.'

She smiled wanly. 'You are still welcome if you change your mind.'

He walked over and kissed her. 'I must go.'

She patted his cheek, but her eyes glistened with tears. 'I hope we will see you tomorrow.'

Once he stepped back out into the winter air, he hurried to his studio and let himself in. He leaned against the door with visions of Tranville hopping from his mother's bed into Ariana's.

Throwing down his gloves and hat, he crossed the room to a bureau where he kept paper. Pulling out several sheets, he grabbed a piece of charcoal and began sketching.

The lines he drew formed into an image of Ariana.

Chapter Four

That evening Ariana sat at a mirror applying rouge to her cheeks and kohl to her eyelids to make her features display well to the highest box seats of Drury Lane Theatre. The dressing-room doors were open wide, so that she and the other actresses could hear their cues to go on stage. In a half-hour the curtain would rise on the evening's performance of *Romeo and Juliet*, and backstage was its usual pandemonium. People shouted. Pieces of set were moved from one side to the other. Actors, actresses and the ballet dancers who entertained between acts ran here and there in all states of dress and undress.

Ariana loved the commotion. She vastly preferred being among it to walking up the stairs to the private dressing room usually reserved for the leading actress. Her mother had demanded that dressing room, and Ariana had not minded in the least. The backstage bustle energised her.

Her mother's reflection appeared behind her in the mirror. Dressed for the comparatively minor role of Lady Capulet, her mother glared at her. 'Have your wits gone begging?'

Ariana set down the tiny brush she'd used to darken her lashes. 'Whatever do you mean, Mama?'

Her mother gestured dramatically in the direction of an invisible someone. 'Lord Tranville pays for your portrait and an entire play and you refuse his escort. You would not even walk with the man.'

Ariana replied to the image in the mirror. 'I was under the impression his financial investment was meant to benefit the theatre, not his vanity.'

Her mother threw up her hands. 'Then you are a bigger fool than ever I imagined.'

Ariana was no fool. She knew precisely what Tranville had hoped to purchase.

She averted her gaze from the mirror. Even if Tranville's motives had merely been gentlemanly, Ariana would not have welcomed his company. She liked being alone with Jack Vernon. She liked the intimacy of it, liked that he could look at her without anyone else as witness.

Ariana held her breath, imagining him raking her with those eyes and rendering on paper what he saw. It felt akin to him touching her.

Her mother tugged at her shoulder, interrupting her reverie. 'Tranville has a great deal of influence here in the theatre. You cannot treat him so shabbily without penalty. You profess to wanting success, but, the way you are bound, you will ruin matters for both of us.'

Ariana did indeed wish for success, success as an actress, not as Tranville's plaything.

The renowned Daphne Blane enjoyed above all things the adoration of men. Her acting career was merely the means of putting herself on display, and her fame came more from the numbers of men with whom her name had been linked over the years than from her roles on stage.

Her single-minded interest in winning the attention of the most prestigious gentlemen had left Daphne Blane little time to be bothered by a daughter. Ariana had been cared for by others.

Theatre people were the ones who showered her with attention. They had dressed little Ariana in costumes, painted her face, even allowed her to walk on stage as part of a scene. The theatre had been where she was happiest. She loved it so much she'd walk on any stage, in any role, merely to be a part of it all.

Ariana drew the line at bartering herself to lustful men, even if they would help her acting career. If that was the price of success, it was too high and too false. She wanted to rise on the merits of her skill, nothing more. She wanted to earn the best roles, the best reviews, the most applause, because her performance deserved it.

Her mother, however, had made one valid point. Ariana might not wish to share Tranville's bed, but she ought not to alienate him completely. He could wield his influence in this theatre for both good and ill.

She turned to look her mother in the eyes. 'Put your mind at ease, Mother. I am well able to manage Lord Tranville. I've managed others like him before.'

'Oh?' Her mother placed fists on her hips. 'Eighteen years old and you are such an expert on men?'

Ariana inhaled a weary breath. 'I am twenty-two, older than you were when you gave birth to me.'

Her mother's eyes scalded. 'Well, one can be very foolish at twenty-two. If I'd had more sense I never would have given birth to you.'

Ariana flinched.

She covered the sting of her mother's words with a tight smile. 'I learn by your mistakes.'

Her mother glanced away, gazing at a tree that seemed to cross in front of the door. Scenery for Act II. 'Well, Tranville attends the performance tonight. Be nice to him in the Green Room.'

Ariana turned back to the mirror and dipped a huge feather puff into the face powder. 'I am always nice to gentlemen.' She merely did not bed them.

Mr Arnold appeared at the dressing room door. 'Ah, there you are, Daphne, my dear. You look lovely as usual.'

Ariana's mother beamed. 'Such flattery. I am dressed as a matron.'

'Nothing could diminish your beauty.' He squeezed her hand and glanced to Ariana. 'Your daughter has inherited every bit of your loveliness. She makes a fine Juliet. Beauty and an acting skill that rivals your own. You must be proud.'

Ariana's mother still smiled, but Ariana caught the hard glint in her eye. 'Yes, I *must* be proud, mustn't I?'

Early the following morning, Jack woke to a messenger bringing him Tranville's first, quite generous, payment of the commission. At least Tranville's money enabled Jack to re-plenish his supplies. He walked the mile to Ludgate Hill where Thomas Clay's establishment offered the finest pigments and purchased enough for several paintings. He returned in time to set up the studio for Ariana's arrival.

As he waited for her, he looked over the several images of Ariana he'd sketched from memory, including the ones he'd drawn after that first fleeting contact with her. The night before he'd filled page after page with her profile, her eyes, her smile; when the light had faded to dusk, he read *Antony and Cleopatra* by lamplight.

She knocked upon his door promptly at two. Jack rose from his drawing table, hastily stacking the sketches. When he opened the door, her face was flushed pink from the winter air.

'Good afternoon, Mr Vernon.' She smiled and her eyes shone with pleasure.

Their impact forced him to avert his gaze. 'Miss Blane, I trust you are well.'

'I am always well,' she responded cheerfully.

He had the presence of mind to assist her in removing her

cloak, too aware of the elegant curve of her neck and, beneath her bonnet, the peek of auburn hair at its nape.

'Were you able to read the play?' she asked, pulling off her gloves and untying the ribbons of her bonnet.

He hung her cloak on a peg. 'I read it all last night.'

She placed her hat and gloves on the table nearby and faced him, still smiling, looking eager for whatever was to come.

His sketches had not done her justice, he realised. He'd not captured that spark of energy, that vivacity that was hers alone. His fingers itched to try again.

But he must attend to the civilities. 'I will make us some tea.' He started for the galley, but she reached it ahead of him.

'I'll do it.' She swept aside the curtain covering the doorway and glanced around the galley. 'There is very little for me to do. You've prepared everything.'

He'd placed the kettle on the fire before she arrived. The tea was in the pot. She poured the water.

'You must allow me to carry the tray,' he said.

She looked up at him with an impish grin. 'Must I?'

He stepped into the space. 'I insist.'

There was no room for both of them, but he thought of that too late. Their arms brushed as she tried to move past him and the mere contact with her caused Jack's senses to flare with an awareness of more than her physical beauty.

She faced him, their bodies almost touching. Reaching up to his face, she gently rubbed his cheek with her finger. 'You have a black smudge.'

Charcoal from his drawings.

He grabbed a cloth and rubbed where she had touched, but he could not erase the explosion of carnal desire she aroused in him. He turned from her and picked up the tray. She followed silently as he carried it to where they'd been sitting the previous day.

She sat in a chair as if that moment of touching had never

happened. 'Where do we begin? Do we discuss how to depict Cleopatra?'

Jack murmured, 'It seems a good way to start.'

She poured the tea and handed him his cup. 'What did you think?'

'Of Cleopatra?'

'Yes.' She lifted her tea.

He placed his cup on the table. 'I was struck by her political ambition. I had not remembered the play that way from my school days.'

She smiled. 'Perhaps you were too romantic as a boy.'

He laughed drily. 'I dare say not, but I understand more of life now. Antony was motivated by passion, but Cleopatra was motivated by ambition.'

She nodded. 'I do agree. She betrays Antony twice. And I doubt she killed herself out of love for him.'

He moved his cup, but did not lift it. 'But his love for her led to his death.'

'And to hers,' she reminded him. 'One could say she was a woman alone merely trying to make her way in the world and that his passion for her led to her downfall.'

He thought of his mother's situation. 'The world has not changed much.'

'Indeed,' she said with a firm tone.

He glanced into her face, remembering it was Tranville who played the role of Antony in her life, not he. The sun from the window shot shades of red through her auburn hair. The look she gave him in return was soft and companionable.

Jack had to glance away. 'It is an odd play. More a history than a romance.'

She laughed. 'It is a good thing. There is enough romancing from Mr Kean in the play as it is.'

He glanced at her in surprise. 'You do not like Kean as your leading man?'

She shook her head. 'Not at all. He smells of whisky and he is too short.'

'The celebrated Mr Kean?'

Her face puckered as if she'd eaten a lemon. 'I dare say he shows more favourably in the theatre boxes.'

Her frank tone made him relax and pushed thoughts of Tranville out of his mind. He felt as if they'd returned to Somerset House.

They began discussing how Cleopatra might be depicted and if she should be seated or standing. Jack was impatient to draw her.

She put down her teacup and sat on the edge of her chair. 'Shall I pose now? Perhaps as Cleopatra on her throne?'

She straightened her spine and raised her chin, instantly transforming herself into a haughty queen who looked down on the rest of the world.

He was intrigued. 'Hold that pose.'

He moved his drawing table closer to her chair and placed a clean sheet of paper on its angled surface. He sketched quickly, using charcoal and pastels, not thinking, allowing the image to come directly from his eye to his hand.

She remained very still, almost like a statue.

He put that sketch aside and replaced it with a fresh piece of paper. 'Stand now and move.'

'Move?'

He twirled his hand as an example. 'Move around in front of me. Like Cleopatra would move.'

The natural quick and graceful movements that had entranced him heretofore were replaced by a regal step, back and forth.

He sketched hurriedly.

'I feel a bit silly,' she said as she crossed in front of him.

'You do not look silly,' he responded. 'This is precisely what I need.'

He tried her in other poses, seated and standing, producing ten pastel drawings that gave him ideas of how a final painting might appear.

He looked through them.

'May I see?' She walked over to stand beside him at the drawing table, bringing with her the scent of rose water. She examined each drawing, one after the other.

'Remarkable!' She looked through them again, setting three of them side by side. 'You were drawing so fast, I never dreamed you could make them look so much like me.'

He sorted through them again. 'They are still not right. I am not sure why.'

He'd set his earlier sketches of her on the floor next to the drawing table. She saw them. 'What are these?'

She picked them up and went through them. When she came to the ones he had done after Somerset House, she looked up at him with a puzzled expression.

'Some sketches I made earlier,' he replied, deliberately vague.

'These are different from the others.' She stared at them. 'I look…' She paused. 'Alluring.'

He did not respond.

She broke into a smile. 'You drew these after the exhibition, did you not?

He would not lie. 'I did.'

'I like them,' she said simply and he felt himself flush with pleasure. 'You make me look enticing.'

'It is not enough.' He was glad she did not question him about why he'd drawn her that day; he was uncertain he could answer her.

She looked at him as if she could see into his thoughts to all he'd felt about her that day, feelings forbidden him now, but he would not think of that. Today he merely wished to paint her.

'Cleopatra must look enticing.' She looked around the

room and found a *chaise-longue*. She pushed it closer to his writing table and reclined upon it, propping herself on one arm and turning to face him directly. The effect was both sensuous and regal.

Jack's breath hitched at the sight of her.

She dropped her role as Cleopatra. 'You do not like this one?' She started to change position.

He held up a hand. 'Do not move. Let me draw you that way.'

She resumed her pose. 'We are doing well today, are we not?'

'Yes.' He concentrated on the lines he was drawing.

'I feel we are rubbing together as well as when we met at the exhibition.'

He glanced up at her, but did not respond.

She went on. 'What happened yesterday, do you think? I was convinced you were unhappy with me. Will you tell me now what it was?'

He stopped. 'There was nothing.'

She tilted her head, then seemed to remember why she was there and returned to her original pose. 'I did not imagine it. My presence distressed you.'

He focused on his drawing. 'Perhaps my mood was due to something else not concerning you.'

'Then tell me what made you unhappy,' she said in a kind, genuine tone.

'I cannot recall now,' he lied. 'Likely it was nothing.'

She remained quiet for a while and Jack filled in the colour of her dress, the flawless tint of her skin.

'Do you have many friends in London?' she asked after a time.

'Not many,' he answered. 'I am from Bath.'

'Are you?' she said brightly. 'I played *The Beggar's Opera* in Bath. Did you see it? That was two years ago.'

He shook his head. 'I would have been in Spain.'

Her expression turned sympathetic, but she did not pursue that topic. 'I do not have many friends in London either,' she said instead.

'Does not your mother live here?'

She waved a hand, then remembered to return to her pose. 'My mother is not precisely a friend. One needs friends for entertainment.'

Jack had little room in his life for entertainment. 'Entertainment.'

'You know. Walks through the park, visiting the shops, sharing an ice at Gunter's—things like that.' She paused. 'There are my theatre friends, of course, but most of their entertainment involves taverns.'

Jack let her conversation wash over him like the water of a clear spring on a summer day. It kept him from concentrating too hard on his work and allowed the lines of the drawing to flow. He replaced one paper with another and began to draw just her face, filling the page with it.

'You and I should be friends,' she went on.

His hand stopped and he stared at her again.

She smiled at him. 'Then I could call you Jack. And you could call me Ariana.'

Before he could form a response, there was a rap at the door. Jack put down his pastel to answer it, but the door opened.

Lord Tranville walked in. 'Well, well, well.' He removed his hat and bowed to Ariana. 'Good day, my dear.' He turned to Jack. 'I thought I would stop by and see how things were progressing.'

'Tranville.' Jack went rigid. 'It is the second meeting. What progress did you expect?' He placed the sketch of her on the *chaise-longue* on the bottom of the pile.

'I should like to see.' Without waiting for permission, Tranville stepped behind Jack's drawing table.

Jack kept his hand on the stack of drawings, so that Tranville could see only the one on top, one of Ariana seated upon the chair.

Tranville glanced over at Ariana. 'You make a lovely model, my dear.'

She did not respond.

He examined the drawing again and shook his head. 'You look nothing like Cleopatra, however.' He turned to Jack. 'For God's sake, she needs to look Egyptian.'

Jack's fingers flexed into a fist.

Ariana spoke up. 'Gracious, my lord. You expect too much of a first day of posing. Did you think I would be in full costume and theatre paint?'

Jack felt fully capable of defending his work to the likes of Tranville. He resented the older man's intrusion, but resented more the reminder of his claim on Ariana.

Tranville smiled at Ariana, and Jack noticed his eyes flick over her reclining form. 'If you are happy with the sitting, my dear, then I am content.'

Jack twisted away, hiding the disgust on his face he knew he could not disguise.

'Jack, when do you finish for the day?' Tranville asked. 'I am here to escort Miss Blane home.'

Jack's shoulders stiffened.

Ariana sat up. 'That is not necessary, sir.'

'I cannot allow you to walk alone.' Tranville tossed Jack the sort of glance that passed between men when they expected to make a conquest.

That Tranville would flaunt his affair with Ariana to the son of his former mistress made Jack's blood boil. Only his promise to his mother kept him from grabbing Tranville by the collar and tossing him out on to the cold pavement.

'We are not finished.' Ariana resumed her Cleopatra pose.

Tranville walked over to a chair and sat. 'I do not mind waiting.'

Jack stacked the drawings and put his pastels back in their box. He would not draw another line with Tranville there. 'We are finished.'

Ariana shot to her feet and glared at Jack. Without a word she picked up the teacups and tray and carried them into the galley.

'You must not do that,' Tranville said. 'It is servant's work.'

'I do not mind.' She used the same inflection Tranville had used previously.

Jack followed her in to the galley. 'I will see to the tea things.'

'We were not finished. Why did you say we were?' She spoke quietly, but seemed to bristle with annoyance.

'I cannot work with him watching.'

She crossed her arms over her chest. 'When do I return, then?'

He shrugged. 'Tomorrow?'

'Very well. I'll arrive at two, if that will be convenient for you.' Her voice was clipped.

'Two o'clock, then,' he responded in kind.

She pushed past him, back into the studio.

Tranville stood with her cloak, ready to assist her. He draped it over her shoulders, his hands lingering.

Jack turned away, pretending to see to his dishes. He did not turn back until he heard the door close behind them.

Chapter Five

Ariana reluctantly took Tranville's arm. The pleasantries he uttered as they walked to the end of the street were no more than an annoying buzz in her ears.

She trembled, so full of anger she could barely contain herself. She did not know who made her angrier, Tranville for intruding or Jack for not tossing him out.

She thought of him as Jack now, already feeling an intimacy with him even though he had only begun to relax in her presence. It had been a most curious experience to sit for him. She felt his every glance, but also felt that the paper, the colours, the lines kept him at a distance from her.

If only Tranville had not swept in—

'What time do you pose for Jack tomorrow?' she heard Tranville ask.

She avoided answering the man, asking a question of her own instead. 'You seem on very familiar terms with Mr Vernon. What is your connection with him?'

He gave a trifling laugh. 'Jack is the son of a friend. I have known him most of his life.'

'Oh?' she said, truly interested. 'Are you a friend of his father?'

Tranville paused for a moment. 'His mother, actually, although I was acquainted with his father before the man's untimely death.'

'I see.' A friend of the mother and merely acquainted with a deceased father? She pumped him for more information. 'When did Mr Vernon's father die?'

He waved a hand, as if the man's death had no importance at all. 'Sixteen—seventeen years past or some such.'

'I would have been only six years old.' Let him be reminded of the differences in their ages. 'Mr Vernon must have been quite young as well.'

He frowned. 'Indeed.'

Had Jack's mother been a conquest of Tranville's? It might explain much about Jack's seeming animosity towards the man. They crossed Maiden Lane. Almost home, thank God.

'You did not tell me what time you were expected at Jack's.' He sounded as if he were trying to disguise his annoyance.

'Two o'clock.' She hated answering him.

'I will come to escort you,' he said.

She halted and released his arm, facing him directly. 'Sir, I would beg you not come at all and certainly do not intrude on the sitting again.'

He looked affronted. 'I beg your pardon?'

'Do not come,' she repeated, saying each word slowly and clearly. 'You ruined the sitting. It broke Mr Vernon's concentration. Could you not see that?'

His face turned red.

Forcing a charming smile, she changed tactics. 'Now do not become cross with me. Anyone entering at that moment would have done the same.' She took his arm again and they began walking. 'I am very cognisant of how much you wish this portrait to be a success for the theatre. In order to achieve that end, the artist will need privacy.'

'Did Jack tell you that?' His arm tensed.

She made herself laugh. 'Indeed not! But anyone who knows anything about posing for portraits realises that privacy is paramount.' She, of course, had only a day's knowledge of sitting for a portrait, but she trusted Tranville knew even less.

Ariana spied a pretty young woman glancing at them from across the street. The young woman's companion was an equally young and handsome man who gazed upon the young woman as if the sun rose and set upon her.

Ariana envied them.

Tranville spoke again. 'Surely I might walk you to Jack's with no disruption.'

Ariana hated that she must cater to this man, merely because of the power he wielded. She sighed inwardly and looked up at Tranville. 'Very well, you may call for me a quarter of an hour before two and walk me to the artist's studio.'

His mouth widened into a broad smile.

She shook a finger at him. 'But you must not arrive to walk me back home, because it is never certain precisely what time we shall finish.'

His brow creased. 'If the hour is late, it will not be safe for a young woman—'

She cut him off. 'If it is late, I shall insist Mr Vernon walk me home.' She made her voice sound as if this was not the circumstance she most desired. 'I dare say it is the least he can do for all that you must have paid him.'

'Very well.' This time he stroked her palm with his thumb. 'I will do as you wish of me.'

She withdrew her hand. They were finally at her door.

'Good day, sir,' she said with a curtsy.

He obviously hoped to be invited inside. He reached for her hand again, but she opened the door.

'Wait.' He gripped the door. 'Will I see you tonight in the Green Room?'

'Perhaps.' She plastered on a smile and hurried inside.

* * *

Jack begged off dinner at his mother's again that evening. After seeing Tranville's manner toward Ariana, Jack could not face his mother. He spent the rest of the afternoon staring at the drawings he'd made of Ariana, forcing himself to think of the task as an artistic challenge.

He finally set them all aside and donned his top coat, needing the brisk winter air to cool his emotions. He burned with anger and resentment.

Head down against the wind, Jack crossed the Strand and strode toward Covent Garden, avoiding Henrietta Street and memories of Ariana's bedchamber and fears that Tranville might have visited it. All he desired was a meal of mutton and ale in some noisy tavern smelling of ordinary men partaking of ordinary pleasures. He wandered to Bow Street and found such a place, seating himself at a small table against one wall.

The man seated at the next table insisted upon befriending him. The man turned out to be an actor, no great surprise since Drury Lane was only a few streets away.

'I perform with Kean and the incomparable Daphne Blane,' the man said. 'You must come to see me perform. I'll get you in.'

It meant seeing Ariana as Juliet again. Jack accepted the invitation.

No one questioned the actor's new friend when they entered the theatre. The man told Jack to stand at a spot in the wings with an excellent view of the stage, albeit a sideways one. Before the play began Jack looked around, expecting at any moment to glimpse her. He saw Ariana in the wings on the other side, but she did not see him.

Jack's newfound friend played Abraham, a Montague servant who had a few lines and a swordfight in Act I. No longer on stage, he stood next to Jack, watching the performance.

'This is an excellent portrayal of Juliet,' the man whispered to Jack. 'Best I've ever seen. Ariana is Daphne Blane's daughter so her acting skill is no surprise.' He laughed quietly. 'The word is that Daphne does not know which of the many gentlemen bedding her at the time sired the girl.'

Everyone knew that theatre people lived by very loose standards, with no expectations to mix in polite society, but Ariana's story seemed a sad one.

Jack watched her on stage, playing a beloved daughter. She was completely convincing as an innocent, trusting young girl about to be thrown into a cauldron of passion and family strife. When Ariana had posed as Cleopatra, she'd been equally convincing, turning herself into a jaded, cunning, sensuous queen.

He wanted his portrait also to reveal what was uniquely her. That she was forthright, unafraid and determined.

He frowned. Perhaps that was merely the role she played with him. Did she play another sort of woman for Tranville?

He ran a hand through his hair. He must not allow himself to care about her. She was a commission, nothing more. He need only create a decent painting.

On stage she recited the lines, '*My bounty is as boundless as the sea, My love as deep; the more I give to thee, The more I have, for both are infinite—*'

Jack closed his eyes. Her words fired his senses. Ever since Spain, he'd numbed himself against disappointment, loss and horror. Ariana threatened to cut through those defences and make him feel again.

Jack suspected his theatre companion could take him to the Green Room if he requested it. But if Tranville was there and fawning over Ariana, Jack could not stomach it.

The play was over and his companion joined the final bows on stage. Afterwards he invited Jack, not to the Green Room, but to return to the tavern for more drink. Some of the other young actors joined them. As they walked out of the theatre, Jack came close enough to Ariana to reach out and touch her. Her mother had her in tow and was so busy talking to her that Ariana did not see him.

He let the opportunity pass.

At the tavern Jack was content to observe his companion with his friends. Jack was included in round after round of drink, but was not really a part of their circle. As he watched, the drink rendered them quicker to laughter, to anger, to maudlin sentimentality. He made note of the expressions on their faces, their gestures, their postures, all tinted in shades of brown in the dim tavern light.

Jack felt the haze of too much drink and eventually bade them goodnight. He walked out to the street and turned the corner into an area that was dark and narrow. Sounds of the tavern's revelry echoed against brick walls.

Suddenly it was as if he was back in Badajoz. The shadowy figures crossing the street in front of him, darting into alleys or standing in doorways, suddenly seemed about to attack. The good-natured laughter from distant taverns sounded like the demented laughter of Badajoz. Happy bellowing turned into screams. Jack plastered himself against the cold wall of a building and pressed his hands over his ears.

He was not in Badajoz, he told himself, but his senses refused to listen. His heart pounded, his muscles tensed, and a voice in his head shouted, 'Run!'

He ran. Ran as if drunken soldiers pursued him as they had in Badajoz. Ran as if he were escaping visions of carnage and brutality and violent lust.

His lungs burned by the time he reached his studio and pulled the key from his pocket. Panting, he opened the door and stumbled inside. Visions of the soldiers holding down the French woman returned. Again her son wailed for them to stop. Again Jack saw the face of Edwin Tranville, smiling drunkenly.

'Come join the fun,' the spectre said. 'Plenty for you, as well.'

Jack staggered into his bedchamber and pulled out the chamber pot. Kneeling over it, he vomited until nothing was left but dry heaves.

The next morning he woke with a start. His mouth tasted foul, his head throbbed with pain, and the room stank of vomit.

He rose, still dressed in the clothes of the previous night, and picked up the chamber pot, retching as he carried it out back to clean it.

Afterwards, he pumped clean water into a large pitcher. He used the water to rinse out his mouth, brush his teeth and wash himself, all the while his head reeling and his stomach threatening to rebel.

After he managed to change into clean clothes, he made his way to his mother's residence to beg for breakfast and pots and pots of tea to rid himself of the hammer and anvil in his head.

Wilson let him in and he went directly to the dining room, expecting to see food set out to eat.

He did not expect to see Tranville seated at the table, cup in hand, reading a newspaper.

'Jack.' Tranville nodded in greeting. He was alone in the room.

Jack put a hand on the doorjamb to steady the growing rage inside him. He did not nod in return.

Tranville chuckled and returned to his newspaper.

The need for food and to prove Tranville could not intimidate him prevented Jack from turning around and walking out. He went to the sideboard and found it more generously filled than usual, kippers and slices of ham, in addition to the usual cooked eggs and sliced bread. The kippers made his stomach reel almost as violently as Tranville's presence. Jack chose two eggs and slices of bread, spreading them with butter and raspberry jam.

He chose the chair directly opposite Tranville and poured himself a cup of tea from the pot in the centre of the table.

'You are asking yourself if I did indeed spend the night here.' Tranville popped a forkful of kipper into his mouth. 'I spent a very pleasant night.'

Jack glared at him, but refused to be baited.

Tranville tried again. 'I did consider your sister's presence, if you are wondering.' He lifted his tea cup to his mouth. 'But I decided she is old enough to know what is what. Old enough for a husband, I dare say.' He laughed again. 'Besides, she had already retired when I arrived. I came after the play was done.'

After the play? Tranville had not spent the night with Ariana, then. Despite his resolve to think of Ariana as merely a commission, Jack expelled a relieved breath. It was quickly replaced with anger that Tranville had come to his mother instead. 'It is a wonder you considered anyone's feelings but your own.'

Tranville's eyes burned with anger. 'Your mother did not mind.'

Jack gripped the edge of the table. He held Tranville's gaze. 'Take care how you speak.' Even a promise to his mother had its limits.

Tranville made a placating gesture. 'Now, now. You know I have the highest regard for your mother.'

'Regard for her?' Jack looked daggers at him.

Tranville's voice turned low. 'What passes between your mother and me is none of your affair and you would do well to remember that.'

Those were almost the exact words his mother had spoken to him.

Tranville slapped his palm on the table. 'Know your place, boy,' he said with more energy. 'Do not question a peer of the realm about his affairs.'

Jack leaned forwards. 'I will not see my mother hurt by you.'

Tranville adopted the expression of a reasonable man. 'Your mother understands my needs, boy. That should be the end of it for you.' He stuffed a piece of ham into his mouth and chewed.

Jack's gaze did not waver. 'She knows you are bedding Miss Blane?'

Tranville gave a half-smile and lifted a finger in the air. 'Ah, but I am not bedding Miss Blane. Yet.' He took a swallow of tea. 'Otherwise I should not be here.'

Tranville had not bedded Ariana? At all? This news stunned Jack. For a moment he felt paralysed. Until he realised Tranville was using Jack's mother to slake his lust for Ariana. It was enraging on all accounts.

Jack pushed his chair back, ready to vault across the table and lunge for Tranville's throat, when his mother swept into the room. 'Why, Jack, I did not know you were here.'

Still trembling with rage, he stood and gave his mother a kiss. 'For breakfast.'

She patted his cheek. 'You are always welcome.'

She walked over to Tranville, who also stood. 'Good morning, Lionel.'

He kissed her on the lips, sliding a glance to Jack as he did so. 'My dear, allow me to serve you from the sideboard.'

He held a chair for her and she lowered herself into it gracefully. 'I would be most grateful. Just an egg, I think.'

He brought her the egg and returned to his seat to pour her tea for her.

Beneath the table Jack's hands were clenched into fists.

Nancy walked in, rubbing her eyes. Never cheerful in the morning, she peered at Jack and mumbled, 'Morning.' Then she noticed Tranville. 'Oh!'

He stood and bowed. 'Good morning, Nancy, my dear. Will you allow me to serve you?'

She looked confused. 'I can do it. Please sit.'

When she returned to the table, Tranville popped up and pulled out a chair for her. 'Did you sleep well?'

'Yes, thank you,' she responded politely.

As she ate, Nancy glanced from her mother to Tranville and back. She turned to Jack, her expression questioning.

He shrugged.

Nancy finished one cup of tea and poured herself another. 'Lord Tranville, I saw you on the street yesterday afternoon. Who was the young lady with you?'

Jack darted a glance to his mother, who merely stared down at her plate.

With no hesitation Tranville responded, 'It must have been Miss Blane. I escorted her back from Jack's studio.'

Nancy shook her head in bewilderment. 'From Jack's studio!'

Jack broke in. 'Lord Tranville commissioned me to paint Miss Blane's portrait.'

Nancy's eyes widened. 'It was the younger Miss Blane, the actress who played Juliet. I thought she looked familiar.'

Tranville leaned towards Nancy. 'I am convinced the young Miss Blane will be a great success, as great as her mother. She will be an asset to the theatre.'

'I see,' murmured Nancy, but she looked uneasy.

Jack rose and put another piece of bread on his plate.

Tranville pulled out his watch, an expensive gold time-piece, and checked the time. 'It is late. I must be off.'

Jack returned to his seat.

'Must you leave so early, Lionel?' Jack's mother appeared crestfallen.

Tranville leaned down and kissed her on top of her head. 'Business, my dear. I'll call upon you again, I promise.' He put his hand on Nancy's shoulder. 'A pleasure to see you again.' He nodded to Jack and walked out of the room.

Jack could not even look at his mother.

Nancy seemed to force a smile. 'Well. It is the younger Miss Blane who sits for you. Tell us, is she as pretty up close as she was on stage?'

Jack fought to keep his expression bland. 'I would say so.'

Nancy went on, sounding determinedly cheerful. 'How exciting. How is the painting progressing?'

'I have hardly begun.'

She kept on. 'I should like to see her up close. When does she next come for a sitting?'

'Today at two.'

'May I come and meet her?' She gave him a look that dared him to refuse her. 'I promise I will not stay and distract you.'

Jack glanced at his mother, whose face had become pinched.

'I can think of no reason to object,' their mother said, looking as if she wanted anything else but to give her daughter permission to meet the woman who was to replace her in Tranville's bed, a woman in the freshest bloom of youth and beauty.

Jack could think of no excuse to keep Nancy away. 'Very well.' His glance went from his mother to Nancy. 'Come at two.'

Chapter Six

Nancy picked through the bundled herbs at the Covent Garden stall, selecting a bunch of lavender and holding it to her nose before placing it in the basket her friend Michael held for her. She reached in her reticule for her coin purse.

'I will pay,' Michael gave the vendor a coin. 'It will be my gift to you.'

'Thank you, Michael. You are too good.'

'It is my pleasure,' he said.

They strolled past vegetable and fruit stalls tended by red-cheeked vendors bundled in wool, their breath making clouds as they hawked their wares.

'Thank you for taking me out, too,' Nancy said. 'I sometimes think I shall go mad sitting in the drawing room all day watching Mama do needlework.'

'Again, the pleasure is all mine.'

She sighed and glanced away as they walked.

'Something is troubling you,' he said.

'Troubling me?' She glanced back at him.

Michael was not quite as tall as her brother. He was thinner, as well, but to Nancy he was a dependable friend and much too perceptive.

'Nothing troubles me,' she stated emphatically.

He threaded her arm through his and looked upon her with his kind blue eyes. 'You cannot fool me, you know.'

His face was so dear, so open and earnest, but she was not even certain she could put into words what troubled her.

'Are you concerned about your mother?' he asked.

She pulled away. 'Why do you think I would be concerned about Mama?'

His smile turned conciliatory. 'A mere guess.'

They walked on in silence, no longer touching. Nancy stopped in front of a stall holding cages of hedgehogs, popular as pets because they ate the beetles that plagued London houses.

She leaned down and touched the snout of a baby hedgehog poking through the slats of his cage. She liked how Michael never pressured her to speak, like Mama sometimes did, wanting to know anything that distressed her. Her mother, like Michael, would also have perceived her upset and she certainly could not confide in her mother.

Nancy glanced up at Michael, who merely smiled with unspoken sympathy. She stood again. 'Oh, Michael.' She slipped her arm through his and they strolled on. 'I am not certain what upsets me.'

He merely squeezed her hand.

They passed by a flower stall. He stopped and purchased a small bouquet of flowers and handed them to her. She smiled. He was always giving her small things. He was her very best friend and the only friend she had in London. Even though she only really met him last summer, she felt as if she'd known him her whole life. Perhaps she could talk to him a little.

'How much do you know of my family?' she asked him.

He did not answer right away. 'I know your father died when you were very young. I know that—' He hesitated and took a breath. 'I grew up in Bath. I know that Lord Tran-ville…supported your family.'

He said it without censure and it gave her the courage to go on. 'It was very wrong for my mother to accept Lord Tranville's help, but I am convinced it is due to the grand passion they have for each other.'

She glanced at him to see if he wore that same sceptical look as Jack. Michael seemed only to be listening.

She went on. 'I was used to his—his visits to my mother from time to time, but last night—' She swallowed. 'I think he spent the night with her because he was at the breakfast table this morning. It bothered me.'

'Did it?' Michael remarked.

She stopped him and looked up into his face. 'Remember yesterday when we saw him with that young lady?'

He nodded.

'That bothered me, too.' Her throat tightened. 'It was that actress, the one who played Juliet. It is she Jack is painting.'

'Jack is painting her?' He sounded surprised.

She nodded. 'Lord Tranville commissioned the portrait. I—I think she may have some designs on Lord Tranville.'

'What makes you think so?' His calm tone soothed her.

'Oh—' she sighed again '—just a feeling. When I mentioned seeing her with Lord Tranville everyone started acting strangely. Jack was there, too, and he acted strangest of all.'

Michael reached up and brushed a lock of hair off her cheek, tucking it behind her ear. 'There is likely some other explanation, but let us formulate a plan to discover what the true reason may be.'

She felt all the tension leave her. 'You will help me?'

He smiled at her. 'Of course I will.'

She took his arm again and started walking. 'What are you doing today at two o'clock?'

Shortly before two, Nancy and Michael rapped on Jack's door.

Jack was still in his shirtsleeves when he answered it.

'I hope you do not mind I brought Michael.' Nancy crossed the threshold and took off her cloak.

'Indeed not.' Jack shook Michael's hand. 'No classes today, Michael?'

'Not today.' Michael set the basket on the table near the door. 'I was at liberty to escort your sister to the market.'

'We brought a tin of biscuits for tea.' Nancy hung up her cloak. 'Shall I put a the kettle on?' She took the tin from the basket and handed it to him.

'You are staying for tea?' Jack did not look happy.

The plan she and Michael had concocted was that they would stay for tea so Nancy would have a better opportunity to assess Miss Blane. 'It will enable us to have a real chat.' She walked to the galley.

Jack followed her. 'You merely wanted to meet Miss Blane, you said.'

She smiled sweetly at him. 'It would be impolite not to chat with her.'

Michael approached Jack. 'My father sends his regards. I received a letter from him yesterday.'

How like him to create a diversion. Nancy gave him a grateful look.

Jack answered him. 'He is well, I hope.'

'In excellent health.' Michael gestured toward a stretched canvas on the floor. 'Do you need any help with that? I'm accustomed to it with my father.'

'No help. I have finished. It only lacks tidying up.' Jack brought out a broom and swept up the scraps of linen and wood that were on the floor.

'I'll get those.' Michael took the dustpan from Jack's hands. 'Is there somewhere for this outside?'

'Out of the door in the galley.' Jack picked up the stretched canvas and set it against the wall.

Michael brushed past Nancy on his way to the door. 'How are we doing?' he asked in a low voice.

'Splendid so far.' Nancy leaned her head out of the galley doorway. 'I can only find three cups,' she called to Jack.

'Look behind the jars of pigment,' Jack responded.

She rummaged through the cabinet and found the extra cups, setting one on the tray. 'Will Miss Blane be prompt? I can pour the hot water now.'

Jack did not look pleased. 'She was on time yesterday.'

Nancy took a breath, refusing to be daunted.

'I need to finish dressing.' Jack disappeared into his bed-chamber.

Michael came in from outside. 'We are staying for tea, I gather.'

Nancy grinned. 'We are indeed.' She carried the tea tray into the studio. 'Help me rearrange the furniture.'

They pushed four chairs into a cosy group with the tea table in the centre. Nancy took out the flowers Michael had purchased for her. 'I'm going to put these out. I'll take them home later.' She found an empty jar to use as a vase and placed the flowers on the table. 'Thank you, Michael. We should have plenty of time to take her measure.'

Jack emerged from the bedchamber still buttoning his coat. He surveyed the scene. 'You cannot stay long, Nancy. I've work to do.'

A knock sounded at the door and Nancy's heart jumped into her throat.

'I'll answer it.' She reached the door before Jack could protest.

When she opened it, it was Lord Tranville she saw first. He stood with Miss Blane on his arm.

'Lord Tranville!' Nancy's spirits fell. This seemed a confirmation of her fears.

'Nancy, my dear.' Tranville gave her a peck on the cheek and stepped aside so Miss Blane could enter.

Miss Blane looked at Nancy and broke into a smile. 'You are the sister—'

'Jack's sister,' Tranville broke in.

Her attention was on Nancy. 'I remember your portrait from the exhibition.' She extended her hand. 'I am Ariana Blane.'

She remembered the portrait? Nancy could not help but be complimented. She curtsied. 'I am Miss Vernon.'

'I am so pleased to meet you.'

Lord Tranville was poised to assist her with her cloak, but Miss Blane took it off herself and hung it on a peg next to Nancy's.

Jack stepped forwards. 'Allow me to present our friend to you.' He gestured to Michael. 'Lord Tranville, Miss Blane, this is our friend Mr Harper.'

'I am honoured.' Michael bowed.

'How nice to meet you,' Miss Blane said, sounding as if she really meant it. 'I believe I saw both of you on the street yesterday. Is that not a coincidence? Oh, look, you have tea.' She turned to Jack. 'You should not have gone to so much trouble.'

'My sister did it all,' he responded.

Lord Tranville immediately chose the best chair and held it out for Miss Blane. 'I cannot stay long.' He took the chair next to her for himself.

Michael fetched a fifth cup and chair while the others sat and Nancy started to pour.

Conversation predictably began with the weather and how they all hoped February would bring warmer temperatures.

Miss Blane turned to Nancy. 'Let me say again how glad I am to have seen the lovely portrait of you. I do not know when I have been so impressed.'

'She's a very pretty girl.' Tranville spoke as if Nancy were not seated across the table from him. 'I believe her looks will bring her excellent marriage prospects.'

Nancy lowered her head in embarrassment.

Jack glared. 'That, sir, is family business.'

Tranville gave him an ingratiating smile. 'Jack, my boy, you know that what concerns your family, concerns me. You may rest assured that I will be on the lookout for suitors for your sister. My position gives me an advantage. I know the best people. I dare say I can discover more than one man who will find her acceptable.'

Nancy's cheeks grew hot.

Miss Blane laughed. 'You jest, sir, surely. It is very plain that Miss Vernon can attract her own suitors.'

Tranville gave her a patient look. 'She looks well enough, indeed. Her looks and youth will make my job easier, I am certain.'

Jack looked as if he would explode. 'It is not your job, sir.'

Even Michael looked angry.

'Stop talking nonsense, Tranville,' Miss Blane ordered in a good-humoured voice. 'Your joke is falling flat. If you were onstage, I would close the curtain and bring out the ballet dancers.'

Tranville looked about to defend himself, but Miss Blane quickly turned to Nancy. 'Tell me, Miss Vernon, have you seen any fashion prints for this month? There seems to be a tendency for dresses to have ruffles at the hem, which I adore. I must order one.'

She had deliberately altered the subject, Nancy realised. 'I think it makes for a pretty change.' Nancy turned to Michael. 'Do you not think so, Michael?'

Michael looked as surprised as Nancy, but he rose to the occasion. 'It is rather like the embellishments one sees in the decorative arts these days, I would say. A new trend.'

Jack seemed also to be staring at Miss Blane in astonishment.

'Michael is a student of architecture at the Royal Academy,' Nancy explained to Miss Blane.

Jack turned to Lord Tranville, but his expression was still

rigid. 'Mr Harper is Sir Cedric's son. You know Sir Cedric, the portrait artist in Bath?'

'The fellow who got you into this business?' Tranville's tone was deprecating. 'Paints the people who come for the waters?'

'He is a member of the Royal Academy.' Jack looked thunderous again.

'Hats…' Miss Blane turned to Nancy again. 'What do you know of the latest in hats?'

Nancy knew nothing of the latest in hats, but she babbled on about ribbons and lace and different shapes until Lord Tranville stood.

'I must be about a matter of important business.' He bowed to Nancy, but more pointedly to Miss Blane. 'Do forgive me for leaving.'

Jack stood, but made no effort to walk him to the door. Miss Blane continued to chatter about hats. When the door closed behind Lord Tranville, she abruptly abandoned the topic.

When Jack sat again, Miss Blane lifted her cup. 'Well, this is lovely.' She took a sip and slid a glance towards Jack. 'Have you showed your sister and Mr Harper our work so far?'

'I have not.' Jack still frowned.

'Oh, do show them,' she pleaded. 'I should like their opinion.'

'I would like to see them,' Nancy added.

Jack was still fuming inside at Tranville's comments about Nancy. The audacity of the man to assume he had any right to arrange Nancy's life. He rose reluctantly. 'The sketches are in the back room. I'll get them.'

He strode into his bedchamber.

Tranville thought some man of his choosing would find Nancy *acceptable*? Jack remembered the men Tranville befriended in the army, men like Tranville himself, more concerned with their own ambition than with the welfare of the men serving under them.

Jack opened the large trunk where he kept his drawings. He riffled through the stack he'd produced the day before, selecting only ten of them. When he put back the rest, he noticed the corner of a large leather envelope peeking out from beneath many other drawings he'd produced. It was the envelope containing his drawings from the war, from Badajoz.

He closed his eyes as images of that night flashed in his mind, as they had so vividly the night before. Edwin deserved to be punished for it and Tranville deserved the shame of having such a son.

Jack slammed the lid of the trunk. He, Deane and Landon had chosen to keep that secret. Jack had given his word.

He wondered again what had happened to the French woman and her son. Had Deane managed to find them a place of safety? Had they survived the war? Did they dream of that night like he did?

Jack shook the thoughts from his mind and picked up yesterday's drawings and carried them into the studio. Michael removed the tea tray and flowers and Jack placed the drawings on the table.

He showed them one by one and the lively discussion that ensued helped bring him back to the world that was his refuge. The world of his art.

'I like the reclining figure,' Michael said. 'Its composition is pleasing. Very reminiscent of Titian's Venuses.'

Miss Blane laughed. 'Mr Harper! Those paintings showed Venus without clothing. I've seen the engravings.'

Michael turned red. 'I meant in the composition, the pose.'

She placed her hand on his. 'I know that is what you meant.' She turned to Jack. 'Imagine if your work was compared to Titian.'

Jack shook his head. 'I very much doubt that would happen.' He stared at his sketch of the reclining Ariana. God help him, he was picturing her as Titian's nude Venus.

'You are good enough,' Ariana said.

He raised his head and his gaze met hers.

Nancy pointed to the picture. 'It is very nice, but there is nothing in it to say this is Cleopatra. I thought you were to paint her as Cleopatra.'

Her comment was very close to Tranville's the previous day. 'This is merely the first step,' he said tightly.

Ariana picked up the sketch. 'I have no idea how an Egyptian queen would appear.' She turned to Jack. 'Would it not be splendid if I truly looked the part?'

Nancy said, 'You must have such a costume in the theatre.'

'I dare say such costumes exist.' She gazed away in thought. 'I should love to look as if plucked directly from an Egyptian vase.'

As they spoke the painting was beginning to form in Jack's mind. Ariana draped in fine linens, gold jewellery adorning her neck and wrists, her *chaise*, an Egyptian sofa, pyramids in the background.

'There are prints of Egyptian friezes and sculptures we could view at the Royal Academy,' Michael said. 'If you wish, we could view them today.'

'You could arrange that?' Ariana asked him.

'Of course, he could!' Nancy jumped to her feet. 'Let us go right now. May we, Jack?'

He liked the idea of using real images from the period to inform the work. 'Give me time to get my sketchbook and pencil.'

Soon they were walking down The Strand toward Somerset House, the wind from the Thames fluttering the ladies' skirts and threatening to whip Jack's hat off his head. Michael and Nancy were ahead, their heads together in deep conversation.

Jack heard a snippet of it. 'It was not at all what I expected…'

Nancy spoke about meeting Ariana, he suspected. Jack should have anticipated Tranville would be with her. This portrait was merely a part of Tranville's pursuit of her, no doubt. Had Tranville bestowed other gifts upon her?

Ariana's manner towards Tranville was a puzzle. She seemed to ignore him, except when deflecting his talk of arranging nuptials for Nancy. The damned audacity of the man.

Ariana held Jack's arm as they walked. 'Those two seem very happy,' she remarked. 'I dare say matchmaking for Nancy's sake will be unnecessary.'

'What do you mean?' It was as if she'd heard his thoughts.

'Those two.' She inclined her head towards Nancy and Michael. 'Surely they are sweethearts.'

He gaped at them. 'They are friends. Michael is our only friend in London.'

'Not your only friend,' she murmured.

'Who else?' he asked.

She gave him a disappointed look, and they walked on.

After a while she asked, 'Is Tranville not your friend? He says he is.'

Jack stiffened. 'He is no friend.'

She shook his arm. 'Jack. Jack. You make me want to ask you what is between you and Tranville, but I doubt you would tell me.'

He gritted his teeth. 'It is a private matter.'

The mood that had been lightening between them darkened again. Jack could not shake the picture of Tranville seated at his mother's breakfast table from his thoughts. It had not been the first time Tranville had so used Jack's mother, only this time she must have had no illusions about it.

Jack walked on, mouth clamped shut.

Ariana broke the silence. 'Every time Tranville appears in person or in conversation, you turn dark and sullen. Did you know that?'

He turned to her and spoke with deep sarcasm. 'Forgive me. I shall endeavour to be more entertaining.'

She hit his arm. 'Stop it. I do not want that.' They walked a few more steps before she added, 'I like you, Jack. I wish to be your friend. If we might be friends, think how enjoyable our time together will be.'

He broke in. 'This is a matter of business between us. Nothing more.'

'It is more to me,' she countered. 'It is my future. Yours, as well, I think. I want this painting to help make me a sensation on the London stage. You must be counting on it to bring you commissions. We both want the money and attention the painting can bring.'

'That is still business, Ariana.'

Her eyes widened and a smile flitted across her face. He realised, then, that he'd called her by her given name, belying all his talk of business.

'Jack.' She spoke his name as if confirming his slip. 'Your drawings are good, but they are not exceptional. You are holding back. I look flat in them, like I am nothing more than a doll. You can do better; I've seen you do better, but we must get over this—this barrier between us.'

'Nonsense. There is no barrier.' Inside he knew she was correct.

'The barrier is Tranville,' she said.

'Then it is an insurmountable barrier,' he shot back. 'Tranville is paying for the portrait. He is as much a part of it as you and me.'

She stepped in front of him, causing him to stop. 'Money doesn't make him part of it.' She put both hands on his arms. 'He is nothing to me, Jack.'

The hood from her cloak fell away and her face was bathed in a soft light, diffused by clouds obscuring the sun. Wisps of auburn hair beat against her cheeks and eyes he knew to be green had turned grey from the sky's reflection. Her eyes pleaded and she raised herself on tiptoe, bringing her face even closer.

His gaze fell to her lips. He tried to memorise their colour in the overcast afternoon, more violet than pink. His head dipped and he noticed the length and curl of her dark lashes.

His hands closed around her waist.

A carriage clattered by and Jack stepped away, shaken out of his reverie.

He glanced past her to see that his sister and Michael had put a great deal of distance between them.

'We had better walk on,' he said.

She held him back. 'Can we be friends, then? Forget about Tranville when we are together and enjoy ourselves?'

He stared down at her, knowing at this moment he wished for more than friendship with her.

Forgetting Tranville would be difficult, but far easier than resisting the desire she aroused in him, yet she looked so earnest, so compelling, he could refuse her nothing at this moment.

'Very well, Ariana.' He looked into her eyes again and again felt the rush of desire for her. He bit down on his resolve. 'I shall try.'

Chapter Seven

Ariana walked out of Somerset House with Jack at her side feeling she could not be happier. Only on stage did she feel similar exhilaration.

True, she had not convinced Jack to confide in her, but he had used her given name, more than once. And he had almost kissed her. It was enough to send her spirits soaring to the heavens.

Inside Somerset House Jack had quickly sketched from print after print of Egyptian art. He'd been so totally absorbed that she, his sister and his friend might well have been invisible. Ariana did not mind. It was fascinating merely to watch him work.

Now that their lovely time at Somerset House had ended Ariana could not bear her day with Jack to come to an end.

They strolled back to Adam Street talking about Egyptian prints.

'I did not like all that I saw,' Ariana said as she walked between Jack and his sister. 'The women looked so strange.' She shuddered, recalling one print depicting a bas relief of a bare-chested queen nursing a boy almost as tall as she.

Michael grinned at her. 'Do you mean you do not wish to

be painted in profile with some strange symbol resting on top of your head?'

'I want to look regal and exotic.' She gazed at Jack, who had lapsed into silence again. 'What do you think, Jack? Am I to be in profile?'

'Not necessarily.' He seemed to be only half-listening.

Michael went on. 'At the Academy we practise designing classical architecture, but we are expected to create buildings suitable for modern use. Jack might use the same principles.'

'Meaning I do not have to be in profile?' Ariana arched a brow.

Jack finally smiled down at her. 'You do not. Cleopatra will be as exotic and regal as you desire.'

His smile made Ariana feel like warm honey inside. She was quite in danger of becoming completely besotted with him.

'Well, I am glad the Egyptian ladies wore their hair down,' Nancy remarked pragmatically. 'You have such lovely hair. It will make a very pretty display.'

Ariana smiled at her. 'Why, thank you, Miss Vernon. What a nice compliment.'

She liked Jack's sister, so fresh and young and full of hope, exactly like the portrait Jack painted of her. It was obvious to Ariana that Michael shared her opinion of Nancy and more.

Ariana turned back to Jack. 'Perhaps you might come with me to look through the theatre's costumes and props for something that will befit our Egyptian queen?'

'That is an excellent idea,' Michael agreed.

'What fun to rummage through theatrical costumes!' Nancy looked at her brother. 'You should do it.'

Jack's gaze touched Ariana again. 'If you wish it.'

Her heart fluttered.

They reached Adam Street, and Nancy pulled at Michael to hurry him on. 'Mama will wonder what has happened to us. It is almost time for dinner.'

Michael was evidently an invited dinner guest.

Nancy and Michael said their goodbyes and hurried off. She was alone with Jack.

'Will you walk me home?' Ariana asked.

'Of course,' he replied without hesitation.

It made her heart soar. 'I enjoyed myself today.'

He did not respond.

She jostled his arm. 'Here now, Jack. There is no harm in telling me you enjoyed yourself as well.'

He looked down at her and his mouth slowly widened into a smile. 'I did enjoy myself.'

She *was* besotted with him, she thought.

When they crossed Maiden Lane, it was all she could do to not dance for joy. What harm would there be if she opened her heart to Jack? She was not the green girl she'd been at nineteen.

When they arrived at her door, she grabbed his hand. 'Come in for a little while.'

He did not ponder long. 'For a little while.'

She opened the door, still holding his hand, giddy with excitement.

Betsy stepped into the hall, carrying folded laundry. 'Miss Blane, there is a gentleman to see you.'

'A gentleman?' She glanced at Jack, who already seemed to have retreated from her. 'Who is it?'

'Lord somebody.'

Her insides turned leaden.

'Tranville,' Jack said.

'I'm sure I don't know, sir,' the maid responded. 'I wasn't the one who let him in. He's been here over an hour, though.'

Ariana felt as if she'd plummeted down a well. 'Is he in the drawing room?'

'That he is,' the girl repeated and hurried up the stairs.

Jack moved toward the door. 'Good day, Miss Blane.'

She still had his hand. 'No, come upstairs with me, just for a little while.'

He glanced toward the closed drawing-room door. 'You have a guest.'

It felt as if a stone wall had suddenly been erected between them.

'He can wait,' she pleaded.

'He must not be reckoned with, Ariana.'

'I will send him away,' she insisted.

He shook his head.

It was no use. 'You will still come to look at the costumes tomorrow, will you not?'

He again glanced at the drawing room door.

'Oh, do not refuse, Jack. Please,' she whispered.

He put his hand on the front doorknob. 'Select any costume you desire and bring it to the studio.'

She covered his hand with her own. 'Please, Jack.'

He looked into her eyes. 'There is much at stake for both of us. You said so yourself. It is best this remain a business matter.'

She tossed her head. 'I can manage him.'

His expression hardened. 'Do not underestimate what that man can do.'

He turned the knob, her hand still touching his. She reluctantly released him as he opened the door.

'Come to the studio tomorrow afternoon whenever you choose.' He turned away and was gone.

Ariana closed the door, her throat tightening. She made a frustrated sound as she tore off her cloak and hat and pulled off her gloves, throwing them down on a nearby chair. She paced the hall for a few minutes, trying to calm herself enough to face Tranville.

Jack was mistaken about Lord Tranville. He was merely full of his own consequence and ruled by carnal desire rather than a rational assessment of his attraction to a woman less than half his age. She could manage such a man.

She squared her shoulders and entered the drawing room.

Tranville sat in a chair, his legs extended and his head bobbing against his chest.

She cleared her throat.

He uttered a loud snort, opened his eyes and sprang to his feet. 'Miss Blane!'

She remained just inside the doorway and spoke in her coolest voice. 'Lord Tranville.'

He took a step forwards. 'My dear, where have you been?'

She lifted an eyebrow, but did not answer him.

He halted. 'I was concerned something had happened to you.'

She gave a shake of her head. 'Why?'

'I stopped by Jack's studio, but there was no answer. Naturally I thought you had come home—' his tone was matter of fact '—so I decided to call upon you.'

'You stopped at the studio?' She was shocked. 'I asked you not to.'

'Oh, I had given you plenty of time. I actually thought I would see Jack.'

Her breathing accelerated. '*You* gave me plenty of time? I did not realise my time was yours to give.'

He answered with a laugh. 'You misunderstand me. I merely happened to be in the neighbourhood and I wanted to see what progress Jack had made.'

'Happened to be in the neighbourhood,' she repeated.

'Indeed.' It now seemed to be dawning on him that she was not pleased. 'So, where were you? Where did you go?'

Ariana walked to the window, pressing her lips together so she would not say something she would later regret.

'You expect me to account to you where I go, what I do?' Her voice rose to a higher pitch.

'Not at all.' his tone was almost cheerful. 'I just wanted to know.'

She swung around to stare at him. This man deserved the biggest dressing down she could deliver.

Her mother's voice—and Jack's—sounded in her head, warning her not to make an enemy of him.

Even so, she must make clear to him he had not purchased *her* along with the portrait. Gentlemen assumed actresses, singers and dancers were like trinkets in a shop, awaiting purchase. Ariana's mother had been a high-priced ornament, but as soon as some new glittering ornament had appeared, gentlemen cast her aside.

Ariana wanted none of that. She just wanted to act.

She turned to Tranville. 'Sir, do sit.'

He had not moved far from the chair in which he had been napping. He lowered himself on to it.

She chose a chair not too nearby. 'I am distressed.'

'Distressed?' He sat forwards in his chair, immediately solicitous.

She wished she could shrink back.

Instead she put on a patient smile. 'I perhaps misunderstood you.' It was always better to act as if the fault was on her part, not the gentleman's. 'I thought you said this portrait placed me under no obligation to you—'

He interrupted her. 'It does not, I assure you—'

She silenced him with a hand. 'And I thought you agreed not to come to the studio.'

He straightened. 'I agreed not to interrupt you at the studio while you were sitting for the portrait, which I assure you I had no intention of doing.'

She tilted her head as if pondering a question beyond her means of comprehension. 'And if I had been there when you knocked, would that not have been an interruption?'

He coloured, but she feared it was not in embarrassment, but in anger. 'But you were not there.'

She must tread carefully. 'The point is, sir, that I either misunderstood you or you are not a man of your word.' She made herself smile again. 'And I cannot believe you are not a man of your word.'

His eyes flashed. 'Of course I am a man of my word.'

She stood. 'Excellent!'

He rose as well.

'Then I may continue to sit for the portrait.' She smiled again. 'Without your assumption that you have purchased my attentions—'

His eyes bulged. 'Purchased your attentions!'

'—and I have your word you will not come looking for me at the studio and intrude on what I consider a most serious endeavour?' An endeavour she wished to make very private.

He had no recourse but to nod his head in agreement, although she could see he did not like it.

She took a few steps towards the door and then stepped aside.

He gaped at her as if not believing she expected him to leave. He did not march out as contritely as she had hoped.

Instead, he walked up to her, his eyes hard as flints. He took her hand and raised it to his lips, and spoke in a smooth voice. 'My dear, I have the highest, the deepest esteem for you. Anything I did, I did because of my regard for you, my desire to fulfil your every wish.'

He still did not believe she was serious.

She curtsied, gently pulling her hand away. 'I am complimented, sir, but I must speak very plainly. My affections are not secured by what favours a gentleman performs for me. I must refuse the portrait if you expect some compensation from me in return for it.'

This was a gamble. If he pulled out of the portrait, she would lose that valuable exposure for her acting career and Jack would lose his commission.

He looked affronted. She'd wounded his vanity, and men whose vanity was wounded were very prone to retaliation.

Placate him, she told herself. Don't lose Jack's commission.

She touched Tranville's arm. 'It is not you, sir. It is merely that I value myself too highly to sell my attentions to anyone. You know how the theatre is. How gentlemen are. In my opinion, it cheapens me to give my heart to the highest bidder.' She spoke honestly. 'I never accept a gift if an obligation is attached.'

His brow wrinkled as if he was pondering what, to him, must seem a mystifying statement. An actress not willing to sell herself to the highest bidder? Was this possible?

'You may still sit for the portrait—'

'Thank you, sir.' She smiled, genuinely grateful she had not lost her gamble. She extended her hand to him. 'I look forward to seeing you at the theatre.' Perhaps he would get the message that his visits to her residence were as unwelcome as his visits to the studio. 'And I shall be happy to share your conversation there.'

He clasped her fingers a bit too tightly. 'I will bid you good evening, then.'

'Good evening, sir.'

He bowed and walked out without another word.

Rid of him at last. She would have felt some joy if not for the fact that Tranville had already driven Jack away.

That evening Tranville walked up the narrow steps leading to Daphne Blane's dressing room, a room that Tranville thought ought to have been given to her daughter who had the lead female role.

He paused, inhaling a deep breath at the thought of Ariana. Such a beauty. Like a fresh, spring day. He felt young again just gazing upon her, and she fired his blood unlike any woman since he'd first set eyes on the youthful Mary Vernon.

It was indeed fortunate Mary was nearby. She had secured

Jack's co-operation, but, more than that, she had indulged his needs. Otherwise he might have been forced to visit a brothel. Ariana's coquettish behaviour had him in a constant state of frustration. The girl drove him mad. He must have her, there was nothing else for it.

Daphne Blane was bound to have influence over her daughter. She was a woman who knew the value of a gentleman's attentions.

He reached her door and knocked.

A maid admitted him.

Daphne Blane lounged on a red brocade sofa, wrapped in a silk robe festooned with peacocks. 'Do sit, Tranville. I am delighted you have come to me.'

She leaned forwards a little and the top of her robe gaped open enough to reveal quite impressive *décolletage*. Her daughter resembled her in that regard, but with breasts young and firm…

'It is always a pleasure to see you, Daphne, my dear.' He took the wooden chair that was nearby, turned it around and straddled it so that he could lean his arms on the chair's back. 'I have come to you for assistance.'

She moved again, exposing a bit of bare ankle. 'My assistance?'

He nodded. 'With Ariana.'

'Ariana.' She leaned back and tightened her robe. 'What has Ariana done now?'

'She is acting as if she will spurn me.' His voice grew low.

She looked aside. 'Spurn you?'

He laughed. 'Values herself too highly, she says.'

Daphne frowned. 'Foolish girl.'

'Intervene with her.' He leaned forwards, but spoke as if ordering his soldiers.

She sighed and tapped a long fingernail on the wooden table next to her. 'The little fool. She is no better than she should be. She plays a game with you, sir.'

His brow wrinkled. 'I detest games.'

Her eyes flashed. 'Oh, I suspect she thinks she is being clever. I dare say she will come running if she feels you have lost interest.'

'I have not lost interest.' He pounded on the back of the chair. 'I am more determined than ever. Tell her I will purchase some jewellery for her, something made up from Rundle and Bridge. Tell me what sort of bauble will tempt her.'

She shook her head. 'You act too eager, sir.' Her eyes shifted in thought. 'You need to teach her a lesson. Stay away from her.'

He began to rise from his seat. 'That is out of the question. I've half a mind—' He broke off.

She seized his arm. 'I am telling you what will work with her. Make her jealous. Give jewellery to some other woman.' Her expression turned shrewd. 'Me, if you like. Let her think you are interested in me. She wants my roles in the plays; she will want you, as well.'

He pondered. The girl was ambitious. He could make things happen for her if she would allow it. He already had.

Daphne crossed her arms over her chest. 'She came to London to take my place on the stage. Without her here, I might have played Juliet. I might have had the role of Cleopatra.'

Daphne had fought hard with Mr Arnold for the role that went to her daughter.

He straightened in the chair and inclined his head to her. 'Help me and I will help you.'

She looked thoughtful.

He put on a pleasing face. 'I would be indebted to you. The next play is yours if you make my desires come true.' As long as her daughter did not want the role, that is.

She considered. 'I will help you, but you need to follow my advice. Let her think she has lost you.'

There was a knock on her door. 'Ten minutes, Miss Blane.'

He stood. 'We have a bargain, my dear. I will not stay for the performance tonight.'

She extended her hand to him. 'Excellent, sir. Have patience. All will come out right.'

He clasped her hand and brought it to his lips. 'Thank you, dear lady.' When he dropped her hands he hardened his voice. 'I am determined to have your daughter, but I will not be toyed with. She will find me a generous benefactor, but a formidable enemy.'

Daphne returned a look equally as hard and determined. 'I am also not without influence, my lord, if you trifle with me.'

He understood her. They were two of a kind, both used to having matters go their way.

Tranville bid her adieu and hurried down the stairs. Not wishing to encounter Ariana, he slipped through the backstage, where people were running to and fro preparing for the curtain to rise. He refused to be publicly snubbed by the silly chit.

Let her think he was succumbing to her wishes by failing to show up for her performance. *Romeo and Juliet*'s run would be over soon. Then Ariana would begin preparing for the April opening of *Antony and Cleopatra*, and Jack would be finishing her portrait. When the portrait was completed and it became his gift to her, he would make his move.

Just to show her his kindness, he'd sweeten the deal with some diamonds or emeralds, diamonds to dazzle her and emeralds to match her eyes.

Tranville walked outside to where the carriages delivering the fashionable theatregoers were moving away. His frustration was so high it needed relieving. When his coach rounded the corner and stopped in front of him, Tranville called to the coachman, 'Adam Street.'

Chapter Eight

The next day Jack delivered Mr Slayton's portrait to the man's bank on Fleet Street. He walked back to save on the coach fare. As he turned onto Adam Street from the Strand, a hackney coach pulled up to his building's entrance.

Ariana emerged—alone—juggling two large bandboxes. She placed them on the pavement and handed some coins to the coachman. Jack watched her retrieve the boxes again and start for his door. He quickened his step.

Her face lit up when she saw him approach. 'Hello, Jack.' The cheerful tone of her greeting made it seem as if the last words they'd shared had not been strained. She lifted the boxes. 'I have raided the costume room.'

He took them from her. 'I see,' was all he could muster.

She followed him inside, unfastening her cloak and hanging it on the peg. As she took off her gloves and hat, she asked, 'Would you like to see the costumes?'

She seemed determined to pretend that nothing had happened between them. No attraction. No invitation to her room. No intrusion by Tranville.

'I would.' He could pretend as well. He carried the boxes to the *chaise-longue* before removing his own outerwear.

She opened one of the bandboxes. 'This one has the gowns.'

She pulled out three gowns and laid them out on the *chaise*. They were made of cloth so thin it floated until resting on the *chaise* in graceful folds. One gown was shimmery yellow silk. The other two were white muslin.

She pointed to the yellow one. 'I thought this looked almost like gold. Gold cloth would befit a queen like Cleopatra.' She rearranged the skirts of the other two. 'These could look like classical gowns, I thought.'

The one looked like no gown at all, but more like a chemise made of a light, sheer fabric that would cling to her body. If Cleopatra wore that gown with nothing underneath, the muslin would reveal the blush of her bare skin, the deep rose of her nipples. The tantalising idea took hold and the artist in him yearned for the challenge of painting such a transparency. The man in him had no business thinking such thoughts of her.

He turned to the other box to distract himself. 'What is in this one?'

She opened it and brought out a golden collar, long lengths of gold chain necklaces, two bejewelled crowns and an assortment of colourful shawls. The chains and crowns were cheaply gilded, the jewels mere glass.

'I thought this might have an Egyptian air to it.' She placed the collar over one of the white gowns, creating the sort of circular collar that adorned the clothing on the Egyptian prints. 'Or perhaps Cleopatra could wear a great deal of jewellery.' She draped the gold chain necklaces over the other muslin dress.

She seemed careful to confine her attention to the costumes, barely looking at him, acting in exactly the business-like manner he'd requested of her. It ought to have put him at ease.

It did not.

Had he gone with her to the Drury Lane Theatre and searched through trunks of costumes, he might have seen her eyes sparkling at each discovery. He might have witnessed her excitement at finding the gold collar. Perhaps she would have held up the jewelled crowns, letting their cut-glass gems glitter in whatever light the costume room possessed. They might have debated which gowns to select. They might have laughed together.

He had missed that chance.

She stood back and surveyed her arrangement of the gowns. 'What do you think?'

He hid his reaction. 'Any of them will do.'

She made a face. 'Any? I was hoping you would tell me which was best.' She touched the yellow cloth again. 'I confess, I could not decide.'

'I do not know.'

He knew. His choice was too scandalous to consider. Only one gown suited him, both the artist and the man. 'Would you be willing to try them on?'

Her determinedly impersonal attitude faltered a bit as she returned his gaze. 'Certainly.'

She gathered the gowns and he opened the door of his bedchamber for her.

As she walked into the room and placed the gowns on his bed, she looked over her shoulder. 'I fear I shall have to ask you to unlace me.'

Had she said the words with any hint of seduction, he would have refused, but she spoke as if he were her maid.

Jack found the hooks at the back of her dark blue carriage dress. As his fingers undid them he brushed the soft skin of her neck. She moved under his touch, like a cat being petted. When he untied her laces, her head lolled against her shoulder.

Desire shot through him at her reaction to his touch. It also brought a surge of pleasure he ought not to allow himself to feel.

As soon as he finished, she stepped away. 'Thank you, sir,' she said brightly. The moment passed.

He left the room and paced the length of the studio until

she emerged wearing the yellow gown. 'I need your help again.' She presented her back to him.

He tied the laces, his fingers now trembling a bit.

She stepped back and twirled around in front of him. 'Well?' The yellow silk swirled around her, creating pretty patterns of light and dark.

He took in a deep breath. 'Try the collar and the jewellery.'

He brought over the full-length mirror he sometimes used when he needed to draw from a reflection. She tried on the collar first and then the jewellery and surveyed herself in the mirror with each.

They repeated this performance with the sheer muslin dress, which tantalised Jack more than he wished to admit, even though it was her shift and corset visible beneath it, not the pink skin he yearned to see, not the image lodged in his brain so vividly it aroused him.

Ariana remained carefully impersonal, enabling him to maintain control over himself.

The second muslin gown was little more than two gathered pieces of cloth joined at the shoulders and tied with a simple cord at the waist. As she walked in it, the muslin billowed like clouds around her legs.

'I love how this gown feels.' She danced in front of him, the fabric moving with her. 'It would be perfect onstage.'

She caught him watching her and stopped, the ghost of a smile on her face.

He glanced away. 'Try it with the collar.'

She picked up the collar and brought it to the mirror. 'I have an idea for this.' She pushed the neckline of the dress lower so that her shoulders were bare and fastened the collar over it. When done, she looked at herself in the mirror before lifting her gaze to his reflection behind her. She waited for his reaction.

He nodded. 'I like that.' It made a perfectly acceptable costume.

'I do as well.' She untied the cord around her waist and replaced it with the gold chain necklaces, looking up to see if he approved.

He nodded.

She smiled and reached up to take the pins out of her hair. Her auburn locks tumbled halfway down her back.

He drew in a breath.

She gathered her hair in her hands. 'I think I can roll it under so it looks more Egyptian.'

As she fussed with hairpins, the light caught in her curls, creating gold highlights that rivalled the gold of the collar and chains. Jack's fingers twitched, wishing to be buried in her curls.

'Leave it loose,' he murmured.

She looked at him through the mirror and he felt the passion flare between them.

He took another breath. 'It wants only a crown.'

He handed her the simplest crown, the one that came to a single point in the front. Three large red jewels decorated it, one at the peak and two lower, enhancing the triangular shape of the gold.

He placed the crown on her head and they both examined the result in the mirror. His hands came to rest on her bare shoulders and their gazes met through the reflection and held.

She whispered, 'Jack?'

The brief contact begged for more. The connection between them could not be denied, only resisted.

Reluctantly he removed his hands and took a step back. 'We have Cleopatra.'

Her expression flickered first with disappointment, then turned into a determined smile. 'I approve. What now?'

He closed his eyes, better able to deal with an image of Ariana on the canvas than the flesh-and-blood woman. He pictured her in white against white. White linen draping the *chaise*, white marble walls behind her and a window showing white buildings in the distance. Hieroglyphics lining the wall would provide some contrast, but the tones would be white, grey and black, except for Ariana, who would shine like the gold of her collar and crown.

'Pose on the *chaise*.' He pushed his writing table over. 'I want to sketch this idea.'

She climbed on the *chaise* and assumed the position he'd drawn before. He took a piece of charcoal and started to draw.

Several minutes passed before she spoke. 'Did Tranville call upon you today?

Tranville again. The mere mention of the man's name broke Jack's concentration. 'He did not.'

'Good.'

They fell silent again, and Jack wondered why she had asked. He did not request an explanation, however; he merely tried to concentrate on his sketch.

After a time she said, 'I told him not to interfere.'

He looked at her. 'Told him?' Tranville did not take well to being told anything.

She explained, 'I reminded him that I'd accepted this portrait with the understanding that it would place me under no obligation to him. I reminded him that my affections were not for sale.'

Jack glanced at her, not quite believing what she said.

She sobered. 'Not every actress wants the attention of gentlemen in the Green Room.'

He nodded, even though he doubted any actress could avoid such attention. 'What was Tranville's reaction?'

She shrugged and the collar slipped lower on her shoulder. 'What could he say? He had given his word to me. He merely needed convincing that I meant to hold him to it. I told him he must not interfere and I am delighted that he seems to have listened to me this time.'

His eyes narrowed. 'Ariana, he is not a man who gives up what he wants.'

She shrugged again. 'He is a man.'

'A ruthless man.'

She stared at him. 'How do you know that?' She held up a hand. 'Wait. I don't suppose you will tell me, will you? What connection you have with Tranville?'

He did not answer immediately. 'He is connected to my family.'

'A friend of your mother's, he told me.'

Jack frowned. 'He told you that? A friend?'

'Yes.'

'A friend is one way to put it,' he said tightly. 'Or at least he once was such. You may then comprehend his connection to me.'

She nodded, clearly understanding his meaning. 'But there is more, is there not?'

He went back to his drawing before speaking again. 'On the Peninsula, he was ruthless in his ambition, caring more for his own consequence than for the welfare of his men.'

'He was a soldier?' She sounded surprised.

'A brigadier-general. Before he inherited his title.'

'A general?' She laughed.

He was puzzled at what amused her.

Her eyes sparkled. 'Forgive me, but it seems a silly thing for a general to suddenly become such an enthusiastic patron of the arts.' She giggled. 'I suspect he is more interested in the actresses than in preserving the cultural significance of the theatre.'

He could not help but smile. Not at her accurate measure of Tranville's character, but at how lovely she looked when filled with mirth.

She gazed at him. 'That is nice.'

'What is nice?' He sobered again.

'You smiled.'

He returned to the sketch, selecting pastels to add colour to her skin and to the gold.

Ariana watched his face as he drew. His concentration on his work was as intense as it had been at Somerset House. This time it felt as if he'd retreated again to that place she could not reach, that place somehow connected to Tranville. It frustrated her and made her sad.

She had indeed become besotted with this moody artist who kept so much inside, yet showed so much in his art. She wanted to unlock the mystery of him and to be someone with whom he could share confidences and engage in little adventures, as their excursion to Somerset House had been.

'Jack, we should visit the Egyptian Hall. Have you been there?' The building on Piccadilly had a façade in the Egyptian style. It would be a treat to explore it with him.

He hesitated. 'I have not been there.'

'We should try to see it, do you not think so? To complete our research.'

He merely continued drawing, using his thumb to smear something on the paper.

She tried again. 'Perhaps your sister and her Michael would like to come with us.'

He stopped drawing, as if he were actually considering her request. 'My sister has few outings. She would enjoy it.'

She smiled. 'Then say yes.'

He paused and it took him a long time to meet her gaze. 'Yes.'

Her insides danced with happiness.

She smiled. 'That is splendid. Will you make the plan? My days are free and soon my nights, as well, when the play ends.'

'When will that be?' he asked.

Some of the ease they'd built together the previous day seemed to have returned. 'Three more performances, the last on Saturday night. Will you come to that performance? As my guest?'

'No.' His expression turned dark. 'Tranville will be there, no doubt.'

She had pushed for too much. It contented her that he agreed to visit the Egyptian Hall.

'Make the plans for our outing. I'm sure I will have nothing to conflict with it.' She would not allow anything to do so.

He put down his piece of chalk and stood back, looking from her to the drawing and back, his elbows akimbo.

Finally he said, 'Come and look.'

She slid off the *chaise* and walked over to stand beside him.

'Oh, my!' In his drawing, he'd transformed the room into an Egyptian palace, complete with an Egyptian view out of a window. She was in the foreground, full body lounging on the chaise. The only colour on the paper came from her skin and features and the gold adornments she wore. As a result, he'd shown her off in a remarkable manner. Still…

'It is but a quick sketch,' he said apologetically.

'It is good.' She gazed at it again, her brow creasing. 'For a sketch.'

He examined it again. 'Speak plain, Ariana.'

She stepped back and turned her head towards him. 'It has no emotion.'

He stared at it again. 'It is merely a sketch.'

'You will make it a marvellous painting, I am certain.' It only wanted the life he could bring to it.

She clasped his arm and squeezed and to her surprise he put his arm around her for a moment as they stood together.

His mantel clock chimed six.

She knew he would say it was time to leave.

'I have already begun to prepare the canvas,' he told her. 'It must dry, so there is no need to meet tomorrow.'

She was bitterly disappointed, not wanting to go a day without seeing him. She averted her head so he would not see.

'Unless,' he went on, 'Nancy wishes to see the Egyptian

Hall tomorrow. It would be a good day to do that since we cannot work.'

She turned back to him, trying not to show how happy the idea made her. 'That would do very nicely, would it not?'

'If you are at liberty to wait, I will take a few minutes to go and see if the plan is agreeable to Nancy.'

'Shall I come with you?' She was perfectly willing to persuade Nancy, if necessary.

'No,' he said sharply. 'No,' he repeated in a softer voice. 'My mother—it is best I dash over there. I can arrange a hack for you while I am out.'

She nodded and wondered if Jack's mother knew of Tranville's interest in her. If so, his mother would certainly not want to encounter her. Ariana's mother resented every man who had left her and every woman who'd replaced her, especially if the woman was younger.

Ariana made herself smile. 'I will change back into my dress. Will you lace it again before you go?'

His eyes darkened. 'Of course.'

She hurried into his bedchamber and quickly took off the crown and the voluminous costume. She donned her carriage dress and returned to the studio. Jack stood at the window, his arms crossed over his chest.

'I need my lady's maid,' she joked, lifting her hair and presenting her back to him.

He made quick work of tying the laces and fastening the hooks.

As soon as he was done he walked over to take his top coat from its peg. 'I will return shortly.'

He seemed in a hurry.

She smiled. 'Take your time.'

After he left, she pinned up her hair and returned to tidy the bedchamber where she'd left the costumes in disarray. She picked up the bandboxes and carried them into the room.

Smoothing out the fabric as best she could, she folded the gowns and placed them back in the bandbox. She repacked the crowns and the gold chains into the other. No need to return them to the theatre until her portrait was completed. After she closed up the boxes, she sat on the bed, fingering the coarse blanket that covered Jack when he slept.

An image of him, all tangled in the blanket, flew into her mind. How lovely it would be to lie next to him, to feel his warm skin all along the length of her, to fall asleep nestled in his arms. She'd always thought that one of the nicest parts of being with a man. If the man were not a scoundrel, that is.

She quickly stood. It would not do to dwell on such matters, especially because things between her and Jack seemed so fragile and tenuous. Best she simply be glad he was willing to make a visit to the Egyptian Hall with her.

She glanced around his room, which was sparse of furniture. The simple bed. A chest of drawers with a pitcher and bowl on it. The room seemed to double as a storeroom with a big trunk in one corner and several paintings leaning against the wall. She placed the bandboxes next to them and could not resist a peek.

All the paintings were of battle. Not the glory of victory like the painting he'd exhibited at the Royal Academy, but paintings of soldiers fighting. She turned them around and lined up three of them side by side.

They were not pretty. The men's faces were distorted with fear and violence and pain. They stabbed at each other with swords and bayonets. Blood flowed everywhere. But, in each painting, Jack had also included something that contrasted to the horror. One painting showed a beautiful church in the background. In another, green fields dotted with sheep. In a third, white stucco buildings on a pretty village street. The street was stained with rivulets of blood, but, even so, something of beauty remained.

She thought her heart would break for him. How awful war must have been.

She squatted so she could better examine the skill with which he'd created the images. He certainly depicted emotion in these paintings, complicated emotion. Such as including the face of a terror-stricken child in one of the village windows.

'What are you doing?' She looked up to see Jack in the doorway, a black expression on his face.

She'd not heard him return, but could not even think of answering his question, not in the presence of these wonderful works of art. 'These are marvellous, Jack. I am in awe of them. Why are they here against the wall? You should display them.'

He crossed his arms over his chest. 'I did not paint them to display them.' His voice was tight.

Why did this disturb him? 'Why did you paint them?' she asked almost in a whisper.

He glanced away from her before walking into the room and facing the paintings. 'It is difficult to explain.'

She did not waver. 'I am capable of comprehending difficult things.'

He reached for the frame of the painting with the church and turned it back against the wall. 'When I came back from war I could not rid myself of what I'd seen. So I painted it.'

'You painted how it felt.' She thought her heart would break for all he'd gone through. She gestured to a cluster of soldiers slashing at each other. 'I cannot see how you endured it.'

His voice dropped deeper. 'These do not show the half of it. I have sketches—' He waved a hand. 'Never mind the sketches.'

'I should like to see them,' she murmured.

He shook his head and turned to the doorway. 'We must go. The hackney coach is waiting outside.'

She followed him out to the studio. He held out her cloak for her and put it around her shoulders.

She fastened it, greatly desiring to dispel the grim mood she'd created by looking at his work. 'Did you find Nancy at home? Did she agree to the outing?'

He barely looked at her. 'She agreed and will ask Michael this evening if he can join us.'

She felt her spirits lift. She would not miss a day with Jack.

'We will meet you at your residence at eleven o'clock, if that is acceptable.'

She tied the ribbons of her hat under her chin. 'At my residence?'

He looked puzzled. 'Should we not?'

She did not know how to answer that. 'Your mother did not mind Nancy coming to a house where actors live?'

'I still do not comprehend.'

She thought it was self-evident. 'Actors and actresses are not respectable, you know.'

He laughed drily. 'Neither are we Vernons.'

He waited at the open door for her to walk through. She could see the hack waiting for her.

She brushed past him, but suddenly turned and looked up into his eyes. 'I do not wish our day together to end.'

His eyes darkened.

'Come with me, Jack,' she murmured, trying not to show how much she yearned for him to say yes. 'Spend the evening with me. Come to the theatre. Be my guest.'

He glanced towards his mother's door. 'I am not expected elsewhere.'

She smiled and touched his cheek. 'Then come with me.'

She watched the ultimate decision form on his face. 'Give me a moment to lock my door.'

Chapter Nine

Jack turned the key in the lock and returned to the street where Ariana waited. She smiled like a child giddy at receiving a much desired toy.

He doubted his company was worth celebrating, but he simply wanted to remain with her, to hold on to her company for as long as he could. That had been his motivation for the Egyptian Hall outing as well. He'd included Nancy as a chaperon. For him.

It occurred to him again that they had no chaperon in the studio, and that he had already engaged in the intimacy of undoing her laces. In the studio he had his work. His art was the chaperon.

Tranville had been at his mother's house again, his mother delighted at his company. It sickened Jack, but helped him make his decision to spend the evening with Ariana. If he remained with her, he would not be thinking of his mother.

Jack assisted Ariana inside the hack and climbed in next to her. 'I told the driver to take us to Henrietta Street.'

'Perfect.' She tucked her arm around his. 'We can eat dinner there and go to the theatre afterwards.'

Tranville had announced that he was not attending the theatre that night. Ariana and Jack would be free of the sight of him.

Jack was surprisingly comfortable sitting close to Ariana during the brief ride to Henrietta Street. After he paid the jarvey, Ariana took his arm again and they walked up to the door. In the evening light, her features were muted in grey, but every bit as lovely as in sunlight. What would it be like, he wondered, to paint her in all different kinds of light?

'I am so glad you came,' she said as they entered the house. 'Come up to my room. We can take off our coats there and be comfortable until dinner is served.'

She held his hand as they climbed the stairs and she pulled him into her room, closing the door behind her. She released him to remove her outer garments, tossing them on a nearby chair.

She turned to help him with his top coat. 'I will be your valet. It is only fair, since you were my maid.'

He was frozen in place, wanting only to gather her into his arms and tumble with her on that nearby bed. There could not be a riskier proposition than indulging in his attraction to her. Even if she had rejected Tranville, he had laid a claim upon her and would lash out if he knew she'd chosen Jack instead. Jack would welcome a battle with Tranville, but he was not willing to risk the man retaliating against Ariana or his mother.

Ariana seemed free of any such concern as she lay his top coat on the bed. She also placed his hat and gloves there. Clever girl. The bed would act as a clothes press at the moment, she'd silently informed him, not the place of his imagined pleasure.

There was a knock on the door and a male voice, 'Ariana! We're having refreshment in the drawing room. One of the girls was given a bottle of Madeira.'

'Marvellous!' She turned to Jack. 'Would you like some

Madeira before dinner? The other roomers here are a friendly sort.'

Better to dampen his temptation with wine. 'I will do as you wish.'

She searched his face and he fancied she could see the battle raging inside him. 'I wish for many things, Jack.'

His brow wrinkled.

She smiled. 'Madeira, I think.'

Jack wanted her with every muscle and vein in his body, every aching of his soul, even though he knew, with Tranville's involvement, his desire could lead to nothing good. Still, she was fresh and vibrant and full of life, and Jack was so very sick of war and death.

He took in a breath and held it for a moment, before gesturing towards the door.

Arm in arm, they descended the stairs and entered the drawing room. The first person Jack saw was the actor who'd befriended him in the tavern and had taken him to watch *Romeo and Juliet*.

'Why, Jack!' The man came forwards, extending his hand. 'What the devil are you doing here?' He turned to the other man there, another actor who had joined them that night after the play. 'Look, Franklin, it is Jack.'

Their greetings were as friendly as if they'd been long-lost friends accustomed to addressing each other by given names. Jack was quickly introduced to two actresses in the room, Susan, who was about Ariana's age, and Eve, a bit older.

Ariana waved a hand, interrupting. 'Henry. Jack. How do you know each other?'

The man, whose name Jack had not learned until that moment, answered, 'Jack and I are drinking companions. Or at least we were the other night.' Henry turned to Jack. 'You, my dear fellow, did not tell us you were privy to Ariana's bedchamber—the first man invited in there, as a matter of fact. At least to my knowledge.'

He was the first?

Ariana broke in, 'Did Jack not tell you he is painting me? He is the portrait artist who is portraying me as Cleopatra.'

The actor clapped him on the shoulder. 'You sod. You did not say a word of it, not even when we were at the theatre.'

'You were at the theatre?' Ariana blinked.

Henry led him to a side table. 'Come on. I will pour you some of this fine Madeira.'

Both the Madeira and the conversation flowed freely until dinner was announced and they withdrew to the dining parlour. At the dining table more wine filled their glasses and the talk was all about the theatre—who'd won what role and how had they secured it.

Henry turned to Ariana. 'The thing I want to know is how you managed to convince Tranville to give you the part of Cleopatra without going to bed with him.'

Ariana fluttered her eyelashes at him. 'On my merits as an actress, perhaps?'

Henry laughed. 'Your mother cursed like a sailor when she discovered the part was not hers.'

Ariana glanced at Jack. 'My mother has a jealous streak.'

Henry rolled his eyes dramatically. 'You are not jesting. She is a fine actress, though, as fine as Sarah Siddons.' He poured Jack more wine. 'Tranville paid a pretty price to get Kean, too.' He winked at Jack. 'But in hiring a portrait artist, the fool hired his own rival.'

Ariana said, 'Tranville is a lecherous old man, as are most of the gentlemen who come to the Green Room.'

The other actresses loudly agreed with her.

Jack attempted to let the talk of Tranville flow past him and just enjoy the free-speaking of these theatre people, such a contrast to his own family where so much went unspoken.

'Tranville has wealth, though,' the older actress remarked in a wistful tone. 'He is a fish worth catching.'

Ariana nodded. 'More my mother's type, I would say.' She turned to Jack. 'Did you know he financed the play?'

It was not as easy for him to speak freely. He hesitated. 'To benefit the theatre he would say, but it was clear whose benefit concerned him most.'

A dark look came over her face. She waved her hand. 'At least I get my portrait painted.'

Quickly recovering her good spirits, she held her own while the others teased her about Tranville. The good spirits in the room were infectious, and Jack almost relaxed.

After dinner they walked as a troop to the theatre, their laughter condensing into little clouds in the cold air. Again Jack was admitted backstage. Ariana presented him to Mr Arnold, who seemed pleased that he was painting Ariana's portrait and made encouraging noises about using him again if the portrait improved ticket sales. Jack was also introduced to Mr Kean, even more deep in his cups than Jack himself.

Ariana left him to dress for her role, and Jack settled in a chair with a view of the stage. Henry produced a bottle of wine for him and a glass. He sipped the wine, trying to hold the backstage commotion and confusion in his memory for later sketching. Jack imagined drawing the scene in the style of a Rowlandson print, busy with activity, colourful people and great humour.

A beautiful woman dressed in costume approached him. Daphne Blane.

'You are my daughter's portraitist, are you not?' She neglected the usual civilities of a greeting.

Jack rose. 'I am indeed. Jack Vernon at your service.' He bowed.

She extended her hand to him. 'Daphne Blane.'

'Your fame precedes you, Miss Blane. I knew you immediately.' He clasped her hand, which felt cold and stiff.

Her smile was equally as icy. She looked him up and down. 'Now I begin to understand.' She shook her head. 'Still, my daughter is a fool to choose you over…' She hesitated. 'Over other gentlemen.'

'I am merely the artist who is painting her portrait.'

Her brows rose at this falsehood. 'Well.' She eyed him again. 'You had best do a very splendid portrait.'

'I will try,' he responded. 'It is a great opportunity for me to paint your daughter.'

She tilted her chin in acknowledgement.

He shivered. What had it been like for Ariana to have such a mother?

Soon the play began. Although Jack was watching it for the third time, this was the first performance he felt free to merely enjoy. Ariana became Juliet, but retained some of herself as well. When she was not on stage or changing her costume, she stood with him in the wings, no longer Juliet, but simply Ariana. The other dinner companions kept him company, as well, passing along more titbits of gossip, which seemed to be their preferred conversation.

When the play ended, Henry suggested Jack and Ariana come to the tavern where he and Jack had first met.

Ariana shook her head. 'I cannot. Mr Arnold wants me to greet some of the patrons in the Green Room.' She turned to Jack. 'Come with me. I will introduce you as my portrait artist.'

Jack finally gained entry to the Green Room, as the guest of the play's leading actress, no less. There had been no Tranville to bar the way. While there, he spoke with as many wealthy men who might be interested in future commissions as he could. Ariana had no shortage of covetous gentlemen wanting to speak to her. Not all of these men were reprobates like Tranville. How long before she would meet one worthy of her?

He shook his head to rid himself of such thoughts.

She rushed up to him. 'I've found a gentleman interested in a history painting.'

Jack was presented to a man about Tranville's age.

'You paint battles, eh? And portraits? I've half a mind to have you paint me in my old Horse Guards uniform.'

'My father was in the Horse Guards,' Jack said.

'Damn me, you don't say?' The man peered at him.

But Jack was distracted. He'd spied Tranville's son, Edwin, in the crowd.

The old rage rumbled inside him.

'Vernon is your name?' the man went on. 'There was a John Vernon in the Horse Guards in my day.'

Jack could barely attend to him. 'My father, sir.'

Finding someone who knew his father would ordinarily have pleased Jack a great deal, but the sight of Edwin, his face scarred now, brought back that night in Badajoz.

Edwin swayed with drink as he leered at a ballet dancer who walked past.

'You do not say.' The former compatriot of his father fell silent for a moment. 'Now I comprehend the connection,' he burst forth suddenly. 'Tranville is paying you to paint this actress, is that not so?'

Jack glanced back to the man. His response was terse. 'That is so.'

Edwin had sidled up to one of the actresses from Ariana's boarding house, Susan, the younger one.

Jack bowed to the former Horse Guard officer. 'I must beg your leave, sir.'

The man looked relieved. He clapped Jack on the arm in farewell.

Jack crossed the room to where Edwin toyed with a long ribbon on the sleeve of Susan's dress.

He rubbed the ribbon against his scar. 'Received this in

the siege of Badajoz—' His eyes widened at Jack's approach.

Jack gave him no greeting. 'I would speak to you, Susan.'

She glanced towards Edwin and fluttered her lashes. 'In a moment.'

'Now,' Jack said.

Edwin seemed to recover some composure. 'Didn't expect to find you here, Jack. Hoped they'd sent you to the West Indies or some such place.'

A posting where soldiers died of fevers.

'Not your lucky day, then, is it?' Jack said through gritted teeth.

'Well, well, you've found me out, Jack. Not even m'father knows I'm in London yet. Was in Paris, y'know.' His words were slurred.

'Paris!' Susan's eyes brightened.

Jack turned to her. 'Come with me, Susan.'

She looked from one man to the other, but did not move.

Edwin favoured her with a white-toothed smile. 'The young lady and I were engaged in a very pleasant conversation. I am loath to have you interrupt me telling her all about Paris.'

An intoxicated Edwin was too dangerous to trust.

'I must interrupt.' He took Susan's arm.

'Now see here, Jack!' She tried to pull away.

At that moment Ariana appeared. 'What is this?' Her voice was tense, but cheerful.

Jack gave her an intent look. 'I need to speak to Susan. Now.'

Ariana smiled. 'Of course you do. I shall entertain this gentleman while you talk.'

Edwin tossed a wary glance at Jack, but he happily returned his gaze to Ariana. 'By all means.'

Jack's gut twisted at leaving Ariana with the likes of Edwin, but he knew Ariana would not leave with the man. Susan might.

She was not happy to be led away.

He took the young actress to a corner of the room. 'Stay away from that fellow, Susan. He is no one you would wish to know.'

She shrugged off his grasp. 'He's Tranville's son. He should have money.'

'He is not worth it. Believe me.'

She put her hands on her hips. 'Why should I believe you?'

Jack leaned down to her, his expression brooking no argument. 'Because I know him to be cruel to women.'

Her hands dropped to her side. 'How cruel?'

'Violent.' He could not say more. 'Trust me on this, Susan.'

She chewed on her lip as if calculating her decision. 'Introduce me to some other gentleman, Jack. Then I'll agree to leave that one alone.'

He introduced her to the former Horse Guards officer, who was equally as delighted to meet her.

Jack hurriedly manoeuvred through the crowd to return to Ariana and whisk her away from Edwin. As he made his way, the rumble of voices around him started to turn into the roaring flames of buildings afire. One man's voice sounded like musket fire. A woman's laughter became a scream. He could not move.

Ariana came to him. 'What is it, Jack? You look unwell.'

The memories of Badajoz were about to engulf him again. 'I must leave.'

She took his arm. 'I will go with you.'

She led him to her dressing room where the maid helped her change into her own clothes again. From behind a screen, she asked him about Edwin. He could only repeat what he had told Susan. The sounds in his head did not abate.

Then they walked outside and headed towards her boarding house, but the noises in his head remained. It had rained and the streets glistened with moisture, making their footsteps echo in the still damp air. The sound reverberated in Jack's head, like ghosts shouting at him. His muscles were taut, ready for flight. Every shadow seemed like a marauding soldier. The air smelled of burning wood.

Ariana glanced behind them. 'Look, Jack, there's a fire!'

He spun around. The scent of smoke had been real. The fire was some distance away, perhaps at a warehouse on the river, but the orange glow was visible in the sky and the smell of smoke had drifted. A crash sounded nearby, a wagon overturning perhaps, spilling its contents.

Suddenly he was completely back in Badajoz.

With a cry he pulled her to the wall of a building, flattening her against its brick surface and shielding her with his body.

She gasped. 'Jack, what is it?'

He pressed against her, the sights and sounds of Badajoz so strong now he could do nothing but act as if they were real.

'Must hide.' His voice cracked.

'What is happening?'

He could not speak, could not explain.

She put her arms around him and held him. He clung to her tightly as Badajoz returned to him once more.

'You are safe,' she murmured. 'You are safe. No need to hide.'

It seemed an endless period of time that he was caught in the living nightmare. She held him until a semblance of reality returned.

He released her and pushed himself away. 'I must be mad.'

'Tell me what happened.' She looked alarmed.

He took off his hat and ran a trembling hand through his hair. 'I was back in Badajoz.'

She touched his arm. 'You had a vision?'

He shook his head. 'I suppose you could call it a vision. You know the paintings of war in my room? It was as if they'd come to life and I was in them.'

She came closer, threading her arm through his and holding him next to her. 'You are not there,' she said soothingly. 'You are in London with me.'

He started to walk—and to try not to run. 'It has happened before. I think I must be mad.'

She did not slow their stride. 'You were certainly frightened. I should think if I had seen war as depicted in your paintings, my memories might sometimes overtake me. It is over now, though.'

They reached a street to cross. He could not even say which street it was. The area looked strange to him, even though they must have walked the same route going to the theatre.

As they crossed, she said, 'We are almost at the house.'

With each step the sounds of Badajoz still rumbled. He thought if he could only make it to her door and say goodnight, he could quickly run to his studio and hope to reach it before the vision engulfed him again.

They reached her door and she pulled a key from her reticule, but she took his hand before opening the door. 'You are coming inside with me.'

'I should not.' The sounds roared louder.

She gripped his hand. 'Until you feel calm again. Just for a minute.'

'Ariana, I should not come in with you.'

'No one will blink an eye about it, believe me.' She opened the door and stepped inside, pulling him in with her.

He followed. The house looked strange, lit only by an oil lamp on a table in the hall. Flashes of the Frenchwoman's house in Badajoz intruded. Again he saw the broken furniture, the papers scattered everywhere, the haunted eyes of the woman's young son.

She led him above stairs to her room, turning a key in the lock after closing the door. 'See? We will be safe here.'

She removed her cloak and gloves and lit a taper from a

coal glowing in the fireplace. She used it to light every candle in the room. He was grateful. The more light, the better he felt. She helped him off with his top coat, but this time did not put it or his hat and gloves on the bed but on the chair. That done, she went over to a cabinet in the corner.

She took out a bottle of brandy and two glasses. 'Sometimes I need this to calm down after a performance so I can sleep.'

She poured for him, not giving him a chance to refuse.

With her drink in hand and the bottle in the other she kicked off her shoes and climbed on the bed, sitting cross-legged. She patted the space next to her. 'Sit with me.'

He removed his shoes and joined her, taking a long sip of the warming brandy.

'Will you tell me of Badajoz?' she asked.

He shook his head, unable to even utter words of refusal.

She did not press him, but merely refilled his glass when he emptied it. The brandy slowly calmed him and he was able to breathe normally again. His heart no longer pounded like the regiment's drums.

'Cannot speak of it,' he mumbled, suddenly exhausted. 'And there are drawings I cannot show. But really I ought to bid you goodnight.'

'In a little while,' she murmured. 'You should rest first. Let us take off your coat and waistcoat so you can lie down for a minute.'

He allowed her to remove his garments and loosened his neckcloth.

'You might as well take off your trousers, too,' she said, unbuttoning them as he lay against the pillows.

The brandy and exhaustion were fogging his mind. He ought not to allow her to remove his trousers. 'I should return to the studio.'

'After a brief rest,' she cajoled. 'I will wake you in ten minutes.'

'Ten minutes.' The bed felt very warm and comfortable. Perhaps it would do no harm to rest for ten minutes.

Ariana smoothed his hair and stared down at his handsome face. As she had anticipated, it had only taken him a minute to fall as soundly asleep as a child.

The vision, or whatever it had been that seized him, had frightened her. He acted as if he'd been in another time and place, as if he saw and heard things she could not. She knew very little about madness, but could not believe him insane. She preferred to think that the fire had triggered a very realistic memory.

Badajoz. She tried to recall what she knew about it. The battle had occurred about three years ago, shortly after she'd left the school to join the theatre company. All she'd been thinking of in those days had been performing on stage. Still, she knew many soldiers had died at Badajoz. Was that the place where the English soldiers rioted and looted the town? She could not remember.

She drew her finger across Jack's forehead and thought of Jack's paintings leaning against his bedroom wall. If the real horror of war was worse than that, she could not imagine what he must have endured. To think she had been consumed by the frivolity of the theatre at the same time he had been living in a nightmare he could not shake even now.

She was pleased he slept peacefully.

She slipped out of her room and hurried up another flight of stairs to the maid's room, waking the poor girl to help her untie her laces and corset.

'Thank you, Betsy,' she whispered to the girl.

Betsy had already lain back down to sleep.

Ariana hurried back to her room, opening the door carefully. Jack's eyes were still closed and his breathing even. She pulled off her dress and slid out of her corset. Sitting at her dressing table, she took the pins from her hair, brushing it smooth before putting it in a plait. Not bothering to change into her nightdress, she put two more coals on the fire, blew out the candles, and climbed into bed next to him clad only in her shift.

She adored being close to him. He rolled over to face her, and she could just make out his features in the dim light that came from the fireplace. Her eyes grew heavy, but she did not wish to sleep. She wanted simply to gaze at him, so peaceful now when a short time ago he had been terror-stricken.

From her first glimpse of him she had suspected he was a complicated man. Tonight she'd seen him in complete control of his emotions one minute, then totally at their mercy at another, lost in a vision that terrified him.

Her last thought as she drifted off to sleep was that she was becoming very attached to this soldier artist of hers.

Ariana woke to a cry.

'Release her!' Jack thrashed in the bed as if he was fighting someone. 'Stop!'

She sat up and reached for him, but he flung his arm so hard he knocked her back down.

Heart pounding in fear that he might end up hurting one of them, she grabbed his arm and held on as he fought her. 'Jack. Wake up. You are dreaming.' Her shift rode up to her waist and her hair came loose of its plait.

'Fire! The building is on fire.'

He'd alarm the house. She managed to climb on top of him, even though she knew her strength was no match for his. She covered his mouth with her hand. 'There's no fire. Wake up.'

He sat up and seized her upper arms.

'Wake up!' She was on her knees, straddling his legs, but there was little she could do when he held her in such a tight grip.

His eyes flew open, wild and confused and terrifying.

'It was a dream, Jack.' She tried to make him see her. 'A dream.'

He blinked and finally focused. 'Ariana?' He suddenly embraced her tightly against his chest.

She stroked his neck. 'Shh. It's over. It was only a dream.' She also needed calming.

'Ariana.' He buried his fingers in her hair and brought his lips to hers.

His kiss was one of desperation, as if she were his very last tether on sanity. She opened her mouth and he deepened the kiss, his tongue thrusting hungrily against hers.

Her one brief affair could not compare to this. Desire swept through her and she kissed him back, tugging her shift up until they broke apart and she pulled it over her head. He removed his shirt and with a swift motion, she was suddenly beneath him. He moved his hands over her, kneading her breasts, rubbing her nipples until she thought she would cry out at the exquisite torture. He slid his hand between her legs, stroking her until she writhed beneath him, slick and ready. She pressed her fingers into his skin, soundlessly begging him to fulfil her need.

He obliged her, thrusting inside her so strongly she gasped, not in pain but in a thrill unlike anything she'd ever anticipated.

She lifted her hips to him, meeting each thrust, the sound of their breathing filling her ears. The attraction that had first drawn them together and the desire that continued to flare exploded between them.

She'd known he possessed this passion, but she'd not known he could unleash the same passion from within her. Their coupling was wild, frenzied, urgent. A part of her understood his lovemaking came from whatever dark place he'd been in his dream, but, if he needed comfort for it, she wanted to comfort him.

They moved as if created for each other, faster, hotter, harder, together.

She needed the end to come, but she wanted this to last for

ever. Just when she thought she could stand no more, her release came and, as attuned as they were, his came at the same moment. She wanted to cry aloud for the joy of it.

He stifled her cry, kissing her in that moment of satiation, that moment they were made one in pleasure.

Collapsing beside her, he lay very still. She nestled against him, pressing her lips to his body, entwining her legs with his.

He put an arm around her, holding her close. 'I should not have done that,' he said, his voice low and rough.

She moved her lips against him. 'Do not say that. I know you liked it as much as I did.'

He lifted her face to his and gave her a long kiss. 'I liked it very much.'

She laughed and slid on top of him. 'It was marvellous!'

He rubbed his hands along the bare skin of her back. 'We should not become lovers, Ariana.'

She put her lips on his forehead, his nose, his chin. 'Why not? Why deprive ourselves of enjoying this while we can? Besides—' she felt his arousal grow again '—it is too late.'

He groaned in reply, and joined with her once again.

Chapter Ten

Jack woke to a chilled room and Ariana's warm naked body next to his. He gazed at her face, so beautiful he wondered if he could ever capture such loveliness in her portrait.

He ought not to be lying next to her, even though this was where he most wanted to be. Waking from that dream, he'd needed her. All resolve to resist her had vanished.

He glanced towards the window. The dim light of dawn peeked through the curtains. He'd spent the whole night with her.

Very slowly he eased himself up. She mumbled something and he froze. She rolled over and he waited until he heard her soft, regular breathing. Carefully he climbed out of the bed. The bare wood floor was even colder beneath his feet than the room itself. He untangled the bed covers and placed them over her, then walked to the fireplace to put more coal on the dying embers. At least she would wake to a warm room.

Jack discovered his clothing neatly folded on a chair, everything but his shirt, which he found beneath her shift on the floor. He dressed as quickly and as quietly as he could, watching her the whole time. Holding his shoes in his hand, he walked towards the door in his stockinged feet.

The bed covers rustled.

'You are leaving?' she murmured, her voice raspy with sleep.

He turned back. 'I tried not to wake you.'

She sat up in bed, her hair a jumble of curls. 'Why must you leave? You are not painting today, and we are not going to the Egyptian Hall until later.'

He glanced at the door. 'The house is still quiet. I will not be seen.'

She grimaced. 'No one here will mind that you stayed the night with me.'

It was not what they thought of him spending the night that concerned him. 'Your friends here all speak so freely. It is one thing for them to talk of me as your guest for dinner, but quite another if it is mentioned that I spent the night. It is best if no one knows.'

She stared at him. 'You are worried that Tranville will hear of it?'

He nodded. 'That is precisely it.' He stepped to the side of the bed and brushed the hair from her face. 'I will see you later when Nancy and I come to collect you.'

She clasped his hand and brought it to her lips. 'Until then, Jack.'

It was all he could do not to taste those lips again, to throw off his clothing and return to the delights of her bed, the delights that banished his demons, at least for that space of time. Jack cared nothing if Tranville became enraged with him, but his choices could hurt people he cared about. His mother. Ariana.

For them Jack must take care with Tranville. He must confine his contact with Ariana to the studio. They must go on as merely artist and subject.

With that resolve, Jack left the bedchamber and walked quietly down the stairs, hearing and seeing no one. Once outside he put on his shoes and started for Adam Street. The city was coming to life with carriages and wagons and workers hurrying on their way. Street vendors carted their wares, crying, 'Fresh pies,' or, 'Dutch biscuits,' when he came close enough to hear.

Jack purchased a spicy gingerbread biscuit, wrapping it in his handkerchief and putting it in his coat pocket to eat with his morning tea. It would save him the trouble of breakfasting at his mother's table and the risk of finding Tranville there again.

The brisk morning air felt good in his lungs, and his ears were free of the whisperings of Badajoz. He could almost feel happy.

When he crossed the Strand to Adam Street, however, Jack's growing good mood fled. Tranville emerged from his mother's door and turned in his direction.

Tranville strode up to him. 'Up early, are you, Jack?'

'As are you, Tranville.' He tried to keep his voice even.

Tranville made the pretence of a smile. 'Your mother's household are all still abed.'

Jack ground his teeth.

Tranville laughed softly, aware, no doubt, that he'd annoyed Jack. He suddenly stepped back, eying Jack as if seeing him for the first time. 'You look as if you slept in your clothes. Where have you been?'

Jack met Tranville's eye. 'If I have slept in my clothes, sir, you may be certain I am too much of a gentleman to discuss it.'

Tranville laughed out loud. 'Been with a woman, eh?'

Jack did not answer.

Tranville glared at him. 'I hope this woman of yours is not keeping you from working on the portrait. I want to see what progress you have made.'

'There is nothing to see.' Jack glared back.

'What?' Tranville's brows rose. 'You've done nothing? Time is of the essence, you know. It is almost March and the play will run in April.'

'I am aware of the timing,' Jack replied stiffly.

Tranville jabbed the air with his finger. 'Well, do not dally.

I wish to know the instant it is finished. The instant I may see the final product. And it had better be soon.'

Jack nodded brusquely. 'You will be so informed. Prepare to bring the balance of my fee at that time.'

'Do what I want when I want it and you will be paid.' Tranville started to walk away, but turned back. 'In fact, I want you to make two portraits. One is my gift to Miss Blane; the other will be mine.'

Jack disliked the idea of Tranville owning even an image of Ariana. He shot back, 'The fee is double, then.' Tranville would be a fool to accept such terms.

'Double?' Tranville huffed. 'It will not take you double the time, I dare say.'

He inclined his head in disdain. 'It will delay me from accepting other commissions. Take it or leave it.'

Tranville's eyes had narrowed menacingly.

Jack added, 'I expect half the sum by tomorrow, or I will have to accept another commission.' A commission he did not have, but Tranville could not know that.

Tranville frowned, but finally waved his hand as if swatting at a fly. 'What is money to me? I'll pay your trifling amount.'

He was a fool, Jack thought.

Tranville waved his hand again. 'I have no more time to waste with you.' He hurried off.

Jack watched him turn the corner on to the Strand.

'Go to the devil,' he muttered before proceeding to the studio.

That afternoon, Ariana checked the window again to see if Jack and his sister had arrived yet. This time she was in luck. She saw them walking up to the door.

She ran into the hallway outside her room and called to the maid, 'Betsy, my guests are coming. Tell them I will be one minute. They can wait in the hall.'

'Yes, miss,' Betsy replied from below.

Ariana hurried back into her room and put on her new deep green sarcenet pelisse that had just come from the mantua maker. A matching green hat and buff gloves completed her costume. She took a quick glance in the mirror, hoping Jack would think she looked well in it.

She returned to the top of the stairs, seeing only Jack gazing up at her. Her senses flared with the memory of his arms stroking her, his body engulfing her. By the time she reached the bottom step, she saw that his sister stood next to him.

'I am all ready.' She smiled at Nancy. 'It is a pleasure to see you again, Miss Vernon.'

Nancy curtsied. 'For me as well.'

Ariana smiled at her. 'Your Michael is not with you?'

'He had to attend his classes.'

'What a pity.' Ariana had wanted Michael and Nancy to have their outing together as well.

She turned to Jack. 'Mr Vernon, thank you for suggesting this outing.'

Nancy looked confused. 'Jack told me it was your idea.'

Ariana grinned impishly at Nancy. 'It was.'

Jack opened the door for them and they stepped outside on to the pavement. 'If you do not mind walking, I suspect it is no more than a mile to Piccadilly.'

'Walking will do,' Nancy replied.

Jack turned to Ariana. 'Miss Blane?'

She took his arm. 'Walking it is.'

Nancy seemed more subdued than she had on their first meeting, but Ariana supposed it was because Michael was not with her. Ariana envied the girl her young love. There was much to be said for being courted by a respectable young man and looking forward to a conventional, predictable life.

She, however, had chosen otherwise and must be content

with what her life provided her. The excitement of performing. The freedom to do as she wished. No one expected an
actress to be chaste. She could choose to share her bed with
Jack, if she so desired. She did, most ardently, desire to share
her bed with him again.

Nancy became more cheerful when the Egyptian Hall
came into view. 'It looks like the prints we saw of the buildings in Egypt.'

The building's façade was intended to resemble the
entrance of an Egyptian temple, its three storeys were made
to look as if they were one. Two huge statues of Isis and
Osiris stood high above the entrance, which was flanked by
two columns as tall as the ground floor. Egyptian symbols,
appearing as if carved in stone, embellished the window
frames.

'It looks grand,' admitted Jack.

He paid their admission and they entered the building,
soon walking into a huge musty room with a display of large
wild animals in the centre, birds and smaller mammals in
cases lining the walls.

Ariana gazed around in disgust. 'They are all dead.'

These creatures, once running, flying, chasing prey, had
been stuffed so that people could gaze upon them. She glanced
at Jack, who returned an understanding look that made Ariana
flush with pleasure.

'Oh, my!' Nancy immediately hurried over to the elephant.
She had to hold on to her hat to look up at it. 'I never imagined
elephants to be so huge.' She walked around the centre exhibit,
gasping at the hippopotamus and the polar bear and the zebra.

Ariana was left standing alone with Jack.

She put her arm through his. 'She seems in better spirits.'

'Better spirits?' He looked surprised.

She tilted her head. 'You and your sister are very quiet today.'

He put his hand over hers. 'There is much I cannot say in front of Nancy.'

She grew warm at his touch. 'I am very much in sympathy with that statement. What is troubling Nancy, though?'

He glanced over at her. 'I do not know.'

She whispered, 'If I can contrive it, I shall try to find out.'

He slid a look towards a wall covered with dead birds. 'I will leave you to it, then, and will become fascinated by these colourful fowl.'

She resisted a strong urge to kiss him. Their gazes caught and she saw a mirror image of her yearning. The desire between them flared with such heat, it was a surprise the dead birds did not burst into flames.

'I had best examine these birds,' he murmured.

She took a breath. 'Yes. I shall keep your sister company.'

She joined Nancy, whose initial enthusiasm for the big animals seemed to have flagged. The girl was staring blankly at the zebra.

'It certainly looks like a horse, does it not?' Ariana said.

Nancy blinked and darted a glance to her. 'Yes. Yes, it does.'

'You seem unhappy today, Miss Vernon,' she began. 'What is amiss?'

Nancy sighed. 'Nothing, really.'

Ariana made Nancy look at her. 'I am not convinced.'

Nancy gazed down at the polar bear. 'Oh, it is just that Lord Tranville keeps talking of finding me a husband.'

Tranville again.

'Does he?' Ariana said in a harsh tone.

They wandered over to look at display cases of dead reptiles.

'I suppose he thinks he is helping,' Nancy went on. 'But I do not think I want to be married yet.'

'Have you explained to Tranville about your Michael?'

Nancy blushed. 'You keep calling him *my* Michael, but we are mere friends.' She sighed. 'Besides, he has a year of studies to finish and then he must work for someone. And—and he may not want me.'

'Not want you?' It was clear to Ariana that Michael was besotted with her.

'Because of my family, you know.'

Ariana did not understand at first, but it dawned on her that outside the theatre world, liaisons with gentlemen made a respectable woman a social outcast. For Tranville, of course, it merely increased his cachet.

Two young men in dandified clothing began casting them impertinent looks, appearing as if they had just about worked up the courage to approach.

Ariana tilted her head in their direction as a warning to Nancy, but the young woman seemed oblivious that she had attracted such attention. 'We had better join your brother,' Ariana told her.

Jack smiled as they walked over to him. Together they left that room in search of one with Egyptian artifacts.

Jack had a chance to ask, 'Did Nancy say what is troubling her?'

'Apparently Lord Tranville is still talking of finding someone to marry her,' Ariana whispered.

'That damned man,' Jack uttered through clenched teeth.

They found a room displaying South Seas curiosities, including preserved insects and reptiles, as well as more dead birds. Ariana was eager to move on to another display, but Jack seemed intent on minutely examining every shell and piece of coral in the room.

'Let us go on,' she whispered to Nancy, taking her arm. She called back to Jack. 'We will be in the next room.'

This housed the American exhibit dominated by a large statue of a red-skinned Indian dressed for battle. Two gentlemen stood examining it. Ariana saw immediately that one of them was Edwin Tranville; the other was an older man who was on the theatre's national culture committee with Lord Tranville. She glanced at Nancy, who frowned and turned back towards the door, but not before the older gentleman, Lord Ullman, saw them.

He waved his hand and approached. 'Miss Blane!'

Lord Ullman was an average-sized man in his forties with thin hair and a thick waistline.

'Miss Blane, how good to see you.' When he glanced at Nancy his eyes grew large. 'May I be presented to your enchanting friend?' He sounded as if he'd forgotten how to speak.

Ariana pursed her lips. Lord Ullman probably assumed Nancy was also an actress, a ripe fruit ready for his picking. She darted a glance at Edwin, who was looking at them but did not approach. One was a nuisance, but the other could be trouble. Jack certainly would not want his sister near Edwin.

She made the introduction Ullman requested, speaking quickly. 'Miss Vernon, this is Lord Ullman, who is known to me from the theatre.'

'Charmed, my dear.' Lord Ullman bowed.

Nancy made a polite curtsy.

Ariana turned to Lord Ullman. 'Nancy is not with the theatre, sir. She accompanies her brother, who is the artist painting my portrait. He is in the next room.' She was confident Ullman would lose interest once he knew Nancy was not one of the trinkets on sale. 'I requested that Mr Vernon bring me here to view the Egyptian artifacts. I want to be certain my portrait as Cleopatra has authenticity.'

Lord Ullman continued to gaze at Nancy. 'I see.'

Ariana added, 'We were about to leave.'

Ullman did not heed her. 'Do you assist your brother, Miss Vernon?'

Nancy's forehead creased in confusion and she darted a wary look toward Edwin. 'When he asks me.' She stepped back towards the door.

Ullman smiled at her. 'I am delighted you assist him today. It is my good fortune to meet you.'

Nancy was saved from responding to this unwelcome flattery by Edwin.

He'd sauntered up to them, giving Nancy an unfriendly glance. 'I seem to be knocking into Vernons everywhere I turn.'

'I am equally as pleased to see you,' Nancy retorted sharply.

Lord Ullman scowled at Edwin. 'Dashed unfriendly of you, young man. I will not have it.'

Ariana curtsied. 'We must leave. Good day to you both.'

She and Nancy hurried to find Jack.

Nancy ran up to him and pulled at his sleeve. 'Jack! Edwin is here, of all people.' She turned towards Ariana. 'He is Tranville's son and we've known him since childhood. He was a hateful boy, always harassing me and picking fights with Jack. He looks terrible with that scar.'

Jack looked out into the hall and saw Edwin in the doorway of the next room. The two men glared at each other.

Jack turned back to Nancy. 'Stay clear of him.'

'You do not need to warn me about Edwin.' Nancy pulled on her brother again. 'I do not want to be here, if he is here. Can we leave now?'

Jack looked to Ariana.

'We have seen enough for me,' she said, although they had not spied even one Egyptian artifact.

They made their way through the building and out of the grand doorway back on to Piccadilly.

'I dislike it that Edwin has seen us together twice now,' Jack whispered to Ariana as they stepped away from the building.

Ariana tried to give him a reassuring look. 'I explained we were doing research for the portrait. I doubt it could be credited as anything more.' Her curiosity burned to know the origins of such extreme reactions to Edwin Tranville. Would Jack ever tell her? she wondered.

'I am just glad to be away from him.' Nancy glanced around at the shops that lined the street. 'Jack, may I visit the perfumer for a moment?' The shop was right there.

Jack checked back at the door of the Egyptian Hall as if to see if Edwin followed them. 'I'll stop in Mr Hewlett's, then.' He pointed to a shop with a sign saying Thomas Hewlett Oil and Colourman. 'And meet you in front of the perfumer's shop.'

Ariana accompanied Nancy into the perfumery, although her mind was not on scent, but on Jack. She cared about him, cared that he was disturbed by Edwin, cared about what happened to him in the past as well as the present. She was surprised at the depth of emotion he aroused in her. She'd not expected to feel so strongly about a man again.

Until she met Jack.

'I should like to buy a throwaway for Mama,' Nancy told her as they walked to the counter.

A throwaway was a small vial of perfume, sold in a small amount so the purchaser could sample many different mixtures of scent. Nancy approached the shop keeper and began discussing fragrances. She pointed to the pretty gilded and enamelled glass bottles that would hold the scent.

Ariana wandered back to the shop's window and gazed out into the street as Nancy's discussion went on and on. After a time, she saw Jack come from the colourman's shop. 'I will wait with your brother right outside,' she told Nancy.

Nancy nodded and lifted one of the slender bottles up to examine it more closely.

'She will be a few minutes,' Ariana explained as she walked out of the shop and Jack approached her. He still looked disturbed.

'I wish Edwin Tranville did not distress you so, Jack.'

He took her hand in his for just a brief moment. 'Forgive me. I am not good company.'

'Being with you,' she murmured, 'is enjoyment enough.'

She checked to see if Nancy was still occupied with the clerk. 'I wish you would come to my room tonight, Jack.'

The lines at the corners of his eyes deepened. 'It would not be wise.'

'I do not care who discovers us,' she said valiantly.

His expression was serious. 'We must not be seen together. Tranville can make a great deal of trouble for you. We should not meet, except at the studio.' He blew out a breath. 'Come to the studio in the morning tomorrow. We can work all day.'

She nodded. He spoke of work, but she longed to repeat the pleasures of the previous night. She pointed to the package in his hand, wrapped with brown paper and tied with string. 'What did you purchase?'

'Some brushes and colours that I needed.' He gave a half-smile. 'A great deal of Cremora white.'

For her portrait.

She smiled back at him and gazed into his eyes. It was as if a spark flared between them, a shared passion that would take little to ignite.

Nancy came out of the perfumery carrying her purchase, even more carefully wrapped than Jack's. 'I chose a lovely blend of rose, violet and jasmine.'

'It makes me yearn for spring.' Ariana smiled.

Nancy looked at Jack. 'I hope Mama will like it.'

Jack put his arm around her. 'Of course she will like it.'

They walked back to Henrietta Street. The day had not at all turned out as Ariana had hoped, and she had the rest of the afternoon, the evening and the night to endure before she would see Jack again.

That night, after what seemed an interminable performance of *Romeo and Juliet*, Ariana did her duty in the Green Room. Tranville was there, deep in conversation with Lord Ullman, his expression quite serious. She chewed on her lip and hoped Ullman had not mentioned she'd been with Jack.

To her relief Lord Tranville did not approach her, although his eyes followed her like a cat watching its prey. She shivered and turned away.

Unfortunately, as she turned, Edwin Tranville, glass in hand, stood directly in her path.

She tried to walk past him, but he stepped in her way and smirked. 'I wonder what my father would think if he knew you were out with the Vernons.'

She lifted her chin. 'I cannot fathom why he would care.'

Edwin took a gulp of his drink. 'Ullman told me all about it. My father, pathetic old man that he is, pursues you. Is that not right?'

She sniffed. 'If you are not in your father's confidence, you can hardly expect to be in mine.'

'*Touché*, my dear.' He laughed and drained the contents of his glass. 'But before you brush me off, let me tell you something about Jack. He may fancy himself above his betters, but his mother is nothing but a common whore.'

She almost slapped him, offended to the core on Jack's mother's behalf. But she would leave Jack out of it.

Ariana leaned conspiratorially towards Edwin. 'Someone called my mother that once,' she whispered. 'Her lover shot him.'

Edwin shrank back.

'Be careful with your words, Mr Tranville. You might find yourself challenged to pistols at dawn.' She strode away and joined a group that included Mr Arnold.

As she glanced back, Edwin made his way to where his father and Ullman continued to converse. His complexion remained deathly white.

Chapter Eleven

Jack rose early the next day, so early he begged breakfast from his mother's cook in her kitchen, discovering from her chatter that Tranville had not shared his mother's bed the previous night. Not knowing if that boded well or ill, he returned to his studio to prepare another canvas while waiting for Ariana.

Dressed only in a paint-stained shirt and trousers, Jack undertook the physical work of constructing the frame and stretching the linen. It was a good distraction from the anticipation of seeing her again. Their time together at the Egyptian Hall had been ruined by Edwin's presence, but today, with any luck at all, there would be no Tranvilles to spoil the work.

Because it must be work, not pleasure, that they indulge in today, although the memory of making love to her still fired his blood. He knew he wanted nothing more than to take her in his arms once again and carry her to his bed, to the devil with his painting.

He laughed out loud.

Whom was he attempting to fool? Painting her excited him almost as much as tumbling into bed with her. He wanted the painting to be everything she wished. He wanted the image he created of her to last for ever, her beauty, her essence, preserved for all time

When Jack finished stretching the canvas, he placed it on his easel and walked into his galley to prepare his paints. He needed to mix up a great deal of lead white to use in preparing the canvas. The more expensive Cremora he would save for the painting itself. On a stone slab, he mixed the pigment powder with linseed oil, adding a few drops of turpentine until achieving the exact consistency he desired. With his palette knife, he scooped up most of the mixture and tied it into a small bladder which he'd prick with a tack to extract small amounts of pigment at a time. The rest of the white he scraped on to his wooden palette.

Returning to the easel, he chose a wide brush and began to cover the linen canvas with thin, even layers of white. When the canvas was totally dry it would be ready.

Some artists now purchased canvases already prepared, but Jack liked the methodical nature of this task, engaging enough of his mind to empty it of other thoughts, but lulling in its simplicity.

It also saved him money.

By the time he'd finished and cleaned up the studio, the streets outside were noisy with activity. He could almost feel Ariana near.

He arranged the *chaise-longue* to make the best use of the light and exchanged the canvas he'd just prepared for the one that was dry and ready.

When he glanced out of the window, he was not surprised to see her on the pavement, looking up at him. Before she even knocked he opened the door to her.

'Jack!' she cried, her face aglow with pleasure.

As soon as he closed the door behind her, she rushed into his arms, raising her face for the kiss he now knew he'd been awaiting since dawn. She kissed him eagerly, laughing beneath his lips, pulling off her gloves and her hat as she did so. Hairpins rained down as her thick hair fell loose. He unfastened the hook of her cloak and it slipped off her shoulders to the floor. Her hands were quickly beneath his shirt, raking the muscles of his back and heating him with urgent desire.

His need for her was intense, not only for physical release but to be joined with her, to feel connected to her, as if they were one.

She pulled off his shirt and placed her moist mouth on his chest. He raised her skirt and pressed her against his aching loins.

As he opened his eyes he realised the windows that flooded the room with light also made it possible to see into the studio. With a groan of frustration for having to delay even a few seconds, he lifted her into his arms and carried her into the bedchamber.

Plunged into relative darkness, Jack blinked until he adjusted to the windowless room. He placed her on the bed, and she swivelled around so her back faced him. 'Undo my dress.'

He put his hand on her shoulder. 'Wait. There may be consequences for what we do.'

She spun around and made a sound of exasperation. 'What consequences if no one else knows of it?'

He took her chin in his fingers. 'I meant…we could create a child.'

Her mouth formed an O. She swept her fingers through his hair. 'I know what to do,' she murmured. 'Do not fear. One cannot be around the theatre and not learn such things.'

He relaxed.

'Will you undo my dress?' she asked again, moving her hair out of the way.

'It will be my delight.' He kissed the nape of her neck before undoing the hooks and untying the laces. He pulled the dress over her head and made short work of the laces of her corset. She pulled off her shift and both items were added to the pile of clothing on the floor. Naked but for stockings and shoes, she was an erotic sight. He scrambled to remove his trousers.

She watched him, her eyes widening in pleasure as he stood before her, naked and aroused. 'Jack, do you know how truly magnificent you are?'

He crouched down to reach her feet, pulling off a shoe. 'It is I who should be saying those words to you.'

She sighed. 'I am too outspoken. I know.'

His hand slid up her leg to reach the garter of her stocking. 'Too beautiful, perhaps. Nothing else.'

She played with his hair while he rolled down first one stocking, then the other. When he stood she touched him, her fingers examining the male part of him, a sweet torture that drove rational thought out of his mind.

He moved on top of her on the bed and began a torture of his own, tasting the elegant length of her neck, the luxury of her breasts, the hair that led him to her most feminine place. He felt a surge of masculine energy as she writhed beneath his touch and he rose above her.

'I want you,' she murmured to him, always speaking aloud thoughts he kept silent.

She was more than ready for him. He slipped into her easily, but forced himself to move slowly, wanting to prolong this delicious sense of oneness, wanting to savour her for as long as he could.

The sensations grew and soon there was no wanting at all, just rushing toward the pleasure. All that existed was Ariana, moving in perfect unison with him. Joined to him. He seized that feeling, clung to it, begged it to stay.

His climax erupted and all thought, all feeling, was engulfed in the explosion of pleasure. He spilled his seed inside her and she convulsed around him. Stars burst behind his closed eyes and heaven seemed in easy reach. Their dual moment of pleasure lasted longer than he thought possible, longer than with any other woman.

When it ended, he almost collapsed on her, but stopped himself before crushing her under his full weight. Instead he slipped to her side and lay on his back, his eyes still closed. He was trying to create in his mind an image of what they had experienced, trying to put shape and colour to it. It resembled illuminations he'd seen at Vauxhall Gardens last summer, wild and bright and joyful.

He turned and held her close, kissing her long and languidly.

'That was—' she began.

He covered her mouth with his fingers. 'Allow me to be the outspoken one. That was…quite nice.'

'Such hyperbole.' She laughed. 'I have almost no experience in these matters, but I believe *I* would describe it as wonderful.'

'Almost no experience?' His brows knitted. What woman spent years in the theatre without such experiences?

'There was only one man, Jack.' She stroked his face to ease his frown. 'An older actor when I was barely nineteen, and it lasted not even a week.'

The pain from that experience showed on her face. 'He taught me a great deal—but nothing of love.' Her voice sounded clipped. 'Indeed, I feared I could no longer be tempted by a man until I met you.'

She had resisted every gentleman in every Green Room? Even the one with the fine carriage he'd seen her with that first day at Somerset House?

His disbelief must have shown on his face, because a wounded look flickered in her eyes. 'My mother is known for her liaisons with gentlemen from the Green Room. I am not.'

He touched her arm. 'I do not doubt you. I'm merely astonished you could avoid such gentlemen.' For years? It did seem unbelievable.

She took a breath. 'I manage them. Turn them down without dealing too severe a blow to their vanity. I am quite skilled at it. That is why I do not worry about Tranville.'

Jack moved away and sat up. 'Be wary of him, none the less. And his son. Was he at the theatre last night?'

Her eyes shifted. 'He was, but he did not speak to me.' She pressed herself against his back. 'Do not allow mention of him to ruin our time together.'

The warmth and softness of her naked breasts against his skin threatened to arouse him again, to persuade him to abandon any thought of painting and simply make love all day.

He took a breath and angled his head towards her. 'We should work.'

'One more kiss,' she urged, coming close and pulling his head to her lips.

Her kiss fired his senses again, but he pulled away. 'We really must work. We'll lose the light.'

She sighed. 'I suppose you are right.'

She climbed off the bed and padded across the room, naked and graceful in her bare feet on the wooden floor, all sinuous lines and muted colour. She opened the bandbox and removed the white muslin gown they had decided upon, draping it over her shoulder. 'You know, the prints at the Royal Academy showed the Egyptian women without shoes. I think I should forgo shoes, don't you? Cleopatra's feet would be bare.'

Bare feet. Bare skin. He thought of the Cleopatra of his imagination, the one who wore the sheer costume, naked underneath, but regal and alluring.

'I have another idea,' he said. 'Put on the other muslin gown.'

'The other one?' She looked surprised. 'I thought we decided on this one.'

'We did.' He left the bed and quickly began dressing. He wanted to see if the sheer costume matched the image in his imagination. 'I should like to see you in the sheer one again.'

She regarded him as if he were crazed. 'Very well, but I thought my stays showed through too much.'

He kept his gaze even. 'Do not wear your stays. Just the gown.'

Her eyes widened.

'Indulge me.' He searched for an explanation. 'The dress is transparent. Show me how it looks this way.'

She appeared wary. 'You wish me to pose without my undergarments?'

It was akin to asking her to pose nude, something even prostitutes considered shameful.

'Not pose. I just want to see.'

A sensuous smile came over her face, the sort of smile his imaginary Cleopatra would make. Ariana removed the filmy muslin gown from the box and slipped it over her head. She turned to face him.

He grabbed a fistful of the gold chains she'd brought from the theatre, and took her hand. 'Come into the studio.'

She allowed him to lead her into the other room, so bright with sunlight that they both blinked. He tied one of the gold chains around her waist and draped the others about her neck. Walking around her, he watched how her skin showed through the fabric, how the transparency played with colour and light. The thought of painting her like this was a challenge that fired his blood, even if it was too scandalous to consider.

She arched one brow. 'Do you wish to paint me in this?'

He stared at her a long time, very tempted to say yes. Instead he waved a hand. 'No, change into the other gown. I just had the desire to see this one.'

The next two weeks were glorious ones for Ariana. Her afternoons were often filled with rehearsals for *Antony and Cleopatra*, and the evenings still required she be at the theatre, where she helped out as needed. She did not even mind attending the Green Room after performances, because she always found a way to mention that Jack was painting her portrait. But the mornings were what made life glorious. Each was spent with Jack, making love in his bed, then sitting for the portrait.

Sometimes when Jack was painting, his concentration was so intense they did not speak at all. At other times they shared the stories of their lives.

Jack seemed to select very carefully which bits of his life he shared. He told about the time before his father's death, but little of afterwards. He talked of Spain and Portugal, of the sights, sounds and smells there, but not of the battles in which he had fought.

Ariana found herself chattering on as she remained posed as Cleopatra. She told him of growing up in a girls' school, of her mother and her mother's lovers, of how she ran off to join the theatre company.

One blot on this idyll was the portrait itself. At first it fascinated her, how her image seemed to float to the surface as the days progressed, but there was something missing in the portrait. She was disappointed in it, and Jack well knew it.

Another distressing element was that the portrait was almost completed. Indeed, she really did not need to sit for him any longer, but neither of them spoke of that.

This day, after she finished the sitting, she stood back and surveyed the painting.

'It is lovely, Jack…' Her voice trailed off.

'But?' He spoke the word more as an accusation than a question.

'You know what I think.' She hated to go over this again. 'It lacks emotion.'

He made a frustrated gesture. 'I am painting what I see.'

His observation was acute. The canvas was mostly white, as if Cleopatra sat in a room of white marble, but the white had subtle shades of colour in the shadows, in the hieroglyphics, in the other details of the room and her clothing. Cleopatra herself blazed with colour. Her skin. Her hair. Her eyes, outlined in black. The gold around her neck sparkled, and, although there was only a peek of red cushions on the piece of Egyptian furniture upon which she lounged, the colour echoed the red of her lips.

She had no doubt this all took great skill, but what made Jack's work special to her was missing. She'd tried and tried to explain.

'You are ignoring the emotion, Jack.' She did not know how else to say it.

He shook his head. 'This is no different from when I painted Nancy.'

'The painting of Nancy made her look alive. You could see all that youthful passion in her face, all her hopes and yearnings for the future.'

He threw up a hand. 'That is nonsense, Ariana. Nancy sat for me and I painted what I saw.'

'Then you see me as flat and lifeless.' Her voice rose. 'You showed how you loved Nancy when you painted her.'

He straightened. 'Do you accuse me of having no feelings for you?'

He had shown her in dozens of ways how he felt about her, but he had never spoken of loving her. It hurt her that he never spoke the word, even now.

'What are your feelings, Jack?' She pointed to the painting. 'You hide them on the canvas.'

He strode towards her and seized her by her shoulders. 'You have to ask me, Ariana?' His eyes showed a depth of emotion that took her breath away. Why was that not in her portrait?

'Why does the painting have to pose the same question, Jack?' she murmured. 'You can do better than this. What do you feel when you are painting me?'

He released her and turned away, raking a hand through his hair. 'That Tranville will possess your portrait and will look upon it every day.'

'Tranville,' she said abruptly.

Would she never rid herself of Tranville? Even though he no longer pursued her, she still felt his eyes upon her when he was in the Green Room and when he sat in his box while she was onstage. Sometimes during rehearsal he sat in the back of the theatre. Watching.

She did not mention that to Jack.

'I will also have a copy of the portrait,' she reminded him. 'I should like it to reflect what has passed between us when I look upon it. I should like other people to see those emotions when they look at engravings of it.'

He averted his gaze.

She turned away and headed towards the bedchamber door. 'I am going to change my clothes. If we are done for the day, I must get to the theatre.' She did not know the target for her anger; Tranville for his intrusion or Jack, who allowed him to be so important.

She pulled off her costume and flung it on to his bed. She'd just started to dress when Jack entered the room.

'Are you able to stay a little longer?' he asked.

She took a weary breath. 'I think I ought to go.'

He walked over to her and put his hands on her shoulders. 'I believe you are right about the portrait. I want to try something.'

His touch melted away her anger. 'What?'

His hands slid down her arms to around her back. 'Pose for me in the transparent gown.' He untied the strings of her corset. 'Without your stays.'

Her brows rose. 'Without wearing anything beneath?'

'Yes.' He was very close to her, his fingers untying her laces. 'From the day you brought the costumes here, it has been the image I yearned to paint. Maybe that is the answer.'

She stared at him.

'I realise you would endure much censure if the final portrait showed your nakedness, but I will paint over it. The final portrait will show you in the other white gown.'

Ariana imagined Jack's eyes, serious and intent, boring into her, perusing every inch of her near nakedness, reaching into the very depths of her soul. The prospect excited her mind and her senses, arousing her as his stroking fingers aroused her in bed. Her heart pounded rapidly.

These were the emotions she'd envisioned in the portrait.

She shrugged out of her corset. 'Let's do it,' she cried. 'Let us start right now!'

Chapter Twelve

Nancy bade Michael farewell at the corner of Adam Street and The Strand. He would have to run to reach his class at Somerset House in time. She insisted he not walk her to the door. They always dawdled when saying goodbye, thinking of one more thing to say before parting.

She watched him rush away, smiling at his limber gait. He turned around and saw her and paused as if he might return and walk her all the way. She moved the bouquet of flowers he had purchased for her to one arm and waved him on.

It would be just like Michael to make himself late because of her.

She sighed. What would she do if it were not for him? Michael was her most faithful friend, a far better friend than her old Bath schoolmates who used to whisper behind her back about her mother and Lord Tranville when they thought she did not know. Michael would never do that.

If it were not for Michael, Nancy would hardly ever set foot out of the London house. Her mother never went out now that Lord Tranville had begun to call. Nancy had begun to dislike Lord Tranville's visits. He always seemed to be assessing her, as if he was trying to decide how he could marry her off.

Nancy lifted Michael's flowers to her nose and walked slowly the rest of the way home. When she reached her door, she heard the clock chime one. She'd told her mother she'd be back by noon.

From the hall she heard Tranville's voice in the drawing room. Hoping to avoid him, Nancy walked quietly to the back of the townhouse, and started down the servants' stairs to the kitchen to put her flowers in water.

Their manservant was on his way up. 'Hello, Wilson,' she said cheerfully. 'Would you mind telling Mama I have returned? I'll be in my bedchamber after I tend to my flowers.'

Wilson looked up at her. 'Your mother asks that you come to her, miss.'

Nancy took one more step down. 'I'll see her later. She has a caller.'

Wilson stood in her way. 'Your mother expressly asked that you come to the drawing room as soon as you returned.'

Nancy sighed. 'Because I am late, I expect.'

He extended his hands. 'I'll take your things and see to your flowers, miss.'

Was her mother that upset with her for being late?

In the narrow space of the stairway, she first handed Wilson her flowers, then her hat and gloves. Finally she took off her cloak and handed that to him as well before turning and stomping up the stairs back to the hall. Realising she was acting in a rather childish manner, she collected herself, smoothed her skirt and hair, and entered the drawing room.

'Nancy, you are home,' her mother said as soon as she stepped through the doorway.

Tranville and another gentleman stood. It was the gentleman from the Egyptian Hall, the one who had looked at her so rudely. Why would he be calling on her mother?

'Ah, Nancy, my dear. How good to see you.' Tranville

strode over to her. He took her hand in his. 'Come, say hello. I believe you have met Lord Ullman.'

Lord Ullman's face was flushed. He bowed to her. 'Miss Vernon. It is a delight to see you again.'

She curtsied. 'Good day, sir.'

Her mother patted the chair between her and Lord Ullman. 'Come sit with us. We have been having a nice chat.'

Nancy did not see why her presence was necessary for them to continue their nice chat, but she lowered herself into the chair.

Lord Ullman leaned towards her. 'How are you this fine day, Miss Vernon?'

'Very well, sir,' she murmured.

'Your mother said you were visiting the shops?' he continued.

'The Covent Garden market, sir,' she replied.

'And did you purchase anything?'

'Flowers, sir.' She could not imagine why he was interrogating her so, and why her mother was smiling.

'We have been talking about you,' her mother said.

Nancy quickly turned towards her.

Lord Ullman reached over and patted her hand. 'Nothing but praises, my dear.'

Lord Tranville stood. 'In fact, Lord Ullman has something he wishes to say to you.' He extended his hand to her mother. 'Come, Mary, let us leave the room for a moment.'

Her mother clasped his hand and let him assist her to her feet, which she could do very well on her own. Nancy's heart thumped painfully. She did not wish them to leave her alone with Lord Ullman. 'Mama, wait—'

Her mother merely tossed her a fond look before walking out of the room. Tranville followed and closed the door behind him.

Nancy glanced in alarm at Lord Ullman. She had never before been alone in a room with a gentleman with the door closed. Not even Michael.

Lord Ullman moved his chair closer to her, so that their knees touched, then he took both her hands in his. 'My dear Miss Vernon, I have thought of nothing but you since that moment—that precious moment—of first seeing you in the Egyptian Hall.'

'I cannot imagine—' she began, trying to pull her hands away.

He held fast and brought one hand to his wet lips. 'I have been in a passion for you—'

'Sir!' A passion? This was shocking. He was nearly as old as Tranville.

He kept making her hand wet. 'I cannot rest until you say you will be mine. I want nothing more in this world than to possess you.'

She jumped to her feet. 'Speak no more! I—I am too young for this.' She could not believe her mother had sanctioned this shocking exhibition. 'I have hopes of marriage, sir. I am too young for an affair. I cannot do it.'

He laughed at her and again put her hand against his wet lips. 'You foolish, darling girl. I would never dishonour you with such a request. It is marriage I seek from you.' He fell to his knees. 'Miss Vernon, will you consent to be my bride?'

Her throat seized in panic. 'Your bride?'

She sank back in her chair. He rose from his knees and pushed his chair even closer. 'I have your mother's approval and Lord Tranville's. It is he who has brokered the matter. All that is wanting is your consent.'

Brokered the matter? What did that mean? Had Lord Tranville sold her? Had her mother agreed to it?

'No,' she cried. Her thoughts were racing. She wanted to refuse him, but would her mother be angry with her if she did? 'No. I—I mean, I cannot answer now. Please do not require me to answer. This is too sudden for me.'

He finally released her and gave her room to breathe. 'I quite understand. You know so little of me.' He smiled indulgently. 'Let me assure you, I am a wealthy man. My title is an old one and my finances are as solid as the Bank of England. I am a widower with two delightful children who are in great need of a mother. I am as healthy as a horse.' He patted his chest. 'And, if I do say so myself, lusty enough for a young wife. It shall be my life's endeavour to please you and see you happy.'

Lusty enough? She cringed. He was nothing like the lovers of her fantasies, of the novels she read. He—he was fat. And old. And he had very little hair.

She could not catch her breath. 'Please…'

He stood, but lifted her chin with his hand. 'I will bid you adieu for this day. Your mother and Lord Tranville will, I am confident, ease your maidenly mind.'

He bent down and actually put his lips on hers. It was like being forced to kiss a raw fish.

He straightened. 'One more assurance I will make to you. I naturally forgo any expectation of a dowry. In fact, I agreed with Tranville that, with our marriage, I ought to assume the financial support for your mother as well as for you, and, I further assure you, I am a very generous man.'

Tranville *brokered* the support of her mother as well? Her mind raced. Why would he do that?

Lord Ullman made a deep bow, turned and walked out of the room.

Nancy wiped her lips with the back of her hand and grasped her throat. She bent over, uncertain if she would faint.

Her mother and Tranville bustled in.

Her mother rushed to her side. 'You did not say yes, Nancy dear? I am so surprised.'

Tranville looked stern. 'He makes you a decent offer. More than you have a right to expect.'

Nancy stared into her mother's eyes. 'Do you want me to accept him, Mama?'

Her mother blinked. 'Why, of course. You will be set for life.'

'And so will you—' she snapped.

Tranville interrupted her. 'Now, now. Never mind that. This is about you, not your mother.'

Nancy gaped at him. Perhaps her mother did not know of that part of the bargain. 'But, you—' she began.

'Hush!' He glared at her. 'Do not be a fool and throw this offer away, girl.'

'It is a wonderful match, Nancy. More than I could ever have dreamed for you.'

She shot to her feet. 'I—I need some time. Give me some time.' She pushed by them and headed for the door.

'He will not wait for ever,' Tranville said.

Nancy stumbled into the hall and whirled around, not knowing what to do.

'Nancy?' her mother called from the drawing room.

With a tiny cry, Nancy opened the front door and ran out into the street, without her hat or her gloves or her cloak, not thinking anything but that she needed to find somewhere she could breathe.

A woman's voice sounded from behind her. 'Miss Vernon!'

Ariana, exhilarated and optimistic about the portrait, had just walked out of Jack's building when his sister rushed by her. If she took time to alert Jack, Nancy might disappear from sight.

Ariana ran after her. 'Nancy!'

The girl showed no sign of even hearing her. She seemed to be rushing straight to the river. Ariana could only think she meant to jump in.

She caught up to Nancy near the water's edge, seizing her arm and pulling her away from where the path led straight into the water.

'What are you doing?' Ariana cried. 'What is wrong?'

It seemed to take the girl a few moments to recognise her. 'It is you, Miss Blane.'

'Were you going to jump in?' Ariana's heart was still thumping.

Nancy shook her head. 'I—I want to go to Somerset House. To find Michael.'

Ariana put an arm around the girl. 'I see.' She spoke in a consoling tone. 'To find Michael. But why do you wish to find him?'

'Oh, Miss Blane!' Nancy flung her arms around Ariana's neck and burst into tears. 'It is so awful. What am I to do?'

Ariana let the fit of weeping die down before asking Nancy to explain. The whole appalling story spilled out. Lord Tranville had arranged for Lord Ullman to propose marriage to her. The poor child! Poor Michael.

'The worst thing is,' Nancy gulped. 'My mother *wants* me to marry him. And he is old enough to be my father. And he is fat!' She burst into another fit of tears.

'There. There.' She patted Nancy's back until she calmed again. 'I am sure there is a way to fix this.'

'Nothing can be done!'

She held the girl longer. 'We must go back and tell Jack.'

Nancy pulled away. 'Jack hates Lord Tranville! He'll fight a duel or something.'

'Jack will help you, I know he will,' she murmured. 'You must tell him about this.'

'No one can help me.' Nancy covered her face with her hands. When she dropped them again, she sighed. 'Oh, very well. We will tell Jack.'

Ariana took off her cloak and wrapped it around the shivering girl. She held on to her as they walked back to Jack's door.

Nancy talked the whole way. 'The thing is, if I marry Lord Ullman, he will be the one to support Mama. Lord Tranville added that to the marriage agreement. If I refuse, then maybe he won't pay Mama any more money and we'll have nothing to live on.'

Ariana almost tripped. 'Lord Tranville provides your mother's support even now? I thought his…connection…to her was in the past.'

'He has always supported us.' Nancy nodded. 'Since my father died. We would be in abject poverty if he had not. It will break Mama's heart when she discovers he doesn't want to pay for her any more.'

It had been clear that Jack's mother had once been Tranville's mistress, but Ariana had not known he'd also provided Jack's family's support. 'Why should it break her heart?'

'Because Mama is so in love with him. Lord Tranville is more important to her than anyone else, even Jack and me.'

Was Jack's mother foolish enough to prefer Tranville over her own children? She thought her own mother was the only one to prefer a man—any man—to her child.

'She gave up everything for him,' Nancy went on. 'But, of course, I believe we would have starved otherwise, even though Jack says not.' The girl looked at her quizzically. 'I thought Jack would have told you all this.'

Ariana would have thought so, too. 'Perhaps he did not think it important.' Not important that his mother was supported by Tranville and in love with him to boot.

Nancy's forehead creased. 'I truly believed Lord Tranville loved Mama, but, if he loved her, he would not want to stop taking care of her. He can afford Mama now better than before he inherited his title. It is as if he wants to be rid of her.'

They reached Jack's building. 'Come, we'll knock on the door.' She sounded the knocker.

Jack was still wearing his paint-spattered shirt. 'Ariana?' He saw Nancy and his eyes grew wide. 'Come in.'

'Oh, Jack!' Nancy rushed inside and flung herself into his

arms, her tears flowing again. He looked over her shoulder at Ariana with a question in his eyes.

She made a gesture for him to wait.

'Sit down, Nancy.' He coaxed her over to the *chaise-longue*.

'I'll make tea.' Ariana left them and went into the galley.

She could hear Nancy's halting explanation and her brother's outraged response. Now she had two upset persons on her hands.

She carried in the tea.

Jack was pacing. 'Tranville has interfered enough. It is time I dealt with him.'

Nancy turned white. 'Mama will not like it if you quarrel with him.' Her eyes grew huge. 'You mustn't fight a duel!'

'It would serve the man right,' Jack muttered.

'No!' Nancy wailed.

Ariana hastily placed the tray down and sat beside her. 'Your brother will not fight a duel.' She stared at Jack. 'Will you, Jack?'

He continued to pace. 'Of course not, but I will deal with him.'

She pointed to the tea. 'Let us drink the tea and calm down a little.'

'I want no tea.' Jack glowered. He headed toward his bed-chamber. 'I need to change my shirt.'

Nancy blinked away tears. 'Are you certain my brother will not fight a duel?

She clasped Nancy's hand. 'I am very certain.'

'He dislikes Tranville so.'

Ariana disliked Tranville, as well, for causing so much un-happiness to these people she cared about.

Ariana poured her a cup of tea. 'Here, drink this. It will help you feel better.'

She took a sip and sighed. 'I wish I could tell Michael about this. I should so like to talk with him.'

'When will you see him next?' Ariana asked.

'Dinner tonight, if he comes. But I probably won't be able to speak with him alone.'

The mantel clock sounded half past four.

Jack stepped out of his bedchamber, still tying his neck-cloth. He looked at Ariana. 'Are you not late for the theatre?'

Nancy looked alarmed. 'I have made you late!'

Ariana patted her hand. 'Actresses are supposed to be late on occasion.' She made Nancy look at her. 'Would you like to come with me to watch the rehearsal? It will be a nice diversion.' She glanced at Jack. 'You could collect her later or I could send her home in a hackney coach.'

Jack turned to his sister. 'Nancy?'

She nodded, wiping away her tears with her fingers. 'I could come back in a coach in time for dinner.' She looked at Jack. 'Will you tell Mama where I am? I—I'd rather not face her right now. Tell her I will not be late.'

'I will.' Jack buttoned his coat. 'Let us leave immediately. I want to catch Tranville if he is still with Mother.'

Ariana gave Nancy her cloak and wore one of the shawls she had originally brought for the Cleopatra costume. Jack walked them to the Strand to put them in a hack. Luckily one waited nearby.

He helped Nancy into the coach and turned to Ariana.

She placed a hand on his cheek. 'Take care, Jack.'

He covered her hand with his. 'That is usually my warning to you about Tranville.'

Their gazes locked for a moment before he helped her into the carriage. As it drove away, she watched his figure recede in the distance.

Perhaps Nancy's prediction of doom had infected her as well, because Ariana could not help but feel her future with Jack had also undergone a dismal change.

Once the feeling took hold of her, she could not shake it.

Chapter Thirteen

Jack hesitated only until the hackney coach was out of sight before walking with a determined stride to his mother's door.

When he entered, Wilson was dressed to go out.

'Mrs Vernon was just sending me to your studio, Mr Vernon.' The manservant peered behind him. 'Miss Nancy is not with you?'

'She was with me until a moment ago,' Jack explained.

He heard his mother's voice coming from her bedchamber at the end of the hallway. 'I am merely concerned, Lionel.'

'Nonsense. She's run to her brother,' Tranville answered. 'Leave her.'

'I merely wish to know for certain.' His mother emerged from her room and saw him in the hall. She rushed up to him. 'Jack? Jack? Is Nancy with you?'

'No, Mother. She has gone with Miss Blane to watch her rehearse.'

'She's gone with Miss Blane?' Tranville emerged from his mother's room.

Good God. Had Tranville taken her to bed while her daughter's whereabouts were unknown? And she had gone? The two of them were abominable.

'She wished to see the rehearsal.' Jack looked from one to the other. 'I see you found something to occupy yourselves in her absence.'

'Jack!' His mother blushed.

'See here, boy—' Tranville began.

Jack held up a hand to silence them. He walked to the drawing-room door. 'I would speak with you both now.'

Wilson gave Jack a very fleeting look of approval before turning to his mother. 'Do you have need of me, ma'am?'

'No, no, Wilson. You may go back to whatever you were doing.' She followed Jack into the drawing room.

Tranville walked in after her and closed the door behind him. 'You have no call to talk to your mother or to me in that tone, boy. In front of a servant, as well.'

Jack spun on him. 'Stubble it, Tranville. The servants can hardly be shocked by anything that happens in this house. I came here out of concern for my sister. I demand to know what is going on with this marriage business.'

'It is a wonderful offer,' his mother said in a weak voice.

'When did you learn of it, Mother?' Jack asked her.

She looked as if he'd asked an odd question. 'Lionel told me of it this morning.'

'Was the settlement arranged when he spoke to you?' he continued.

'Of course.' She lifted her chin. 'Lionel saw to everything.'

Jack turned to Tranville. 'You negotiated a marriage settlement for my sister without discussing it with her family first? What gave you that right?'

Tranville's eyes flashed. 'A regard for your family. Is that not sufficient for you?'

'Lord Ullman is a wealthy man,' his mother interjected.

'That may be so,' Jack replied to her. 'And if he is a man of good character and Nancy desires him, I can find no objection. But we know nothing of Ullman. Tranville made these arrangements without a word to you, to Nancy or to me.'

Tranville took a step towards him. 'How dare you question me, sir? Ullman is a gentleman. I made the arrangements because I saw a way to help your sister and I seized upon it.'

'Nancy will want for nothing married to him,' his mother explained. 'She will have security.'

Jack ignored Tranville. 'As I understand it, Mother, *you* will want for nothing if Nancy marries this gentleman. *You* will have security.'

'See here,' barked Tranville. 'I've had enough of this.'

'*I* will have security?' his mother repeated. 'I do not comprehend your meaning.'

Jack inclined his head toward Tranville. 'The marriage settlement included an arrangement for Lord Ullman to assume your financial support. Did Tranville neglect to explain that part to you?'

She turned to Tranville, her eyes wide. 'Is this true, Lionel?'

Tranville gave Jack a murderous look, but he spoke to Jack's mother in a placating tone. 'Mary, I did not wish to trouble you with such details—'

'My mother is Nancy's guardian.' Jack countered. 'She should have been told *all* the details, especially the one that so involved her.'

His mother wrung her hands.

Tranville clasped her fingers. 'I thought only of how you dislike dealing with numbers.'

'But I should like to have known this.' His mother's voice was barely audible.

'You could have included me on the numbers,' Jack countered. 'As Nancy's brother, it would be logical for me to deal with the financial part of her marriage settlement.'

'You?' Tranville laughed. 'What do you know of such matters?'

'I have lived in the world. I know its costs.' He had supported himself on his half-pay and his art commissions for almost two years now. 'And I know my sister.'

His mother blinked rapidly as she looked up at Tranville. 'I did not know you wished to be rid of my support, Lionel.'

He reached for her again, but she stepped back. 'Mary, my dear girl. I would never renege on my promise to you. I made this request by design. It *fulfils* my promise. Otherwise I should not have made it.'

'It saves you a great deal of money,' Jack added in a sarcastic tone.

Tranville turned on him. 'That is of no consequence. It is your mother's reputation I was thinking of.'

'My reputation!' she cried.

'By having Ullman take over your support, I restore your good name.' His tone was mollifying.

She returned a very sceptical look.

He stepped forwards and stroked her arm, speaking soothingly. 'You see, no one could perceive anything untoward about your son-in-law paying for your support. In this manner, I erased any obstacle to your daughter's acceptance in polite society. Or yours. Ullman marrying Nancy and taking over your support removes any taint of impropriety.' He smiled patiently. 'Surely you cannot argue with that.'

Her expression remained wounded. 'You have not expressed concern about impropriety before this.'

'Indeed, it seemed the least of your concerns,' Jack inserted.

Tranville shot him an angry glance, but put an arm around Jack's mother. 'My dearest, surely you understand how the situation has changed. I have an obligation, with my title, to marry again—'

She wrenched free. 'Marry again?'

'Of course I must marry again.' He made himself look regretful.

Jack stepped forwards. 'You damned hypocrite. You are *planning* to marry.'

It seemed clear to Jack now why Tranville had so suddenly dropped his interest in Ariana. He was courting some society miss and keeping his nose clean of mistresses in the meantime. Explaining Jack's mother's support to the young lady's wealthy papa might have created a nasty problem for him. Ullman had come to the rescue.

Jack shook his head. 'You took it upon yourself to negotiate with Ullman so you could rid yourself of any further connection with my mother and marry without impediment.'

Tears welled up in Jack's mother's eyes. 'Is that true?'

Tranville glared at Jack before focusing back on her. 'I must marry, Mary. I must keep the title in my family and that means ensuring the heir will be of my blood. I must sire more sons. Do you not see that the war almost took my only one? Edwin's injury could have cost him his life.'

Only because Jack and two other soldiers had refrained from killing him in Badajoz.

'I need more sons. You must see that, my dear,' Tranville pleaded. 'It is my duty.'

'I'll hear no more about it.' She pulled away from him. 'If—if you will pardon me, I—I must speak with Cook about dinner.'

Jack frowned as his mother rushed out of the room. It pained him to see her so wounded, but it was long past time she recognised Tranville for the man he was.

As soon as she was gone, Tranville wheeled on him. 'That was not well done of you at all.'

'Not well done of me?' Jack laughed. 'The responsibility rests on your shoulders, Tranville.'

Tranville's eyes bulged. 'I refuse to apologise for arranging a proposal for your sister that is far better than she deserves. Nor for negotiating a marriage settlement that protects her and your mother.'

'Cut line, Tranville. You do not have my mother's interests at heart. You embarked on this plan to rid yourself of any ties to a former mistress so some young lady equally as hapless as my sister will think you promise fidelity.'

'You malign me greatly. Do you not remember who I am?' he shouted in outrage.

'I do indeed know who you are,' Jack's voice turned low. 'You are the man who keeps my mother tied to you, in case you should ever have need of her.'

'You cur!' Tranville's face turned red. 'This is the thanks I get for using my position to help your family. Let me tell you, your sister is damned lucky any man would want to marry her, let alone a peer of the realm.'

Jack leaned into his face. 'My sister would do credit to any man. She is a fine person.'

'She is tainted by her mother.'

Jack's hand curled into a fist. 'And, you, sir, are the man who tainted my mother.'

'You ungrateful wretch,' Tranville shouted. 'I rescued your mother from poverty.'

'Even if that were true, you could have assisted her without requiring she repay you in bed.' Jack's anger filled every pore of his being. He was hard pressed to keep control over his fists. The last time he experienced such anger had been at Badajoz, finding Edwin.

The emotion sparked the rumble of cannon fire in his ears.

Spittle dripped down the corner of Tranville's mouth. 'It was my money that sent you to school and purchased your commission—'

Jack ignored the pounding of the guns in his head. 'Because my mother saved for it—'

'Because I was generous enough that she could afford it.'

Jack turned away, forcing his mind to stay in the present time. The battle he needed to wage at the moment was with Tranville.

'Do not profess generosity.' Jack raised his voice above the din in his head. 'My mother continues to repay you. At your whim.'

Jack's mother had left the door ajar and their voices carried far enough for the servants to hear every word. Jack could not care. He was fighting on two fronts, the war in his mind and the one with Tranville.

Nancy climbed down from the hack and walked up to her door. From the drawing-room window she could hear Jack and Lord Tranville's raised voices, but she could not hear what they were saying. She cringed, hating angry words, but she must involve herself in this shouting match. It was about her.

She'd been a coward to run away from her mother and Lord Tranville. A grown woman would see it as her responsibility to deal with them. It was her marriage they were planning, her future. She must act on her own behalf.

By the time she and Ariana had arrived at Drury Lane Theatre, Nancy had calmed enough to remember that a woman had the right to refuse a proposal. All she need do was say no. She told Ariana she wanted to return home to tell her mother. She knew Jack would support her wishes.

Nancy hurriedly opened the front door and entered quietly. In the hall, the voices sounded even louder. She froze.

'Do not try to tell me, Tranville,' she heard Jack say, 'that Ullman suggested taking over Mother's support. It was you, thinking of your own plans to marry.'

Nancy frowned. Lord Tranville was planning to marry? That's why Lord Ullman would be supporting her mother?

'I have explained enough to you, you insolent puppy!' Tranville responded. 'I did this for your mother and your sister, because of my esteem for them both.'

'Drivel,' Jack shot back. 'And what happens if my sister

refuses Ullman? What then? Do you continue to pay my mother's support?'

'Your sister would be a fool to refuse his offer,' Tranville cried, his voice rising to a shrill sound. 'In fact, you can tell her this. I will cut off your mother's funds if your sister refuses Ullman.'

Nancy gasped. Cut off her mother's funds? What would happen to her mother then? She'd have no money. Worse, her heart would be broken.

'This is how you honour your word to my mother?' Jack's voice was scathing.

'As far as I am concerned, I fulfil my promise by making this arrangement with Ullman. I've ensured her support and that is what I promised her.'

Lord Tranville was forcing her to marry Ullman. Nancy started backing towards the outside door.

Jack went on, 'As far as I am concerned, both my mother and sister are well rid of you. I will support them.'

'You?' Tranville laughed. 'We will see about that. I can ruin you with a word—'

Nancy put her hands over her ears and groped for the doorknob, opening the door enough to slip out. Again outside, she covered her head with the hood of Ariana's cloak and walked slowly and mournfully to the Strand. Her legs felt as if they were weighted with rocks and her heart felt even heavier. If only she could curl up in a ball in some alleyway. Perhaps she would freeze to death by the morning.

She lifted her chin. That was ridiculous and childish, and it was time she set aside childish thinking. If nothing else, today was forcing her to grow into a woman and to face the world as it really was.

Lord Tranville was not the man she'd believed he was her whole life. If he loved her mother, he would not leave her without a penny and marry someone else. He just wanted to bed her mother, that was all.

Nancy covered her mouth and breathed rapidly against the sick feeling that idea created.

Tranville used her mother merely for carnal reasons, and Lord Ullman, with all his talk of being lusty, wanted her for the same reason. This was not *Romeo and Juliet.* One meeting with a person could not create love. Ullman could not possibly love her.

Neither her mother nor her brother could protect her from her fate. Lord Tranville held the strings and was playing them all like the puppets she'd seen at the fair.

If she refused Ullman's proposal now her mother's heart would be broken, Jack's career as an artist would be ruined, and they'd all be poor.

For once in her life it was her responsibility to take care of the family. She must accept Lord Ullman.

Tears rolled down her cheeks and she felt terribly alone. She walked toward Somerset House. At this moment, she was in great need of a friend.

She wanted to see Michael, to tell him how her life had changed since their carefree walk through Covent Garden that morning. Unlike earlier that afternoon, she was not rushing blindly to Michael's side. She merely wished him to know what she must do, for if she did not, what would happen to them all?

She walked solemnly, tears silently falling. When she crossed Southampton Street, a man coming from the direction of Covent Garden brushed against her, then caught her arm, and pulled her so she was facing him.

'Well, if it isn't little Nancy Vernon.' The scarred face of Edwin Tranville looked malevolently down upon her. His breath smelled of whisky. 'And walking the streets all alone.' He laughed. 'A street-walker. My lucky day.'

'Let me go, Edwin,' she snapped.

But he did not let her go. Instead he dragged her against the wall of a building. 'I want a kiss from the street-walker.'

'Stop it, Edwin.' Nancy squirmed.

She lifted her leg and slammed her heel down hard on Edwin's foot. He let go of her and she struck his face. With no gloves on, her nails scraped his scar.

He gave a cry of pain and immediately cupped his cheek. Nancy gave him a hard push and he careened into the brick wall of the building.

She ran, frightened now, because she realised how danger-ous it could be to walk on the street alone. She heard Edwin shouting behind her, but she did not look back. She ran all the way to Somerset House and hid in one of the doorways before checking to see if he had pursued her.

It did not surprise her that he was nowhere in sight. Edwin always ran away crying if someone fought back.

Nancy leaned against the wall and tried to catch her breath. She was afraid to emerge from the doorway, but afraid she would miss Michael if she did not.

The sun had dropped low and the shadows had grown to ominous lengths. It should be near time for Michael's in-structor to release him. She stepped out of her hiding place.

Students started to pour out of the building. Some of them eyed her as they walked past, making her frightened all over again, but then she saw Michael laughing at something a com-panion said to him. She could not see his blue eyes from this distance, but she was certain they twinkled with amusement and their corners creased with tiny lines. She knew she was safe.

She waited until he was closer. 'Michael?'

Several eyes turned to her, all very speculative. Some of his companions made catcalls.

'Nancy?' Michael walked over to her. He turned to the others. 'Stubble it, fellows. This is a friend.'

There was more laughter, but Nancy did not care. She'd found Michael.

'What are you doing here?' he asked with a worried frown. 'Is something amiss?'

'Will you walk me home, Michael?' She was eager to get away from these spectators.

'Of course.' He waved to the others. 'I shall see you all tomorrow.'

'Have a good night!' one of them called. The others laughed and hooted.

He led Nancy away, but waited for her to start speaking. She would not tell him about Edwin. She'd pretend that had never happened. Taking a breath she began to explain why she'd braved the dangerous streets alone to see him. She told him everything, including what she'd heard Lord Tranville say about denying her mother financial support.

'What else can I do, Michael?' she asked him. 'Do you think I am right in saying I'll marry him?'

'I cannot advise you about this.' He answered in a voice she hardly recognised.

His face was stiff and unfriendly. He looked so…different.

'Do you want to marry him?' he asked after another pause.

She shook her head. 'I had not even thought of marriage before this.' Marriage had felt like a *some day* sort of thing, a distant dream, one or two years away, at least. 'I think I must marry him for my mother's sake.'

'He is wealthy,' was his only comment.

They walked on, but Michael watched his feet more than where they were headed. Adam Street was only two roads away. Once inside her house again she would not be able to speak freely with him.

He broke their silence. 'I should beg off dinner tonight.'

'No!' she cried. 'Why?' She could not bear it if he were not with her when she had to face her mother and brother.

'Your family has much to discuss.' He pressed his lips together into a grim line. 'I would intrude on your privacy.'

She was suddenly afraid that if Michael said goodbye to her right now she would never see him again. Her heart beat as fast as when she'd been running. She could no longer breathe. Everything turned black and her legs gave way.

'Nancy!'

She felt his strong arms around her, holding her.

'I need to sit down,' she gasped.

He kept her in his embrace. 'We are near Savoy Chapel. We might sit there.'

He helped her to the chapel, which was dark. The door was unlocked, however. They went inside and sat in a back pew.

She tried to catch her breath. 'Don't leave me alone, Michael. Don't leave me.' Tears poured from her eyes. She tried very hard not to sob aloud.

'I shall not leave you,' he murmured consolingly. 'I will see you safely home.'

'No. That's not what I meant.' She could not speak until she caught her breath. 'If…if I marry, will you still be my friend?'

He wrapped his arms around her and held her very tight. 'If you must marry—' It seemed as if his voice cracked. He took a deep breath. 'You shall always be in my heart.'

His answer calmed her even though she was uncertain what it meant. To be always in Michael's heart seemed a good thing, though, especially as her own heart was breaking.

Jack tried returning to his studio to work. After Ariana had left, he'd made great progress on the new version of her portrait, but he could not continue now, not even if he lit every lamp and candle he possessed. There was too much disquiet inside him.

He decided he would collect Nancy at the theatre. He needed to see Ariana, needed her comfort and optimism. Jack hurried out of the door and strode quickly to the Strand, but there were no hackney coaches in sight. He walked to Charles Street and the Drury Lane Theatre, thrusting away the internal rumblings of Badajoz.

He entered the theatre through the back door and made his way through the labyrinth that was the backstage to the wings. No one questioned his presence.

Ariana was on stage with Edmund Kean, rehearsing a scene from Act One. '…I'll seem the fool I am not; Antony will be himself.'

Kean responded, 'But stirr'd by Cleopatra. Now, for the love of Love and her soft hours, Let's not confound the time with conference harsh.'

These were not soft hours, Jack thought. He glanced around and did not see Nancy, but he felt in control of himself again.

Ariana saw him as she left the stage. She hurried up to him. 'I did not expect you,' she murmured. 'What transpired with Tranville?'

The pleasure of being with her surged inside him. 'I confronted him and my mother. He did not like it. That is all really. Where is Nancy?'

Her eyes widened in surprise. 'Why, she never came here. She had the hack take her back home.'

He stared at her. 'She did not come home.'

'Oh, Jack!' She looked away. 'I should have stayed with her, but she seemed calm. And she was determined to return home.' She grasped his arm and pulled him towards the door. 'You should go back. Find Michael. I wager she went to him.'

He wrapped his arms around her, not caring at the moment who might see them. 'This has been a hellish day.'

She hugged him back, holding him tightly. 'I cannot help you search for her; I am in tonight's performance.'

'I know,' he murmured. 'Come tomorrow, as early as you

like.' He took her face in his hands and kissed her, hungry for her lips.

When he moved his lips away, she caressed his cheek. 'She will be at your mother's home when you return. With Michael at her side, you can bet upon it.'

He nodded, but could not believe it. Today he could only believe in unhappy endings.

Chapter Fourteen

The next morning Ariana rose early and hurried to Jack's studio. She'd been so worried about Nancy and Jack, she'd slept little. It was odd to care so much about other people, to think of them before thinking of herself.

She passed the door to Mrs Vernon's apartment, hoping Nancy was safe in her bed and not in some terrible mischief. Ariana never should have let Nancy go home alone.

She quickened her step to reach Jack's door, letting herself inside with the key he had given her.

He stood at his easel, in stockinged feet, dressed in his painting shirt, brush in hand. She'd almost forgotten about the portrait, so much had happened since she'd sat for him in a costume more scandalous than posing in one's nightdress.

He looked up at her entrance and smiled. 'You did come early.'

She pulled off her pelisse and hung it on a hook. 'I could not sleep.'

She rushed to him and was gathered into his arms, forgetting to care if paint got on her dress. His mere warmth, his scent, was comfort to her. 'Tell me. I have worried so. Did you find Nancy?'

He released her and nodded. 'It was as you predicted. She was at my mother's place by the time I returned there.'

She released a relieved breath. 'What happened to her?'

'Nothing. She took a walk, she said.' He still held her.

She examined his face and found only worry there.

'She changed,' he said. 'Somehow between here and my mother's house, she changed. She said she'd decided to marry Lord Ullman after all, giving as her reason a desire to be respectable and to wear pretty gowns.'

Ariana was aghast. 'But what did she say of Michael?'

'She did not mention him, except to say he'd left word he would not be at dinner.' His brow creased. 'I must conclude you are mistaken about Michael and Nancy. He has not declared anything more than friendship to her, ever.'

'Oh, I am not mistaken,' Ariana insisted. 'Nancy and Michael have a grand love for each other, although they may not know it yet.'

'If so, it is a doomed one.' He rubbed his face. 'I must have argued with her for two hours. She would not hear anything I said. She just insisted she wanted to be a countess.'

'I do not believe it,' Ariana said.

Jack frowned. 'My mother dispatched a message to Tranville to bring Ullman to call this afternoon. Nancy will accept his proposal.'

Ariana leaned against him again. 'This is too dreadful.'

Jack's voice rumbled in his chest. 'This is all Tranville's doing and my mother is going along with it. Even after—' He stopped.

'Even after what?'

He released her and picked up a brush. 'Tranville plans to remarry.'

Ariana's jaw dropped. 'Remarry!' She could not be more surprised. There had been no talk at the theatre about him courting anyone.

Jack turned back to the canvas and she looked at it for the first time since the previous day. 'Oh, my!'

He gazed at it as well. 'What do you think?'

The portrait was a long way from being complete, but already it was a vast change from the first one. She was Cleopatra lounging in the same pose as before, but the expression on her face simmered with sensuality, as if this image were indeed casting her gaze upon her lover.

'It promises more than I ever dreamed,' she whispered.

He made a gratified sound. 'There's much more to be done. I need to work more on the transparent effect of the gown.'

Jack had so vividly depicted a blush of skin beneath a thin wash of white pigment Ariana could almost feel the silkiness of the fabric. Because he'd draped it to conceal the dark pink of her nipples and her most feminine parts, the portrait did not look bawdy; it appeared reverent.

'It is remarkable.' She hugged him from behind. 'You have done it!'

He turned to her. 'I need to finish the background, refine the rest. I wish I could use every bit of daylight, but I want to be present when Ullman calls on my sister.

She touched his cheek. 'Even if Nancy accepts Ullman today, she still can change her mind before marrying him.'

He frowned. 'I cannot see that as likely.'

She gazed at the portrait again. She'd almost despaired of Jack ever transforming the work into a great painting, but he had done it. It seemed a terrible shame to cover over the sheer gown with the other one. It suited this sensual Cleopatra.

She gave Jack a swift hug. 'Let us not waste the day. Come and help me with my laces. I'll change into the costume, and you can get back to work.'

Never had a painting emerged from Jack's brush more quickly. Exhilarated, he worked until the afternoon advanced, wanting to seize every second of time. The clock chimed the half-hour and he realised it was near the time to go to his mother's. He wiped his brush and dropped it in a jar of turpentine.

'I surmise we are done for the day.' Ariana uncoiled herself from her posed position.

'I wish it were not so.' Jack covered his palette with a cloth. 'But I am expected at my mother's.'

'For Lord Ullman to call,' Ariana finished for him.

He and Ariana had spoken very little the whole day. He'd been so absorbed by the work he'd almost forgotten to give her breaks. Time passed without his being aware of it.

At this pace both the portrait and a copy could be ready to deliver in two or three weeks. If Tranville still wanted them, that is. His marriage plans might have changed matters. If so, Jack would willingly forgo the balance owed him.

Ariana stretched. 'I wish I could speak to Nancy. Maybe I could discover why she has changed her mind so completely.'

Jack covered his palette to keep the paint moist for the next day. 'I wish you could as well.'

Ariana walked over to the canvas. 'I am amazed.'

He pulled off his paint-streaked shirt and put an arm around her. 'It is as if I am transported. Nothing exists but the painting and you.'

She turned and wrapped her arms around his neck. Her kiss drove even the painting from his mind. Beneath the thin fabric of the costume she was warm and soft and he was consumed with desire for her.

Her lips still touched his. 'Do we have time?' she murmured.

'We have time.' He lifted her into his arms and carried her to his bed.

Their lovemaking was swift and sensuous and thrilling in its intensity. They were attuned to each other now, each expert in knowing the most arousing way to touch, the most erotic way to move. Rushing against the clock lent a new intensity to the lovemaking. When their passion was spent, Jack held Ariana in his arms, loath to release her and proceed on his undesired errand.

The clock chimed the quarter-hour.

'You must hurry,' Ariana said. She slid from his arms and the bed and gathered their clothing from the floor.

He groaned and rose to dress for the meeting with Ullman. They'd become as expert dressing each other as in making love. Ariana pulled fresh linens for Jack from the chest of drawers. He assisted her with her corset and the laces of her dress. While he donned his clean shirt and his good trousers, waistcoat and coat, she folded his painting trousers and her costume, putting it away neatly into the bandbox.

He tied his neckcloth. 'Will you be late to the theatre?'

She shook her head. 'Not at all. I have plenty of time.' She pinned up her hair. 'I would wish you good luck this afternoon, but I have no idea what good luck will mean in this situation.'

They hurried out into the studio where a sudden cloud darkened the room. He closed the curtains. 'Perhaps we will all be struck with lightning and our worries will be over.'

She shook him. 'Do not say that! Not even as a jest. I want nothing to happen to you or your family.'

Jack felt a surge of tenderness for her. 'Forgive me. It was not a good jest.'

She squeezed his arm. 'You must tell yourself that somehow things will work out well.'

He gave her a sceptical look.

'Do say it,' she insisted.

He kissed her again. 'Somehow things will work out well.'

She smiled approvingly and put on her hat.

When they stepped outside, Jack said, 'I'll walk with you to get a hack.'

She shook her head. 'Go to your mother's. I shall be fine.'

When they reached Jack's mother's house, Tranville and Ullman approached in the opposite direction.

'I'll not leave you now,' Jack said under his breath.

Lord Ullman broke into a smile and quickened his pace. 'Miss Blane! How delightful to see you.' He glanced at Jack with a quizzical look.

Ariana stepped forwards. 'Lord Ullman, allow me to present Mr Jack Vernon.'

Jack inclined his head to acknowledge the introduction.

Lord Ullman broke into a smile and thrust out his hand for Jack to shake. 'Of course. The portrait. I could not put together the connection. Delighted to make your acquaintance and I am delighted to be calling upon your lovely sister. Delighted.'

Tranville's expression was less than friendly. 'You promised the portrait soon, Jack. When will it be done?'

'Two weeks,' Jack responded. So much for Tranville forgetting about it. 'If you pay, that is.'

'I'll pay.' Tranville glared at him.

Jack nodded to Ullman. 'I will be at my mother's directly. As soon as I've seen Miss Blane to a hackney coach.'

Tranville stepped to her side. 'I will escort Miss Blane, Jack. You go with Lord Ullman.'

Jack turned toward Ariana. 'I think not.'

'Do not cross me, Jack,' Tranville snapped.

Jack's hand formed a fist. He was ready to do battle.

Ariana stepped between them. 'Go with Lord Ullman, Jack. See to your sister. Her needs take precedence this day.'

Tranville smirked.

Jack could not disagree with Ariana.

Ullman lifted his hat. 'Good day to you, Miss Blane.'

As Tranville walked away with Ariana, she turned and gave Jack an approving smile.

Jack gestured towards his mother's door. 'Come inside,' he said to Ullman.

Wilson took their things, and Jack ushered Ullman into the drawing room. The man looked eager and nervous, more like a fifteen-year-old at his first ball than an earl of mature years.

Ullman was a portly man whose face was the sort that would sport jowls in ten years. Jack imagined he would shrink with age until Nancy towered over him. It sickened Jack to think of Nancy with such a man.

Ullman glanced at Nancy's portrait, which hung on the drawing-room wall. 'So lovely.' A thought seemed to occur to him. 'Did you paint that?' He sounded surprised.

Jack felt the insult even though Ullman seemed oblivious of having made it. 'Yes. An early work of mine.'

Ullman walked over to the portrait and examined it closer. 'Upon my word. It is good.'

This was not making Jack like him any better.

'Please sit, sir.' Jack did not know how much time he had before Nancy and his mother walked in. 'And tell me of this interest in my sister.'

A beatific expression appeared on Ullman's face. 'I cannot explain it. That day in the Egyptian Hall when I saw her it was as if I had seen an angel. I could not get her out of my mind. I confess I dared not hope to see her again until I remembered the—the—the connection between your family and Lord Tranville, so I began discussing with him how to proceed.'

Jack looked him in the eye. 'I wonder that you did not seek me out for that discussion.'

Ullman turned red. 'I—I—I—Tranville acted in your stead, he told me.'

Jack merely nodded. There was no use to travel that road one more time, not when Nancy intended to accept the man.

He did, however, skewer the man with a pointed gaze. 'Tranville vouches for your character, but bear in mind if you mistreat my sister in any manner, you will answer to me.'

Ullman's eyes grew fearful.

Jack added, 'I spent ten years in the army. I am able to defend my sister in countless ways.'

Ullman nodded vigorously.

At that moment Jack's mother entered the room, and the two men stood.

'Lord Ullman, how nice to see you again.' She glanced around the room. 'Lionel did not come with you?'

'He will be here shortly, Mother.' Jack said, his tone clipped.

'I have asked Wilson to bring tea,' Jack's mother told Ullman.

Wilson served the tea, and while Jack's mother poured, the three of them engaged in a conversation that thoroughly covered the weather, past, present and to come. Jack was almost grateful when Tranville finally did walk in.

Jack's mother greeted him with cool politeness, a contrast to his spirits, which seemed inordinately high.

Into the already tense atmosphere walked Nancy, pale as paste, dark circles smudging her eyes. Jack wanted to whisk her out of the room.

'I am so sorry to keep everyone waiting.' Her voice was no more than a whisper.

Jack glanced over at her portrait. The contrast was so striking it might not be the same person. Gone was the innocence, the eager hopefulness, the sheer excitement of being alive, the essence of Nancy that Ariana insisted he had captured in the image, the very qualities of the painting that had led Ariana to speak to him that first day.

Ullman stepped over to her, taking her hand and leading her to a chair. 'Miss Vernon, the wait was a trifle when the reward is seeing you.'

Nancy indeed looked as if she needed assistance to cross the room.

'Well, well.' Tranville clasped his hands together. 'I believe we should leave Nancy and Lord Ullman alone for a time. They have matters to discuss.'

Jack forgot to care that Tranville was managing things. His concern was for his sister.

'Nancy—'

Her gaze met Jack's and she shook her head very slightly.

Tranville and his mother were almost to the door. Tranville turned. 'Come, Jack.'

Jack leaned down under the pretence of kissing his sister. He whispered in her ear, 'You do not have to do this.'

But her eyes were filled with resignation.

He tried again. 'I can take care of you and Mother—'

She shook her head and waved him away.

'Listen to me—'

'No, Jack,' she whispered angrily.

'Jack?' his mother called.

He reluctantly left the room.

In the hall, his mother said, 'We can wait in my sitting room.'

The room was off her bedchamber. Tranville walked in and went directly to a cabinet, producing a bottle of port and a glass.

'Would you like a glass, my dear?' he asked her.

She shook her head and turned away from him.

'Jack?' Tranville lifted the bottle.

Jack would welcome some drink, but not his mother's port at Tranville's invitation. 'I think not.'

Jack's mother sat and picked up some sewing.

Tranville pulled some papers from the inside pocket of his coat. 'Do you wish to read the settlement, Mary?'

She shook her head. 'Jack, will you read it and let me know if it is adequate?'

He read it through. Twice.

The document appeared thorough and detailed, every possibility addressed, all to the advantage of his sister.

'It appears to be in order.' He folded it up again and placed it on the table.

Tranville gave him a smug look.

'She will be secure for life?' his mother asked.

'She will,' Jack was forced to agree. Ullman could give Nancy more than Jack could ever dream of doing.

'Should I sign it, then?' she asked.

'Wait.' Perhaps Nancy would not go through with it.

They waited in silence, except for Tranville's tuneless humming, which nearly drove Jack mad.

Finally a mournful-looking Wilson came to the door. 'Miss Nancy says you may return to the drawing room.'

Tranville snatched up the settlement papers and they all headed for the drawing room.

When they walked in, Nancy turned to them, her eyes glistening with tears. 'Mama,' she said in a weak voice, 'you may wish me happy.'

Chapter Fifteen

That evening Tranville patted the pocket of his coat, feeling the velvet box inside. He smiled to himself. He'd intended this event to take place later, but seeing Ariana that afternoon had persuaded him that there was no need to delay.

He'd waited long enough. Playing it cool with her had not worked at all. Ariana had seemed perfectly content without his attentions.

His plan had been to wait until her portrait was complete, at which time he would formally make it his gift to her, but Jack was dawdling. Tranville decided not to wait even two more weeks. The time was now.

Tranville crossed the foyer of the theatre. He was early and only a few people had arrived for the evening's performance. Ullman was supposed to meet him here.

Ullman was a good sort, well-humoured and harmless. At least Ullman had been the spur for Tranville's renewed campaign. He felt like clapping his hands in delight.

Tranville made his way to his box. He would not show himself backstage. Better he approach Ariana later, in the Green Room. All he required was to be private with her.

He glanced around the theatre, at the lavish gilt, the rich

red curtains, tier after tier of boxes. He imagined the theatre filled with three thousand people, all applauding Ariana in her role as Cleopatra. He imagined being congratulated in the Green Room afterwards, complimented on his foresight regarding London's newest sensation. He even imagined Kean approaching him to thank him for the opportunity to perform with her.

Everyone would know she belonged to him.

Ullman entered the box with a furrowed brow. 'Good evening, Tranville.'

Tranville blinked. 'I expected you to be in raptures this evening. Do not tell me something has gone wrong with your engagement.'

Ullman shook his head. 'Not at all. It is just that I met Lord Darnley outside. Apparently there are considerable rumblings about the Corn Bill. He is exceedingly worried about riots.'

Tranville waved a dismissive hand. 'Fiddle. He is being alarmist. The people would not dare raise a commotion.'

Ullman looked unconvinced. 'I wonder if I ought to send Miss Vernon—I mean, my dear Nancy—to the country. She and her mother could stay at the country house. Get acquainted with the children.'

Ullman was making this molehill of unrest into a mountain peak, Tranville thought, but it might work to his advantage to have Mary out of town.

She was the one person who depressed his spirits with her refusal to face facts. Surely she could comprehend how his life had changed, how a vigorous man such as himself needed a young wife to beget more children. His departed wife had banned him from her bed when she'd still been capable of bearing sons. What a great disappointment his wife had been, so lacking in sensitivity.

Mary had once perfectly understood his masculine needs, never complaining of other women in his life. She used to accept that a man of his nature needed variety. He had no idea what had turned her so sour.

He waved the thought of Mary away and imagined Ariana dressing for the performance tonight. His loins ached.

Soon, he promised himself. Soon he would seat himself on a chair in her dressing room and watch the tantalising process of her donning a gown.

He clapped Ullman on the shoulder. 'I am certain Mrs Vernon and Nancy would enjoy a visit to the country.'

'Thing is,' Ullman went on, 'I must stay here. These matters before the Lords are too vitally important.'

Tranville nodded in agreement, although he could not see a man like Ullman affecting the decisions that needed to be made on the Corn Bill. 'You could send the ladies without you if it makes you feel easier.'

Ullman rubbed his chin. 'I am considering a special licence and marrying her right away. It would be so much better for her to go to the country as my wife.'

At that moment Edwin entered the box. 'Did I hear you talk of a wife? Are you marrying, Ullman?' He sat next to his father and leaned a foot against the box's railing. 'Who is the lady?'

Ullman beamed. 'You were present when I first laid eyes upon her. I am marrying Miss Vernon.'

'Nancy Vernon!' Edwin sat up straight. 'Good God.'

Tranville grabbed his arm and leaned into his ear. 'You will keep your mouth shut or I'll cut off your quarterly portion.'

Edwin blinked. 'Lovely girl,' he muttered to Ullman.

'I am considering a special licence and marrying without delay.'

Edwin gave him a lascivious look. 'You have reason to rush?'

Ullman began to prose on about the Corn Laws and the threats of unrest in the city. Edwin looked alarmed.

While those two fools fretted over unrest that would never

come to pass, Tranville consulted the programme in his hand, looking for Ariana's name. The play was a comedy, *The Country Girl*, and Ariana had a minor part.

He threw down the programme in disgust. She was not listed. That sort of treatment would soon change when she, not her mother, played the leading role.

Three hours later Mr Arnold stuck his head in the dressing room. 'Ladies, time to make your appearances in the Green Room. Some haste, if you please.'

The performance had gone well, and Ariana and three of the other actresses who had walk-on parts lounged in their dressing room. The other three roused themselves at Mr Arnold's directive, and now hurried to clean their faces of stage make-up and dress in their prettiest gowns. Ariana remained in her chair, feeling no compunction to move.

Mr Arnold gave her a severe look. 'Ariana, enough dallying. I expect you in the Green Room in five minutes. The gentlemen are waiting.'

'Yes, sir,' she replied.

After he left the other girls laughed. 'You care nothing of the waiting gentlemen, do you?' one said to her.

Her housemate Susan said, 'She's too moon-eyed over her artist.'

Ariana smiled. 'Can you blame me?'

'He's handsome enough, but he'll never have as much money as Lord Tranville,' Susan admitted. 'I saw Tranville in his box tonight. His son was with him. I do not see why your artist dislikes the son so.'

'I would heed his warnings, none the less,' Ariana said.

Susan nodded. 'I will, but only because the fellow drinks too much. Are you still resolved to break the father's heart?'

Ariana sighed dramatically. 'He has transferred his interest to another, I have heard.'

'Well, she's a lucky one,' another of the actresses said. 'I wish I could persuade him to look my way.'

Susan laughed. 'You have been trying that all season.'

She was welcome to him, Ariana thought. All she wanted was to go home and crawl into her bed. The sooner she slept, the sooner morning would come and she could go to Jack and find out what had happened with Nancy.

She dallied longer than five minutes and wound up walking to the Green Room alone.

As soon as she entered, Tranville approached her. 'May I speak to you, Miss Vernon?'

She had no wish to converse with him, but Mr Arnold had taken notice of her late entrance and would not like it if she cut such an important gentleman.

'Of course, sir.' She stepped away from the doorway.

'Speak with me in private,' he said. 'I beg you, allow me a few minutes.'

He intended to tell her he was to be married, she thought. Foolish of him to think it would matter to her. All that mattered was his marriage would free her to be openly seen with Jack.

'Very well,' she responded.

She thought they would speak directly outside the room but he brought her back into the theatre, leading her into his box. There were still some candles burning there, but the light was dim.

He bade her sit down.

To her surprise, he dropped to his knees and pulled something from beneath his coat.

A velvet box.

'This is a gift for you.' He placed it in her hands.

She felt a surge of anxiety. 'You must not—'

He put his hand over hers, his face inches away. 'Open it,' he demanded. He felt dangerous at that moment. As Jack had warned her he could be.

She opened the box.

Inside was a bracelet, sparkling with diamonds and emeralds. She gasped. 'This is not for me.' He was merely showing it to her, for her opinion perhaps.

'It most certainly is for you.' He lifted it out of the box. 'See? It matches your eyes.'

She pushed his hand away. 'I do not accept gifts.' He *knew* that. 'My position is unchanged on the matter.' She stood.

He seized her wrist and made her sit again. 'You misunderstand me. This is a mere sample of what I am able to give to you.'

'I want nothing from you.'

He tossed the bracelet aside and grasped her other hand. 'Let me explain.' He paused as if searching for words. 'Ullman made me think of it.'

Ullman?

He peered directly into her eyes. 'I am not asking you to be my mistress. I am proposing marriage.'

'Marriage!' she cried.

'Marriage.' He nodded. 'Do me the honour of being my wife, becoming my baroness.'

Her stomach turned. *She* was the woman he planned to marry, the woman for whom he would cut off Jack's mother's allowance.

She grasped at straws. 'You cannot marry an actress.'

He laughed and patted her hand. 'Why not? Did not Elizabeth Farren marry Lord Derby?'

Ariana remembered being told that the actress-turned-countess, Elizabeth Farren, had bounced her on her knee when she'd been three years old. 'No matter. I cannot.'

His voice dropped and his eyes grew flinty. 'Has Jack spoken against me?'

'Jack?' His manner alarmed her.

He held her hand so tightly it hurt. 'He turned you against me, did he? I swear I'll ruin him.'

He must not blame Jack. Her mind raced. She had to remedy this.

She put on an indignant expression. 'This does not involve my portrait artist, sir. It involves *me*. My acting career.'

He loosened his grip. 'Do not fear. You shall have your chance on stage. You will be a sensation in *Antony and Cleopatra*. I would not deprive you of that moment of glory.'

'And afterwards?' She already knew the answer. A baroness did not appear on stage.

He laughed. 'As my baroness, you will be far too busy with important matters to think about the theatre. We shall become a powerful force in London. You for your beauty, and me for my influence. You will hold grand balls and be hostess at important political dinners. We can travel. To Paris. To Naples. To Vienna.'

It sounded like death to her. One whole night with Jack would be worth more than a lifetime with this man, and Jack was the only man she knew for whom she would consider giving up the stage.

She took a deep breath. 'Lord Tranville, you, indeed, do me an honour. I must consider your proposal very carefully.'

'You cannot say yes?' His brows rose.

She needed to tread carefully. 'Not an immediate yes.'

He released her. 'I will take that as a yes.'

'Please do not. But I shall consider your offer in all seriousness.'

'I do not see any reason for delay.' He spread out his hands. 'I can give you the world.'

She moved away. 'You would not wish me to say an impulsive no, would you? Giving up the stage is no trifling matter to me.' She must consider a way out of this, a way to make him not want her. 'I must be certain.'

'You will not miss being an actress. How can I convince you?' He grabbed her in his arms and kissed her.

If he thought his kiss would convince her, he was mistaken. It almost made her gag.

She pushed him away and spoke sharply, 'If you take liberties with me, sir, I shall not believe your intent is honourable. I will not be tricked into a liaison.'

'It is no trick.' He responded with a hungry look. 'I want you for my wife and nothing will stop me.'

She stood. 'I wish to leave now, sir. If you will pardon me.'

He stood as well and thrust the velvet box with its valuable bracelet into her hands. 'You must accept my gift.'

She handed it back to him. 'If I accept your offer, I will accept your gift. Now please escort me back to the Green Room or move out of my way so I may return there alone.'

He pressed himself against her. 'I will escort you, my dearest love.'

Somehow she bore his company back to the Green Room. He would not leave her side, and to her dismay, he whispered his intention into her mother's ear. Her mother's immediate reaction was displeased shock, but later she took Ariana aside when Tranville was distracted by Mr Arnold.

'You fool,' whispered her mother. 'You did not accept him right away? We could be set for life.'

We?

Of course. Her mother would relish such a close relationship to a baron, especially one with deep pockets.

'I have no wish to give up the theatre,' Ariana explained.

Her mother laughed, and some people turned their heads at the sound. She came even closer to Ariana's ear. 'The theatre is nothing. Say yes and marry as quickly as you can before he comes to his senses.' Her mother flounced away.

Ariana interrupted Tranville's conversation with Mr Arnold. 'If you gentlemen will pardon me, I bid you goodnight.'

She moved quickly and had almost got away when Tranville caught up with her. 'My carriage awaits you, my dear.'

She was forced to ride with him and when it pulled up to her residence, he manoeuvred her into another kiss. Ariana finally escaped and hurried inside.

From a gap in the curtain of the drawing room, she watched for his carriage to pull away.

She walked slowly upstairs without any idea of what to do and wishing it was not the middle of the night. She would have to wait until morning to tell Jack.

Jack entered the Seven Stars near Lincoln's Inn Fields, the latest tavern on a search through at least a dozen dark and noisy taverns starting near Somerset House. He'd been searching for Michael all night, through the dark London streets in a widening circumference. The rumblings of Badajoz pursued him each step of the way, but he ignored them.

Nancy's happiness depended upon it.

Michael had not attended his classes that day, Jack had discovered. He'd not been in his rooms. One of his fellow architectural students told Jack that Michael had been with a young woman the day before, the same day he'd failed to come to dinner, the day Nancy had made her decision to marry Ullman. It did not take much to surmise that Nancy, when missing, had gone to Michael and had told him of her plans.

Jack made his way through the narrow tavern, searching each table, suspecting it would be to no avail. He seriously considered giving up his search, but was not eager to brave the dark, shadowed streets again and the memories that assaulted him there.

In the very farthest corner of the room, he saw Michael, sitting alone at a small table, a tankard of ale in his hands. He did not even notice Jack's approach.

'I have been searching for you.' Jack lowered himself in the seat across from the elusive man.

Only then did Michael look up. 'Jack.' He lifted his tankard. 'Have some ale.'

Jack gave his order to the tavern girl and turned back to Michael. 'No one has seen you all day.'

Michael shrugged. 'I took a very long walk. Through Mayfair, actually. A personal study of the architecture there.' He took another sip of ale. 'Mount Street has some interesting townhouses. I wished to examine the style and construction of them.'

Mount Street was where Ullman's townhouse was located.

Jack's ale was set down before him. 'Your conclusion?'

'I could assess the residences as being quite fine.' Michael's expression was pained. 'But I cannot aspire to live in one of them.' He drained his tankard and asked for another.

Jack peered at him. 'Are you foxed?'

Michael gave him a wan smile. 'I wish. Unfortunately, I have been doing more walking than drinking.'

At least Jack would be able to reason with him. 'I came to talk to you about my sister.'

Michael looked away.

Jack persisted. 'I know Nancy sought you out the other day, so I surmise she told you of Ullman.'

A muscle in Michael's cheek flexed. 'I wish her happy.'

Jack leaned forwards. 'She is not happy. She cannot be. She is miserable, but I cannot talk her out of this folly.'

'It is not folly to marry a man who is able to give her every luxury in life,' Michael countered in a mournful tone.

Jack dismissed his words. 'Would you marry a woman for whom you have no regard, simply for her money?'

Michael looked defiant. 'I might.'

'You would not, and neither should Nancy marry Ullman.' Jack levelled a direct gaze at him. 'You know my sister's character. You know her romantic nature. This engagement to Ullman fulfils none of those romantic notions of hers. It is wrong for her, and I want to know what you intend to do about it.'

'I?' Michael's brows rose. 'I can do nothing. I have nothing to offer any woman. I must complete one more year of study and even after that it will take time for me to earn a creditable income.'

So he had been thinking about it. Jack was encouraged. 'You know wealth means nothing to Nancy. She is doing this to please my mother.'

'More than to please her mother.' Michael drank again. 'Do you not know that Tranville will cut off your mother's funds and ruin your chances as an artist if she does not marry? She is in a desperate position, Jack.'

Nancy knew of Tranville's threat?

He waited until Michael looked back at him. 'Listen to me. We must not allow Tranville to blackmail us into sacrificing Nancy's happiness. I will take care of my mother, Michael. You must take care of Nancy.'

'I cannot—'

Jack would not hear it. 'I will help you as much as I can. I suspect your father will as well. Nancy would not mind if all she had was one miserable room as long as she shared it with you. Indeed, she would find such a situation romantic.'

Michael shook his head. 'She has never indicated anything of the sort towards me. No romantic feelings—'

'She ran to you first, did she not? She told you more about her reasons for marrying than she told her family. Why else would she do that unless she felt a romantic attachment to you?'

'It is friendship she feels.' He lifted his tankard to his lips.

'Fustian.' Jack pushed Michael's hand down. The ale splashed on the wooden table top. 'Listen, Michael. You, me, Nancy, my mother—we will all muddle through somehow no matter what Tranville threatens. I am persuaded we will have food enough to eat, clothes on our backs and roofs over our heads. Life will improve as time progresses.'

Michael averted his gaze.

Jack was losing patience. 'Michael, look me in the eye and tell me you do not love Nancy, and I will walk out of here and never trouble you again.'

Michael looked him in the eye. His words were clear and deliberate. 'I love your sister more than I love my life.'

The intensity of emotion in Michael's words stunned Jack and echoed inside him. He could not help but glance away.

Michael's father had once told Jack to look for a revelation in his art, that moment when he knew what separated his work from that of other artists, that piece of truth that was uniquely his. He'd thought Sir Cecil was merely spouting nonsense until Ariana had shown him the truth in his art.

Jack felt his whole body go warm, as if he'd been suddenly bundled in a blanket. He knew the truth in Michael's words was the truth in his heart.

He loved Ariana more than he loved life.

He wanted to be with her always, could not imagine a day without seeing her smile, without basking in her energy and optimism, her belief that everything would turn out right.

He almost jumped off his chair. He wanted to dance on the table to tell the world he loved Ariana and would happily live with her in one miserable room as long as they were together.

He looked back at Michael and it was all he could do to contain his excitement.

Michael gripped his tankard as if he were gripping a life line. 'I will say it again, if you did not hear. I love Nancy more than life itself. I love her enough to do what is best for her. I love her enough to respect her wishes, even if it puts a dagger through my heart, even if it means I must let her go.'

These words dampened Jack's enthusiasm.

Jack looked him in the eye again. 'Do not confuse desire with duty, Michael. My sister thinks she must martyr herself for our mother and for me, but do not delude yourself into thinking she desires being Ullman's wife. Look beyond what she has said to you into what is in her heart. She has this romantic notion that she is the only one who can save her mother and brother, but you, Michael, are the only one who can save her. The question is, are you man enough to try?'

Michael looked miserable. 'I cannot answer you now, Jack.'

Jack knew his own answer. He would allow nothing to end his time with Ariana. He intended to ask her to share all her tomorrows with him. He intended to ask her to marry him.

If he could only convince Michael to do the same. 'You do not have much time. Nancy seems determined to rush into this marriage. You must act swiftly.'

Chapter Sixteen

Ariana let herself into Jack's studio early the next morning. To her surprise, he was not standing at his easel. The curtains were still drawn and the room was empty. She hung her pelisse on the hook by the door.

The sounds of loud breathing came from the bedchamber.

She smiled and tiptoed across the studio. Quietly she stood at the side of his bed and gazed down at him. He lay on his back, one arm flung above his head, the covers twisted between his legs. As when they made love, he wore nothing. Her eyes lit on the scars here and there on his chest, reminders that he had not always stood behind an easel.

She sat on the bed and gently traced each mark of some Frenchman's sword with her finger, glad, at least, that he need never face the horror of war again.

He turned his head and mumbled something unintelligible. His eyelids twitched and opened. It took him a moment to focus on her.

Then he smiled and reached for her.

She fell into his arms willingly. 'Good morning, Jack.' She'd intended to walk into the studio and immediately tell him of Tranville, but she could not bear to speak of it upon his awakening.

'You are a welcome sight.' His voice was raspy with sleep.

He pulled her down into a long deep kiss and she vowed that she would somehow make everything right for them. Rid them of Tranville's interference in their lives.

She wanted to love Jack for a long time, so long that she refused to think of their ever parting. He might never speak the words of love to her, but he showed the emotion whenever he looked at her, touched her. In his painting of her.

Between kisses, he undressed her, tossing her clothing off the side of the bed. His lips against her breasts were as familiar to her as breathing and his hand caressing her flesh was now a recognisable thrill. He knew exactly how to give her the greatest pleasure possible. She could only hope she gave him the same in return.

Today's lovemaking took on a special poignancy for her. Their relationship, already so complicated it had to be kept secret, was bound to become even more difficult now that Tranville had proposed to her.

Jack's skill at arousing her drove those worries from her mind. When he groaned in pleasure at her touch, she felt triumphant and powerful. It was like a dance between them, first her move, then his, then they moved together.

Some unspoken communication between them set a leisurely pace, unhurried, but as intense and sensuous as it had been the day before when they'd rushed through lovemaking.

Ariana gasped when he entered her. She pressed her hands against the firm muscles of his buttocks, holding him fast lest the connection between them be broken. As their passion grew, she stopped thinking and merely lost herself in the dance, which became faster, wilder as he drove into her and the intensity of sensation grew and grew. She heard her own voice making urgent sounds, begging him to move faster.

When she thought she could bear it no more, the pleasure reached its crescendo and she cried out. A second later he spilled his seed inside her, his convulsing also as endearingly familiar as a dance's final bow.

Ariana seemed to float back to the bed, again feeling the texture of the bed linens against her back, the cool air on her skin. He made a partially successful attempt to cover her with a blanket and nestled her in his arms.

'I could get used to this way of waking up.' His voice sounded full of emotion.

An emotion she shared.

She kissed his bare skin. 'I am surprised you were still asleep. I expected you to be at the easel.'

He nestled her closer but paused before speaking. 'I was out very late last night.'

'You were?' He'd been avoiding the streets after dark. 'Did you have a repeat of your visions?'

'Almost.' He held her close. 'I heard the sounds. I could almost feel the visions pressing against my brain.'

She hugged him. 'But it was not like before?'

'No.'

They lay entwined in each other's arms for a few more precious moments. She thought she felt a tension build in him.

Finally he said, 'We must get up. Get to work.'

He rose from the bed and walked to the pitcher and basin on the bureau to wash. Ariana pulled out the sheer muslin dress.

'Why were you out so late?' she asked, putting the dress on over her head.

He watched her, his eyes warm. 'I was looking for Michael.'

'Did you find him?' She fixed the gold chains around her waist.

'I did and I tried to convince him to talk Nancy out of this marriage, but I am not at all certain he will do it.' He put on his painting shirt and trousers. 'He admitted being in love with her.'

She smiled at that, a sad smile because love seemed so complicated for all of them.

He went on. 'When Nancy left you the other day, she went to Michael.'

Ariana was not surprised. 'She was running to Michael when I first found her.'

When they were both dressed, they walked out to the studio. Jack opened the curtains and set up his easel. Ariana made tea in the galley. She discovered some biscuits in a tin for Jack's breakfast. He ate quickly and began readying his paints, poking the small bladders with a tack and squeezing paint from them onto his palette.

She put the tea things away and leaned against the galley doorway. 'I have to tell you something.'

He smiled over at her. 'I have to tell you something as well, but you must go first.'

'I discovered who Tranville intends to marry,' she began.

His expression turned sour. 'Who is it?'

She inhaled a very deep breath. 'It is me.'

Jack stared at her in stunned silence, not believing his ears. 'You?'

She nodded. 'He proposed last night.'

He could barely make himself speak. 'What reply did you give him?'

Her posture went rigid and her eyes grew wide. 'I told him I needed time to consider his offer.'

He could only stare at her.

He'd just begun to hope for a future between them. He had been about to agree they could declare their attachment openly. He intended to propose marriage to her himself. Now it all seemed impossible.

She stared back at him. 'Jack. I am not going to accept him.'

He turned away, but said, 'He is wealthy. You would become a baroness.'

Her voice was tense. 'If you do not think those things should matter to your sister, why should they matter to me?'

He had no counter to that.

Suddenly his hopes for a future with Ariana seemed dashed. What would Tranville do to Ariana if she refused him? What would he do to Jack's mother if she chose Jack?

He faced her again. 'What does Tranville threaten if you do not marry him?'

'Threaten?' Her voice rose very high. She cleared her throat. 'His only threat is to end my career on the stage if I do marry him.'

Jack would never have asked her to give up the theatre.

He turned back to the easel. 'We should work.'

She walked over to the *chaise-longue* and assumed the pose she'd used for both portraits. Her expression, however, was troubled.

Jack dipped his brush in some of the white and dabbed at the canvas. His brush seemed to move at random.

'I will make him change his mind,' she said. 'I will make him think it is his idea, not mine, and then he will have reason to feel guilty instead of vindictive.'

Jack could not see a way back to her. If she married Tranville, she was gone, but even if she did not, Tranville would never sit still for Jack being the man who stole her from him. He would find a means of taking away everything that meant something to her.

'Do not be too upset, Jack.' Her voice was low. 'Please.'

He tried to focus on the painting. 'This is not good news, no matter what you decide.'

'No matter what I decide!' Her voice was indignant. 'There is only one choice.'

Somehow they got through the morning but it had been a quiet, mournful time. When the mantel clock struck one,

Jack declared their session over. Ariana said she had a rehearsal to attend.

Helping her dress into her street clothes was a difficult intimacy to endure. He was tempted to thumb his nose at Tranville, his family, the theatre, even art itself, and jump back into bed with her.

Instead, he did not even kiss her. 'I will not need you tomorrow,' he told her. 'I can finish this in a day or two.'

She responded with a questioning look. 'You told Tranville two weeks.'

Because he wanted as much time with her as possible.

'To put on the finishing touches and to make the copy, I will need two weeks. It is not crucial for you to pose for me.'

She looked wounded and confused.

He tried to mollify her. 'I am engaged most of the day tomorrow with Lord Ullman,' he explained. 'Ullman apparently wishes to show us his townhouse and God knows what else.'

'Very well,' she murmured.

A few minutes later as Jack watched her walk up the street towards the Strand, he had a notion he understood how Michael had felt after parting with Nancy.

Nancy was seated in her room, wrapped in a woollen shawl because the fire was merely one measly dying coal, the coal bucket was empty, and she did not want to rouse herself to get more. She just sat, staring into the flame of one candle on the table beside her. All she wanted was to sit alone and be miserable.

There was a knock on the door and Wilson's voice. 'Mr Harper has called, miss.'

Michael! She bounded out of the chair.

'I will be there directly, Wilson,' she called through the door. 'Tell him to wait. One minute.'

She turned around, looking down at her gown, wondering if it was good enough, but changing it would only delay seeing him.

It would have to do.

She brought her candle to her dressing table and hurriedly tidied her hair. To think she'd almost refused to have the maid pin up her hair this morning. She peered at her face in the mirror and rubbed at the dark smudges under her eyes and pinched her cheeks to put some colour in her face. She looked terrible. She should not even show her face to Michael, she looked so awful.

Once when she had almost refused the chance to walk to the shops with Michael because she looked a fright, he told her it was foolish to think she could be anything but pretty.

The memory made her smile.

She hurried downstairs, but slowed as she approached the drawing room. It would be so painful to see him, painful to part from him again.

She peeked into the drawing room. He stood with his head bowed, so very still. It frightened her a little. He looked like the man who had come that day to tell Mama that Papa was dead. She'd been very little, but she remembered.

'Michael?'

He lifted his head and smiled a bittersweet smile. 'I had no classes. I came to see if you would like to take some air.'

Just like before, when they'd been carefree friends.

'I would like that very much,' she replied.

Wilson must have been hovering because he appeared with her cloak, hat and gloves. They were soon on the street.

'Where would you like to walk? To the shops?' He sounded almost like the Michael who used to take her on walks.

She sighed. 'Do you know what I would wish? I wish there was somewhere to walk like the park in Bath by the Royal Crescent, somewhere with lots of trees and greenery. I want to smell spring in the air.' *One last time*, she almost added.

It felt as if life would end when she married Ullman.

Michael did not answer right away. 'I suppose we could walk to St James's Park. There is much greenery there.'

'Oh, let us go there, then!' She took hold of his arm.

Michael frowned. 'I am not certain your mother would approve, though. The park has a reputation.'

She blinked up at him. 'A reputation?'

He tilted his head. 'Well, let me say that two people might be very private there.'

She stared into his eyes. 'My mother need not be told of it.'

They walked in silence for a while until Michael spoke. 'I saw Jack last night.'

'Did you?' She did not wish to talk to him about Jack.

'He said you are to marry very soon.'

She did not wish to talk of that either, *especially* not that. 'We are to be married by licence. It is faster.' The banns would not have to be read in each of their home parishes for three consecutive Sundays and no Certificates of Banns would be required as proof.

'You could marry in two weeks, then,' he murmured.

That is exactly what she had been fearing, but she and Michael often had the same thoughts at the same time.

They fell quiet again until reaching Charing Cross.

'This is such a romantic place,' Nancy said.

'Romantic?' Michael sounded sceptical. 'It marks the spot where the coffin of Queen Eleanor last rested before she was entombed in Westminster Cathedral.'

She pushed him a little. 'It was romantic for King Edward to mark all those places with crosses. This was the last.'

He laughed. 'That is romantic? I must take your word for it.'

She shot him a vexed glance. 'Oh, you are teasing me.'

He touched her hand. 'I have missed teasing you.'

Nancy's eyes stung with tears. She blinked them away. 'Let us hurry to the park.'

Hand in hand they ran the short distance to the park and were out of breath when they reached its wide path. Some others were taking advantage of the fine day, but the park was by no means crowded.

Nancy looked up at the trees, holding on to her hat as she did so. The trees were tall and showed spring buds. The lake was dotted with geese gliding in its shimmering blue water. It took Nancy's breath away.

'We must find a bench so that you can rest,' Michael said.

She did not at all feel fatigued, but she let Michael lead her to a bench facing the lake. Fragrant green shrubbery surrounded them. When they sat Nancy could no longer see the other people on the path. It felt to her like no one else existed in the world except her and Michael.

'I am glad you brought me here, Michael,' she whispered to him. This would be a memory to cherish for a lifetime.

'I wanted to be private with you,' he murmured, his voice both enticing and sad. 'To talk to you.'

She did not want to talk. What could she say to him? She just wanted to be with him, to pretend that this moment would never pass.

He gazed into her eyes. 'I need to make certain you are happy.'

'Happy?' Her voice rose and her tears could no longer be blinked away.

He gazed at her with such anguish, she thought she could not bear it. It seemed as if time had slowed down, as if he moved very slowly, putting his arm around her back, enfolding her against his strong chest. He held her like that for the longest time.

While her ear rested against his heart, he spoke, 'If—if I had anything to offer you I would not let you marry Ullman. I would marry you myself, but I have no money at all while I am finishing my studies and no prospects for the future if I do not finish.'

She felt the timbre of his words through his body, words she longed to hear, but words that could change nothing.

'I love you too much to cause you the sort of suffering you would endure if I claimed you for my own,' he went on. 'But it is killing me to think of you with any other man.'

She slid her arms around his neck and looked into his face. 'You do love me, Michael?'

'With all my heart.'

He took her chin in his fingers and seemed to consume her with his eyes. She felt such a rush of feeling, feelings she had never felt before. That morning she'd thought she'd been dying, but now, this touch, this gaze from Michael made her feel more alive than ever before.

She took a breath and inhaled his so-familiar scent. He smelled wonderful. 'I—I thought you were my friend, Michael. Now I know I was wrong. You are my love. My only love.'

His eyes sparked with pain but, still holding her chin, he leaned down and placed his lips on hers.

Her first kiss, she thought, dismissing Lord Ulmann's slobbering attempt. Michael's was the kiss of which romances were created.

He kissed her again and again, doing lovely things with his tongue. Who would have guessed a man's tongue in one's mouth would be so thrilling? The kisses made her feel all achy inside, but in a wonderful way.

Abruptly he pulled away and set her at an arm's length from him. It felt as if he'd suddenly travelled as far as the West Indies.

'I cannot trust myself, Nancy. We must take care.' He was breathing harder than when they'd been running.

She suddenly understood something. These were the sorts of feelings men and women experienced before they tumbled into bed with each other. She understood as a woman what the pleasures of lovemaking could be.

With the right man.

Her tears erupted once more. 'I do not want to stop, Michael,' she cried. 'I do not want to ever part from you, but what am I to do?'

His lip trembled and his eyes turned red. 'I cannot offer you anything but my love. I have no money. No position. No prospects until my studies are done.'

'And then you will go back to Bath, to the position that awaits you?' He had told her many times that an architect in Bath, a great friend of his father's, was willing to take him into his firm.

He seemed to brace himself. 'Yes.'

In the short space of a year Michael would be ready to marry. She tried not to sob. 'If only I were not trapped.'

He looked into her eyes. 'Jack says you are not trapped, that he can support you and your mother.'

'I know he thinks that.' She pressed her hand against her forehead. 'But Tranville vows to ruin him and he has cut Mama off without a care.' For all she knew, Tranville could ruin Michael as well. 'Can I take such a chance with their futures? I should never forgive myself if I caused them suffering.'

Michael glanced away. 'If only I could help all of you. If I had even one year, I swear I could support you and your mother. My father could help Jack find work, as well.'

'You are so dear.' She dared to take his hand in hers. 'How I wish all this would disappear and we could be back in Bath.'

He made a crooked smile and squeezed her hand. 'Nancy, we never knew each other in Bath.'

She fluttered her lashes. 'But we should know each other now.'

'Where is Lord Ullman's estate?' he asked, his voice cracking.

'Lincolnshire.' Far away from Bath. She would never see Michael. If only she could live near him, see him sometimes, speak to him, she could fight off despair, but he would never come to Lincolnshire.

Tears flowed again and Michael held her once more. 'I am so sorry, Nancy. So very sorry.'

Chapter Seventeen

Ariana spent a miserable afternoon. Luckily Mr Kean pleaded illness and ended the rehearsal even before it began, so no one discovered she could not remember her lines, her marks, or anything, really, except that Jack had avoided looking at her when she'd left the studio.

She wished she could be rid of Tranville once and for all. He blanketed everything and everyone with misery.

That evening she avoided the Green Room and instead asked Henry to walk her home. Swearing him to secrecy, she confided in him about Tranville's proposal. She did not tell him of falling in love with Jack.

'The best *on dit* of the century, and I must not speak of it.' He rolled his eyes and sighed.

She laughed. 'It is not quite that important.'

Loud voices came from inside a nearby tavern. There was an atmosphere of tension in the streets that had been absent when she and Jack had walked this same route. It was all about the Corn Bill. The House of Lords was debating a bill to prevent the price of grain dropping. Now that the war had ended, grain from Europe was driving down the prices and landowners' ability to sustain their estates was threatened. Unfortunately the bill being debated would increase the cost of bread.

Ariana heard 'We need bread!' coming from the tavern. She felt a shiver of fear, reminding her of when Jack had been overcome by his memory of Badajoz.

Henry strolled along as if oblivious to the disquiet of the streets. 'You should have kept the bracelet, you know,' he mused.

She gave him an exasperated look. 'You know I do not accept such gifts.'

He shook a finger at her. 'You should. Selling that bracelet would yield enough to support yourself for a year or two.'

She laughed. 'Believe me, it would have cost me much more to keep it. Tranville attaches himself like a leech. Even if you do not give him an inch, he takes an ell.'

As they passed by another tavern a man burst from the door, practically colliding with them. He was full of drink. 'We'll send those lords to the devil, you mark my words.'

Ariana jumped away in fright.

Henry manoeuvred them away from the man and continued as if nothing had happened. 'You must do something scandalous if you wish to be rid of Tranville. Something that would make him look buffoonish. Gentlemen despise looking buffoonish.'

She tried to compose herself. 'What would make him look buffoonish?' She added sarcastically, 'He is an important man.'

He grinned. 'You could have a wild, public affair with someone totally his inferior, such as—' he paused '—an artist or some such person.'

He and their other housemates often teased her about Jack, although she admitted nothing to them.

'How could I be certain Tranville would not take out his wrath against the artist?' Her question was rhetorical.

Henry threw up his hands. 'Then do something outrageous. Dance naked in a fountain or something!'

She gave him a playful punch. 'The weather is still too chilly for that.'

They dropped the subject, but the word *naked* hung in her mind.

The next day Ariana had a message delivered to Tranville asking him to meet her at Jack's studio to view the portrait. Jack would be away with his mother and sister at Ullman's townhouse.

She let herself in to Jack's studio, as she had done so many times before. The curtains were drawn and this time no sounds of sleep could be heard. She peeked into the bedchamber and her heart lurched at the site of the tangled bed linen. She walked over, running her fingers over the blanket, resisting the temptation to make up the bed. She lifted the pillow to her nose and inhaled the scent of him.

She wanted him. Was desolate without him.

Wrenching herself away, she hurried out to the studio and opened the curtains to bring in the light. Carefully she took the cloth off the canvas and gazed at her image. Cleopatra, nearly naked.

The clock chimed three, the time she'd asked Tranville to appear. He kept her waiting fifteen more minutes. Finally she saw his carriage draw up to the entrance.

When she let him inside, his face was flushed with excitement. 'I am eager to see the portrait at last. There is no time to waste to get it to the engraver.'

She helped him off with his top coat, hating touching even the cloth of his clothes.

'Where is Jack?' He clapped his hands together and looked around.

'He is attending to a family matter,' she replied.

'Ah, yes.' He nodded. 'Calling on Ullman.'

'Should we have waited for him?' she asked.

He gave her a mooning look. 'Not at all. I relish the chance to be alone with you.'

She cringed.

He followed her over to the easel, breathing audibly in his apparent excitement.

She stopped him before he reached it. 'I warn you, it is unlike any portrait you have ever seen.'

He smiled knowingly. 'How can it not be when it is of you?'

She made herself laugh gaily. 'Not of me, recall. It is Cleopatra.'

She stepped out of his way so he could view the canvas.

He stared, unmoving, not speaking.

'Is it not grand?' She exaggerated the excitement in her voice.

He still did not speak. His complexion grew even redder, and she felt triumphant. He was reacting in the way she had desired.

'I cannot wait to see it on playbills and magazines and print shops,' she went on, rubbing it in as vigorously as she could. 'Will it not bring hordes of people to the play? Will not everyone talk of it?'

He still stared.

The painting looked even more wonderful than the last time she had seen it. Cleopatra lounged on the chaise, facing the artist, her expression showing precisely how Ariana felt when Jack was about to make love to her. Her hair was loose about her shoulders as if ready for bedding, and her lips were red and slightly pursed for kissing. The pink of her skin showed through the transparent gown, leaving little to the imagination. There was no doubt at all that Cleopatra was naked under the sheer fabric.

Tranville finally spoke. 'What is the meaning of this?' His voice sounded like a growl.

She pretended to misinterpret him. 'See? It shows Cleopatra, the seductress. Most artists show Cleopatra dying with the asp, but I thought that would be too dreary. This portrait depicts the queen's power over men and her own ambition. Do you not like all the nuances of white Jack painted? It is such a contrast to her earthiness, is it not? Was that not brilliant?'

His fingers flexed. 'You are naked.'

She laughed, acting as if he'd made a joke. 'I am hardly naked. Except for my feet.'

Her feet were bare but for a gold ring Jack had painted on one of her toes.

'You undressed for Jack.' He suddenly sounded dangerous.

She made herself smile patiently. 'I dressed as Cleopatra.'

'Whose idea was this? To—to pose naked,' he sputtered. 'Was it Jack's?'

Inside her anxiety grew, but she made herself sound gay. 'It was my idea, of course. What would Jack know about Cleopatra?'

Tranville swung away from the portrait to face her. 'What has been going on here while you forbade me to visit? I did not pay Jack to bed you.'

She took a step back. 'Bed me? Do not be ridiculous, sir. You commissioned a portrait, which you promised was to be *my* possession. I told Jack what to paint, and I like what he did.'

'Do not lie to me, Ariana. I do not take well to lies.' His eyes bulged with anger.

She had to pretend not to be affected. 'Now you are being ridiculous. You are the one who decided to attach yourself to me. I am an actress and I shall always behave like an actress. This painting is perfect for me. It will interest people in coming to see my performances. They will talk of me and write about me, as they did my mother in her grandest days. That is what I want.'

'Are you trying to flummox me?' He advanced closer. 'Because if you are, I will not be pleased.'

She put her acting skill into play. 'I am not flummoxing you,

Lord Tranville. This is the portrait of Cleopatra that will catapult me into fame. I shall be London's latest sensation—'

'This is Jack's doing,' he muttered. He pointed to the portrait. 'He convinced you to pose for this. He told you that nonsense about success.'

She stared him down. 'Of course he did not. It was solely my idea—'

He peered into her face. 'I have no doubt Jack made you think so. He wants to make me look like a fool.'

'How can *my* portrait make *you* look like a fool?' She made her voice incredulous, even though she wanted the portrait to do precisely that.

'Because it is no secret that I am determined to make you my wife,' he shot back. 'And no wife of mine will pose in the nude.'

Ariana lifted her chin. 'I have not accepted you, Lord Tranville.'

He glared at her. 'But you will. Because I will see you never work on the London stage again if you do not marry me.'

She put her hands on her hips. 'You cannot scare me, sir! There are other theatres. If I am a sensation elsewhere, you can hardly stop me from returning to London.'

'Consider this, then.' His voice was deceptively mild. 'If you do not agree to marry me, I will ruin Jack. I will make certain he never paints again. Do not doubt I can do that.'

She did not let her gaze waver, but inside she wanted to scream in protest.

He straightened. 'Furthermore, I will prevent his sister from marrying Ullman. I arranged that betrothal and I can undo it—'

That was no threat.

Droplets of spittle spewed out from his mouth. 'Jack's mother has been dependent upon my generosity since her husband died. I will withdraw my financial support from her. Jack will be forced back into the army, and I'll have him sent to the West Indies where he will likely die of the fever. His mother and sister will wind up in the poor house—'

Ariana wanted to weep, but, none the less, she held up her hand in defiance. 'I do not see how this affects me.'

He leaned into her face with a dangerous look. 'Mark my words, I will do it! Unless you get rid of that painting and marry me, I will exact my revenge upon Jack and his family as well as on you.'

She made herself give him a sarcastic expression. 'You will cause those people unspeakable suffering unless I agree to marry you and destroy the portrait?' She threw her head back and laughed, covering her growing despair. 'How very lover-like of you, my lord.'

The door suddenly opened. Ariana looked up to see Jack staring at her in angry surprise. His sister stood behind him.

'What are you doing in my studio?' he asked.

What could get worse? 'Why, hello, Jack.' She forced a cheerful voice. 'I am showing Tranville my portrait.'

He removed his coat and hat and walked towards her, looking precisely like a stalking cat. 'You did not have my permission to be here or to show my work.'

She waved a dismissive hand. 'Oh, but it is my portrait. I used my key to enter.'

'I gave you the key for my convenience, not yours.' His eyes shot daggers at her.

Tranville bustled over. 'See here, Jack. You ought to be flogged for painting this portrait of Ariana. I'll not have it. I'll have none of it.'

'Why, what is wrong with it?' He walked around to the other side of the easel and gave Tranville a defiant glare. 'It is my best work.'

Nancy walked over, darting a quick glance to Ariana. 'Let me see.'

Her eyes widened.

Ariana's misery grew. All she'd strived for was falling into tatters at her feet. She was desperate to mend things. She walked over to the canvas against the wall and turned it around. 'This is the portrait Jack wanted. I insisted on the other one.'

Her pose was the same, but no pink skin showed beneath the gown. Gone was the seduction in her expression, replaced by a blank face.

'That is more like it.' Tranville nodded in approval.

Ariana wanted to protest. This portrait was leached of all life and emotion. All love.

Tranville looked relieved. 'Well, well, I am very pleased with this one. Very pleased, indeed.' He levelled a stern look at Jack. 'But you must answer to taking liberties in creating the other portrait. You led this young lady into a scandalous position.'

Jack pointed to the portrait on the easel. 'This is the better painting.'

Ariana felt a pang inside as he defended his work.

Tranville raised his chin. 'You allowed Miss Blane to pose for you like this.'

Jack's jaw flexed. 'She did not.' He pointed to the other portrait. 'She posed like that. The other is my contrivance.'

Ariana felt tears sting her eyes. She was trying to protect Jack, and Jack was trying to protect her.

Tranville glanced towards Ariana. 'Why did you tell me it was your idea?'

'It is the portrait I want to show the world,' she said.

'Nonsense,' Tranville barked. 'It will be destroyed. See to it, Jack. The one against the wall goes to the engraver. When will it be ready?'

'A few days,' Jack replied.

'Send word and I'll have it picked up,' Tranville made a signal with his fingers, the sort gentlemen make when ordering servants about.

Jack looked him in the eye. 'You owe me for two paint-ings. Pay my money or you will get nothing.'

Tranville made a wheezing laugh. 'You will be paid, but I want a new copy made.' He started to walk to the door, but stopped halfway and barked at Nancy, 'Did you accept Ullman's invitation to the theatre?'

'Yes,' she replied.

'And your mother and brother will also attend?'

'Yes. He invited all of us.' She looked puzzled.

Tranville smiled. 'Excellent! Miss Blane and I will be sharing the box. She does not perform tonight.' He gave her a significant look. 'Come, my dear.'

His voice alone made her skin crawl.

She cast a glance at Jack, who returned one of anger and injury. She could not blame him. If she stayed to explain to him why she'd brought Tranville here, she would make matters even worse. Her only choice to preserve the illusion that Jack was merely an artist doing her bidding was to leave with Tranville. She believed Tranville's threat and intended to do everything in her power to keep Jack and his family safe from his wrath. If she only knew what to do.

Before she walked out of the door with Tranville she sent Jack one more look, pleading for understanding and begging his forgiveness. He simply turned away.

On the street, Tranville said, 'My coachman was told to circle round. He should be here soon.'

She started off. 'I will walk.'

He seized her arm. 'We have more to discuss.'

Once in the carriage, he reached into his coat pocket and took out the velvet box containing the bracelet. 'I expect you to wear this tonight.'

She pushed it away. 'I've not accepted your invitation to the theatre or your proposal of marriage, sir.'

He handed it back to her. 'Take it. You will go tonight or I will carry out the ruin of your friends. I have no doubt that will influence your decision.' If this were a play she would have said he paused for dramatic effect. 'And you will accept my proposal of marriage.'

Dear God. What was she to do? She accepted the bracelet. 'I will take it as long as it does not obligate me.'

He laughed, a diabolical sound. 'It is not the bracelet that obligates you.'

Jack sat with his head in his hands. He'd considered the portrait a private matter between him and Ariana, not to be shared with anyone, least of all Tranville. Showing Tranville the painting had been like inviting him into their bedchamber.

Jack burned inside. She had betrayed him in the deepest way, using his art to achieve her ends. She wanted the scandal that painting would create. She wanted people to talk about her and to come to the theatre to see her. Had she really thought that Tranville would go along with her plan?

All Jack had wanted was for the people he loved to be happy. He shook his head. That was not true. He wanted to paint and he wanted people to admire his paintings as Ariana had done that first day he'd met her. She was not the only one with ambition. His ambition had led to the portrait as well as hers.

He heard Nancy walk back to the easel. 'Jack, you never even hinted about this painting. Why did you keep it such a secret?'

He rose and joined her. 'Is it not obvious?'

She took a step back and regarded the painting again. 'It is obvious she posed for this.'

He nodded. 'I thought it best not to admit that to Tranville. I never meant it as the final portrait.'

'But it is marvellous.' Her voice was awed. She transferred her gaze to the other one. 'This is not as good.'

He rubbed his face. 'Nancy, you ought to be scandalised.'

She returned a world-weary look. 'You forget that we grew up in scandal.'

He'd once hoped he could keep the scandal from touching her, his dear little sister. Now look what hand life had dealt her.

He ached for her. 'Nancy, one more scandal will not kill us. You can still refuse Ullman—'

She turned her head away. 'Speak no more of it. My mind is made up.'

'But—'

She swung back at him, eyes flashing. 'Do not tease me more! I am going to marry Ullman and there is nothing more to say on it.' She turned back to the portrait, as if doing so shut the door on the topic. 'Do you know why I like this one better?'

He shook his head.

'You—' Her voice cracked. 'You poured your love for her in it.'

His heart broke for her. 'Nancy—'

She shook her head, but smiled sadly. 'We are talking of you now, Jack. You cannot deny that you love her, not with this evidence before me.'

He also could not admit it, not without putting even more unhappiness on Nancy's shoulders. 'It is a painting, Nancy.'

She walked over and sat beside him, holding both his hands, and looking into his eyes. 'Do something for me, dear brother. Do not deny that you love Ariana, and if you have pretended not to love her, you must tell her of your true feelings.' She shook his hands. 'You *must*.'

'It is complicated,' he protested.

She laughed, but it was a depressing sound. 'I am beginning to think all love is complicated.'

Chapter Eighteen

Ariana sat unhappily in the theatre box, Tranville triumphantly at her side, his son with him. She despised them both.

'This is a cruelty, sir,' she whispered to him. 'I was given to believe you had a fondness for Mrs Vernon.'

He looked surprised. 'I am fond of her. Exceedingly fond. That is why I included them in this invitation.'

She had difficulty believing her ears. 'Do you not think it painful for her to be forced into my company?'

He continued to look baffled. 'I do not see why it should. Mary understands that I must marry.' He waved a hand. 'Mary is a good sort. She has always understood me.'

She shook her head. 'And you would repay her good nature by cutting off her money and sending her to the poor house?'

His expression lost all affability. 'That would be at your hands, my dear. Yours and Jack's. The two of you decide that matter.'

'I do not understand why we must sit with any of the Vernons,' Edwin complained.

She turned her head away.

The door to the box opened. Nancy was the first to enter,

followed by a very handsome woman Ariana guessed at once was her mother.

'Lawd, here they come,' Edwin Tranville muttered.

Lord Ullman entered after the ladies. 'This will be a delightful evening!' he exclaimed. 'A theatre party.'

Nancy brought her mother over to Ariana, just as Ariana glimpsed Jack entering the box and remaining inside the door.

'Mama,' Nancy began. 'May I present to you—'

Tranville took Ariana's arm and pulled her closer to him. 'My dear Ariana, allow *me* to present to *you* Mrs Vernon, who I understand you have not met.' He turned to Jack's mother. 'Mary, this is Ariana Blane, my intended bride.'

Ariana felt her cheeks burn with anger on Jack's mother's behalf. She curtsied. 'Mrs Vernon, it is I who should be presented to you.' She glared at Tranville. 'And Lord Tranville misleads you. I have not accepted his suit.'

'She will accept me, Mary. I have every confidence,' Tranville said smoothly.

Poor Mary Vernon looked ashen. 'It is good to meet you.'

It struck Ariana too late that she had inflicted additional injury on Mrs Vernon. How much worse it must feel to be thrown over for a woman who refused Tranville than for one who'd accepted him.

Tranville took no notice of Mrs Vernon's distress. He gestured to a table at the back of the box. 'Jack, pour us all some champagne. We shall make this evening a celebration.'

Jack glowered at him. Ariana could see that every muscle in his body protested against doing something Tranville requested of him.

Mrs Vernon started to sit in one of the back seats.

'Please sit in front, ma'am,' Ariana said to her. 'You will have a much better view of the performance, which, I assure you, I do not require.' If Tranville had not had her pulled from her very minor part in the play, Ariana would have been on stage. Besides, the very least she could do for this poor woman was prevent her from having to witness Tranville fawning over his intended bride.

Ullman ushered Nancy to another chair in front. 'You may sit between your mother and me, my dear. Would you like that?'

'Thank you,' Nancy said in a flat voice.

Jack silently handed glasses of champagne all around.

Tranville lifted his in the air. 'I propose a toast to our betrothed couple. May you always have wedded bliss.' He turned to Jack. 'To the beautiful portrait of Ariana.' Next he raised his glass to Ariana. 'To the portrait's subject, as well, and to the future I am certain she will embrace.'

Edwin gave a dry laugh. 'We all need to drink after that toast.' He downed the entire contents of his glass in one gulp.

Ariana took the smallest sip. Never had a drink tasted so sour, although it was fine French champagne. She glanced at Jack, who never put the glass to his lips.

It was a relief when the play began, although Jack sat behind her she was acutely aware of every shift in his posture, every nuance of his breathing. He'd said nothing to any of them, yet he was the only one she wished to speak to. With Tranville at her side there was little chance of that.

Nancy sat stiff and unmoving in her seat. She reminded Ariana of a porcelain doll with blank eyes and an expressionless face. She imagined Ullman having to move her arms and legs to change her position. It was a heartbreaking contrast to the girl who laughed with her Michael. That Nancy had been the young beauty Jack had painted in the portrait at the Royal Exhibition, the portrait that first gave Ariana the excuse to speak to Jack.

It seemed so long ago. She fingered the diamond-and-emerald bracelet Tranville insisted she wear. It felt as cold and lifeless as poor Nancy.

Watching Mrs Vernon was also painful. If Nancy were a

doll made of porcelain, her mother was one made of rags. It seemed remarkable that the poor woman could remain upright.

To make matters worse, Ariana's mother, playing the lead part, had seen her in the box with Tranville and had given her a look that was both approving and somehow vexed. Undoubtedly Ariana's mother would have something to say to her when next they met.

On the pretext of adjusting her shawl, Ariana glanced back at Jack and found him staring, not at the stage, but at her. If she could say only one word to him she would feel more at ease, but her best means of protecting all of them was to treat Jack as if he did not matter in the least.

Somehow they all endured the first half of the play, ironically a comedy. When intermission came, Ullman took Nancy out to display to his acquaintances. Edwin drank the contents of one whole bottle of champagne. Jack sat next to his mother, and Tranville forced them all to listen to him pontificate on the theatre, a subject on which he fancied himself an expert.

During this soliloquy of Tranville's Jack took his mother's hand and held it. The tenderness of the gesture made Ariana want to weep.

There was a knock on the door and servants delivered a plate of cheese and fruit and pretty pastries. Ullman and Nancy returned and Tranville urged them all to eat.

Ullman pulled Tranville aside. 'I have heard news of unrest—'

Ariana took the opportunity to approach Nancy.

'Use this to make yourself happy,' she whispered. Ariana unclasped the bracelet and put it in Nancy's palm. 'Do not make a foolish mistake, Nancy, I beg you.'

Nancy glanced down at her palm and up again at Ariana. At least there was some expression in her face, even though it was shock. Nancy hurriedly stuffed the bracelet into her reticule.

Ariana took a plate of food for herself as if that had been

why she had risen from her chair. She'd given Nancy the means to be with her Michael. Two years, Henry had said the bracelet could support someone. That should be all the time they'd need.

Jack was suddenly behind her. She sensed him even before she turned to him.

'Pardon me,' he said in a stiff voice.

'Jack.' She could not disguise the yearning in her voice.

He avoided her gaze. 'I am here on my mother's behalf. I would not have her or my sister endure this alone. Please step aside so I might serve my mother.'

She glanced over to see Tranville still involved with a gesticulating Ullman.

'Jack, please forgive me—'

His expression hardened even more and she stepped aside.

Tranville was suddenly making his way towards her. 'Get me a plate, would you, my dear? Ullman has invited us to his townhouse after the performance for a nice supper, but I am famished now.'

She felt like shouting in frustration. She wanted to talk to Jack, to explain. Tranville prevented it and also contrived to extend the night's agony even longer. How much more did he intend for them to endure?

On the way to Ullman's townhouse, Jack glanced out of the window of the carriage, immediately sensing something different in the air, an odd energy in the streets. The hairs rose on the back of his neck and the sounds of Badajoz echoed in his ears.

'We must be watchful this night,' Ullman remarked. 'I heard rumours of gangs angry about the Corn Bill. Tranville assured me it will come to nothing, but I am not so certain.'

Tranville's carriage had pulled out ahead of them with Ariana inside.

They crossed Princes Street, moving toward Piccadilly. Jack kept a vigil at the window, watching men gathering in groups here and there. He sat up straighter. 'There's trouble afoot.'

Ullman's hands flew to his chest. 'Good God!'

The carriage continued into Mayfair where throngs of men grew thicker.

Inside Jack's head the screams and gunfire of Badajoz mixed with the rumblings of these men on the street.

'Are we safe, Jack?' Nancy asked nervously.

He turned around to her. 'I will keep you safe.'

The coachman suddenly stopped the carriage. Jack opened the slot to speak to him. 'What is it?'

'They are attacking the carriage up ahead,' the coachman cried. 'I dare not go on.'

Jack opened the carriage door and leaned out. Several men swarmed around Tranville's carriage.

He ripped off his top coat and hat. 'You take them home now,' he ordered to Ullman.

Jack jumped down.

'Jack, come back!' his mother cried.

Jack called to the coachman, 'Drive to Adam Street and do not stop for anything.'

'Yes, sir!' The coachman signalled the horses to move and turned the carriage on to a side street that would lead them back to Piccadilly, away from the marauders.

Jack ran toward Tranville's carriage where about a dozen men had encircled it and were rocking it back and forth. The coachman was attempting to fend them off with his whip and keep control of the horses at the same time.

Jack heard shouts of 'Down with the Corn Bill!' and 'We need bread', but the words suddenly muffled in his ears. As if someone had taken him by the collar and thrust him aside, Jack slammed against a wrought-iron fence in front of a townhouse. He was no longer in Mayfair, but in the fortress town of Badajoz and the men shouting in the street were red-coated soldiers.

'It is not Badajoz,' he said aloud, pressing his hands over his ears.

'Stop!' he heard Ariana cry. 'Leave us!'

At the sound of her voice Jack pushed himself away from the fence and advanced on the attackers, shouting a Celtic war cry that had once sent Frenchmen fleeing.

Some of the attackers ran off, but one of them spun around and swung his club at Jack's head. He ducked and the club struck the carriage with a loud thud. Then he seized the man's wrist, bending it until the weapon fell to the ground. Another man caught him from behind, restraining him so the first man could pummel him with his fists. Jack twisted, trying to get loose. He knocked the man's hat off, but could do little but try to block the man's punches.

'Jack!' Ariana appeared at the window.

'Get back!' he shouted.

She did not heed him. She leaned out of the window and grabbed the man's hair. The man tried to wrench away and almost pulled her out of the carriage completely.

Jack shouted again. 'Tranville! Hold on to her.' He could just glimpse Tranville trying to beat off the attackers on the other side of the carriage.

Ariana still gripped the man's hair when Tranville pulled her back inside. The man lost his balance and let go of Jack.

Jack lunged towards the other man, landing an uppercut to the man's jaw and sending him into a spin. A third man came at him, and the man Ariana had grabbed reached for his club. Jack seized it first.

'Get rid of him, boys!' the man shouted.

The few men left came after Jack.

Jack called to the coachman, 'Go. Now.'

'No!' Ariana cried as the horses began to move.

Jack wielded the club as he'd once used his sword, striking out with such ferocity, his attackers backed away. As soon as they did, he turned and ran for the moving carriage.

'He's getting away.' Jack felt them at his heels, the sounds of their laboured breathing loud in his ears. One man tried to grasp his coat. More hands groped at him, but he jumped towards the open window of the carriage and hung on.

'Off! Off!' A new attack. Tranville struck Jack's arms with his walking stick.

Ariana snatched the stick from Tranville's hands. 'It is Jack, you fool!' She climbed over Tranville and took hold of Jack. 'Do not let go.'

The carriage rocked and swayed as Jack searched for a foothold. He managed to wedge his toes into the gap between the folded step and the body of the carriage.

The carriage did not slow until they reached the gas-lit street of Pall Mall. 'Where should I go?' the coachman asked Jack.

'Henrietta Street,' Jack told him. 'Take Miss Blane home.'

Jack climbed inside the carriage, where Ariana threw her arms around him. 'I thought they were going to kill you.'

'I am not so easy to kill,' he told her.

Jack tripped over Edwin, who was cowering on the carriage floor, protecting his head with his hands.

'You bloody coward!' Tranville shouted at his son. He hit Edwin with his stick. 'You shame me!'

Tranville took no notice of Jack and Ariana. Jack collapsed in the seat facing her. She sat next to Tranville.

'Sit up, you gutless recreant.' Tranville pulled Edwin up by the scruff of his neck.

Edwin took the seat next to Jack. 'Leave me alone,' he wailed.

Edwin's father, however, directed a string of invectives at him, until he fully realised Jack's presence. He straightened his clothes and merely glared at his son.

'Where are we going?' Tranville asked.

'To take Miss Blane home,' Jack answered.

The carriage clattered more sedately over the cobbles and Jack's breathing slowed to normal. Ariana fished a lace-edged handkerchief out of her reticule and reached over to dab above his eye. 'You are bleeding.'

Tranville seized Ariana's wrist. 'Where is your bracelet?'

It took her a few seconds to answer him. 'I do not know.'

'Those cursed ruffians must have pulled it off you.' Tranville huffed. He turned back to his son. 'See? While you were snivelling and weeping like a girl, those ruffians stole the bracelet. Cost a fortune, I'll have you know.'

Ariana stared at her empty wrist. 'I hope they put it to good use.' She relaxed against the cushions, and Jack thought he saw her smile.

The carriage stopped in front of her building and Jack jumped out to fold down the steps. He gave Ariana his hand to help her down.

Tranville yelled at Edwin, 'Move out of my way. I must see Miss Blane safely inside.'

Jack closed the carriage door. 'I'll do it.' He turned to the coachman. 'Make haste. I hear more ruffians approach.'

'No!' Edwin cried, 'Let's get out of here!'

The coachman grinned. 'Yes, sir!' He cracked the whip above the horses' heads and they started off before Tranville could protest.

Ariana did not wait for the carriage to be out of sight. She threw her arms around Jack. 'Thank God you are safe.'

He held her tightly against him. 'I've been through worse.' He took her face in his hands. 'But you were foolish to put yourself in such peril.'

She gazed up at him. 'I could not sit by and do nothing.'

He laughed. 'Apparently Edwin had no such qualms.'

He enfolded her against him.

Shouts and the sound of breaking glass still rang out in the distance.

He released her. 'You should not remain on the street.'

She grasped his hand. 'Then you must come inside with me. Don't walk these dark streets alone tonight.'

He'd banished the ghosts of Badajoz. 'I am no longer afraid.'

She pulled at his coat. 'Come in anyway.'

He followed her inside and up the stairs to her room. Once in her bedchamber she tossed away her shawl and lit some candles from a taper.

She helped him off with his coat. 'They have torn it.' She poked her fingers through a seam to show him.

'It is of no consequence.' He cared nothing about his coat, not when he was consumed with the desire to hold her in his arms.

She took his hand and led him to the bed. Unbuttoning his waistcoat, she said, 'Let me see what they have done to you.'

He felt a pang of pain as he shrugged out of his waistcoat.

She lifted his shirt over his head and gasped. 'Oh, Jack!'

He looked down at his chest and could see multiple marks of angry red. By tomorrow, he knew from experience, they would turn blue and purple. She touched one of them and he winced.

'They seem a bit tender,' he said, though in truth they ached like the devil. 'I do not believe any ribs are broken, however.'

'What can I do for you?' Her voice was filled with helpless concern as she touched one mark after the other.

He grasped her hand and brought it to his lips. Still holding it, he asked, 'Do you have brandy?'

She moved away from the bed. 'An excellent idea.'

It took her less than a minute to retrieve a bottle and two glasses. She climbed on to the bed with them and poured a full glass for him.

The warming liquid felt very welcome, indeed. Jack let his

gaze rest on her as they sipped the brandy. When she looked up their gazes caught and held. He drained his glass.

'Jack, I am so very sorry.'

He blinked in surprise. 'For what?'

She wiped a hand across her forehead. 'For all the pain I have caused you and your family. At every turn, I have only made matters worse.'

He put aside his glass and reached for her. She came willingly into his arms. 'Tranville is to blame. We can even blame him for putting you in danger tonight. He ignored the warnings of unrest.'

She sighed against his chest. 'I despise him. I shall never marry him, but how I shall prevent him from impoverishing all of you and sending you to the West Indies, I do not know.'

'Is that what he held over your head?' His muscles tensed. She nodded.

Jack had to hold his mother culpable for some of this. He would have dispatched Tranville long before had she not extracted that promise from him.

It was time to break his promise.

He removed the pins from Ariana's hair and combed it loose with his fingers. She sighed with contentment as he did so.

'I will discover a way out of this, Jack. I swear I will,' she murmured. 'I have been waiting for some opportunity. As with your sister—' She clamped her mouth shut.

He moved so he could look into her face. 'What about my sister?'

'Nothing,' she said, but her eyes were wide, as if she was forcing herself to keep them steady.

'Tell me.' He used a firm voice and a firmer expression.

She leaned against him again. 'I found a way to help her, if she chooses it, that is.' She lifted her wrist.

He stared at it. 'You gave her your bracelet.'

She kept her eyes wide. 'Tranville said the ruffians snatched it.'

He laughed and hugged her against him once more. She twisted around and straddled him, burying her fingers into his hair and kissing his lips, his neck, his ears.

A moment before he'd been weary and sore, but now there was nothing but the erotic feel of her lips against his skin, her eager body demanding to join with his. He swiftly rid them both of the rest of their clothing and soon they were naked in each other's arms once more.

Their lovemaking was a wild feast, as if they'd both been without food for days and days and suddenly were given a banquet.

He needed to touch her all over, to taste her, to cherish the feel of her, the scent of her, the sounds she made as their passions heated higher and higher. All the while his mind flashed with images of her. As the seductress Cleopatra in his painting. The innocent but passionate Juliet on stage. The smiling joyful girl who turned a walk to the Royal Academy into a lark. The courageous fighter who had come to his aid tonight. The beautiful, confident, intelligent young woman who stood next to him gazing at a portrait in the Royal Exhibition and dared to speak to him about it.

He wanted to paint all these images of her, and discover more to paint in the future. He wanted some day to paint her holding his child in her arms.

That was his last coherent thought before sensation overtook him and they devoured the last ounce of pleasure together. Moving in unison, their passion built until it exploded inside them, a sparkling dessert of joyous intensity that suspended itself in time.

He knew they would experience such loving again and again. He'd vanquish their enemies, embrace family and friends, and live a happy life.

With Ariana.

He kissed her, his seal of resolve, although he spoke none of it aloud to her. Only four words did he speak as the candles burned to nubs.

'I love you, Ariana.'

Her eyes filled with tears and she clung to him. 'I love you, too, Jack,' she cried, her voice cracking. 'I will love you for ever.'

He squeezed her tightly against him.

Her breathing slowed to the even cadence of sleep, but for Jack a flood of pain remained, the physical pain left from multiple strikes of clubs and fists.

Jack lay awake, aching all over, making use of his sleepless time by considering how to bring their troubles to an end. All plans he conceived led down the same final path.

He must deal with Tranville, once and for all.

Chapter Nineteen

The next morning Jack struggled to get into his waistcoat, trying not to make sounds that would show Ariana every move was an agony. He was not successful.

She hurried over. 'You are still in pain. Let me help you.' She guided his arms through the armholes and slid the waistcoat on to his shoulders. He started to button it, but she stopped him. 'I will do that.'

'I am not so debilitated I cannot button my waistcoat,' he protested, but he liked having her close and fussing over him.

'I do not mind helping you.' She reached for his neckcloth.

He remained still while she wrapped it around his neck and tied it with a neat Mathematical that almost disguised its having been worn in a fist fight the night before.

She patted his chest when done. 'There. Now give me a moment and I will finish mending your coat.'

He carefully lowered himself into a chair near hers and enjoyed the domestic image of her pushing the needle and thread through the ripped seam of his coat.

Another Ariana he wished to paint, he thought.

When she finished she helped him on with his coat. 'I do wish you would allow me to come with you.'

He put his arms around her and leaned his forehead against hers. 'It is best I see Tranville alone.'

He must fight it out with him.

She frowned. 'I know I have made things worse. It is no wonder you do not wish me there.'

He lifted her chin and looked into her eyes. 'If no one is with me, he will not have to fear losing face. It will be just him and me.'

She sighed. 'Very well.'

'I will come to you afterwards, I promise.' He touched his lips to hers.

She threw her arms around his neck and kissed him back, a kiss that almost made him forget his errand with Tranville and the soreness of his muscles.

When the kiss ended she continued, 'I could at least come to the studio with you and help you change your clothes.'

He shook his head. 'I need to stop by my mother's and assure her I am in one piece. I'll manage.'

He knew she would not wish to inflict her presence on his mother.

Jack supposed any happiness came at some cost. In order to make things right for Ariana, for himself, for Nancy and his mother, he needed to break his promise and have it out with Tranville, once and for all. He must also inform his mother that he was in love with Ariana.

She put her arms around him and held him.

'Time for me to leave,' he murmured.

The descent down the stairs brought new aches, which Jack attempted to ignore. Ariana walked him to the door and gave him a final kiss.

As he opened the door and was about to walk outside, she pulled him back. 'Jack, I have a bad feeling about this.'

He kissed her again and held her close for a moment. 'Say somehow things will work out well.'

She smiled, recognising her words to him. 'Somehow things will work out well.'

He left her, glancing back once to see her watching him from the doorway. He waved and hurried on his way, the exertion of the brisk walk actually easing his stiffness and making the aches more bearable.

Wilson let him in his mother's door. 'Master Jack, you are unhurt.'

Jack smiled at Wilson's reversion to the name he'd called him in childhood. 'You heard of my adventure, I see. I came to reassure Mother, as well. Is she up?'

'In the dining room,' the manservant replied, lines of worry returning to his face.

Jack hurried into the dining room.

At the table with his mother sat Tranville.

Jack was stunned. 'What the devil—?'

His mother rose from her seat to embrace him. 'I was so worried about you.'

'Yes, I knew you would be.' He kissed her on the cheek and whispered in her ear, 'What is he doing here?'

She led Jack to a chair. 'Lionel came here last night.'

Jack stared at him. 'You spent the night here?'

Tranville gave him an incredulous look. 'Of course I did. I could not go back to Mayfair after all that rioting business.'

'What about Edwin?'

Tranville frowned. 'I sent him off with the coachman.'

Jack turned to his mother. 'You allowed him to stay, after all that has transpired?'

Her cheeks turned red, but it was Tranville who responded, 'Your mother is an excellent woman.'

A foolish one, thought Jack, appalled at his mother's behaviour.

'Come, have breakfast,' his mother said.

He shook his head. 'I merely came to assuage any worries you might have had over my welfare.'

His mother glanced toward Tranville. 'Lionel told me you were not seriously hurt.'

'I am glad you were spared distress.' Jack said stiffly. He turned back to Tranville. 'I want to speak with you. Not here. Name the hour and I will call upon you.'

Tranville wiped his mouth with a napkin. 'No need. I will call upon you when I am finished eating.'

Jack nodded his agreement. 'I will expect you soon, then.' His mother did not look at him as he left the room.

Wilson met him in the hall, an anxious look upon his face. 'Tell me what to do. Your sister is missing.'

'Missing?'

'The maid thought she was abed when she came to tend the fire earlier, but, when she peeked in a moment ago, she realised the bed was filled with pillows.' He handed Jack a folded piece of paper. 'She left your mother this note.'

Jack peered at him. 'You read a note addressed to my mother?'

Wilson lowered his head. 'It was not sealed. I thought only to protect your mother. And your sister.'

Jack opened it and read:

Dearest Mama,
I have run away. Do not try to find me and do not worry. I shall be kept very safe. Forgive me, but I cannot marry Lord Ullman. You will not be poor, though, for you will always have a home with me. I will write to you very soon.
Your affectionate daughter,
Nancy

Nancy had wasted no time, he thought. He folded the note again.

Wilson asked, 'Do I show it to your mother—?'

'Show it to her after Lord Tranville has left,' Jack told him. 'And tell her I will come back and talk to her about it.' He clapped Wilson on the shoulder. 'Do not worry, this is good news.'

Wilson looked relieved. 'If I may be so bold, I did not think Miss Nancy was happy in her betrothal.'

Jack smiled at him. 'I heartily agree.' He pointed to the note. 'She will be happy now, though.'

Wilson turned to a chair in the hall. 'I have your hat and top coat.' He helped Jack on with his coat.

Jack walked back to his studio and opened the curtains to let in the light. He went over to his easel where Ariana's portrait still remained. He aimed it into the light and gazed upon it as he waited for Lord Tranville to arrive.

Ariana paced her room, looking out of the window at every round to see if Jack was coming back. She very much disliked not knowing what was happening.

There was a knock on her bedchamber door. The maid Betsy called through the door, 'Someone is here to see you, miss.'

Ariana gasped. How could she have missed seeing him arrive?

She flung open the door and rushed past the maid.

'Thank you, Betsy,' she cried as she ran down the stairs.

The hall was empty so she hurried into the drawing room, ready to fling herself into Jack's arms.

Instead she came to an abrupt halt.

Nancy and Michael, fingers entwined, turned at her entrance.

Nancy immediately rushed over to her. 'I know it is unforgivable for us to call at such an early hour, but we do not have much time before our coach departs.'

Michael came to her side and grasped Ariana's hand. 'I do not know how to thank you—'

Ariana looked at them both in bewilderment. 'But why are you here?'

'To thank you,' Michael began.

'And to convince you not to make the same mistake that I almost made.' She gazed adoringly at Michael. 'I might have given up on happiness if not for your gift.'

Ariana smiled. 'The bracelet?'

It was a good revenge on Tranville to give Nancy the bracelet and a much better gesture than seeing her in the poor house.

'I suggest you not sell it in London, though,' she told them. 'Tranville discovered it missing and thinks the ruffians last night took it from my arm. He will be looking for it to be sold here, I suspect.'

'We shall heed your advice and sell it later,' Michael assured her. He cast a worshipful glance at Nancy. 'I have funds enough to see us to Gretna Green.'

Ariana surmised that was where their coach was headed.

'But you must promise me something,' Nancy said, a pleading look on her face. 'You must promise not to marry Lord Tranville.'

Ariana laughed. 'That I most certainly will promise.'

Nancy continued, 'You must marry Jack.'

Ariana sobered and looked down at the carpet. 'I—I cannot promise that, but I do assure you I love Jack with all my heart.'

'Then you must marry him!' Nancy insisted.

Michael put his arm around Nancy. 'Let it be enough that she will not marry Tranville. She and Jack must work out the rest.'

Nancy blinked up at him. 'You are so wise, Michael.'

Ariana thought them quite endearing. And quite young. 'Whatever happens,' she said, 'do not worry. Just be happy.'

'We will!' cried Nancy. She bit her lip. 'Perhaps you had better not tell Jack where we have gone.'

She hugged the girl. 'Do not fear. He will not stop you. He loves you both.'

Nancy sniffled. 'I should be desolated if my brother was angry at me for this.'

'He will not be,' Ariana assured her.

Michael glanced at the clock on the mantel. 'We had better make haste.'

Ariana hugged them both and wished them well once more, and watched them depart with tears in her eyes.

When Tranville's knock sounded on the door, Jack was seated on a wooden chair, his hands steepled against his lips.

He was ready.

He rose and walked slowly to the door and opened it.

Tranville entered hurriedly, already removing his hat and top coat. 'See here, Jack. I must speak to you—' Jack walked away from him '—about Edwin.'

'Edwin?' He was taken aback.

Tranville gave him a pleading look. 'No one must know of his cowardice. It is a terrible shame upon our family.'

Jack turned away. Could it be Tranville was giving him the means to rid them all of Tranville, once and for all?

'Do you want more money for the portraits?' Tranville sounded desperate. 'I will pay you more money.'

'I do not want money.' Jack was calculating. How far could he go?

Tranville lowered himself into a chair and put his face in his hands. When he looked up it was with a resentful expression. 'You always were the one to show off and make Edwin look cowardly. Even when you were boys.'

'I did not make Edwin a coward.' Jack pointed to Tranville. 'You reared him, not I. But you will not speak to me in this manner ever again. I am finished with your abuse and Edwin's. Do you wish the world to know the extent of Edwin's cowardice? I will be delighted to oblige.'

'No!' Tranville looked aghast. 'I will be a laughingstock.

Me, a *general*. A peer of the realm. To have such a son—' He shook his fist. 'It was his mother's doing! She turned him into a namby-pamby.'

And who was responsible for that poor lady's unhappiness? Jack wondered.

'Very well. I will keep silent.' Jack glared at him. 'In exchange I want you out of my family's lives. I want you to settle a sum on my mother that will pay in interest what you dole out to her quarterly. I want you to resign from your damned theatre committee and make no further effort to see Miss Blane. You will not involve yourself in my life, my mother's life, my sister's nor Miss Blane's. Do you understand me, Tranville?'

Tranville's face turned red. 'You overstep your bounds.' He rose. 'No inferior tells me who I see and what I do. Go ahead and tell the world my son is a snivelling coward. Who would believe you?' He started for the door.

'Wait,' Jack cried.

Tranville stopped.

'I have proof.'

Tranville's expression was scornful. 'Proof of what?'

'Of Edwin's cowardice.' He paused. 'Of more than his cowardice.'

Tranville looked concerned.

'Wait a moment and I will show you.' Jack left him and went to gather a packet from his trunk. He'd broken his promise to his mother and now he would break his word. He returned to Tranville.

'What is this nonsense?' Tranville barked.

'Badajoz,' Jack said.

He opened the packet and lay the pages in a row on the floor. Strung together they told the story of Badajoz.

Tranville stared at them. 'That looks like—'

'Edwin.' Jack continued to lay them down.

Jack had drawn his memory of the incident, from his first

glimpse of Edwin trying to rape the woman, to him choking the boy, to Edwin's being slashed in the face by the boy's mother.

Tranville took a step back. 'You made this up.'

Jack kept his gaze level. 'It happened. Edwin was too drunk to know I was there.' He lay down the last pages, showing the two officers who'd also witnessed part of the scene. He'd not drawn their faces or shown their uniforms. 'As you can see, I was not the only one there.'

Tranville kicked at them, scattering them. 'Fabrication.'

Jack picked up one of the papers and showed Tranville the back, correspondence in French with a date a month before the siege.

Tranville threw it aside. 'Edwin's face was cut storming the wall of the fortress.'

Jack spoke quietly. 'You and I both know Edwin hid at the bottom. I saw him, cowering among the dead.'

'You are lying!' Tranville lunged at Jack, knocking him to the floor, scattering the sketches.

Tranville put his hands around Jack's neck and tried to squeeze the life from him. Jack dug his fingers into Tranville's eyes and he let go. Jack sprang to his feet, but Tranville grabbed his ankles and knocked him down again. The two men rolled on the floor, hitting with their fists. They smashed into the canvas and Ariana's portrait fell on top of them. Jack pushed it aside, and got to his feet again, seizing Tranville by his coat and slamming him against the wall.

'Stop this, Tranville,' Jack shouted. 'You cannot win. It is time to give up.'

But Tranville's eyes burned red and he tried to lunge at Jack again. Jack stepped aside and Tranville fell against a table, smashing it to pieces.

He got back on his feet. 'I'll kill you!'

There was some pleasure for Jack in feeling his fist connect with Tranville's jaw, but the fight would solve nothing.

Tranville grabbed a leg of the table and swung it at Jack, who ducked and managed to put his hands around the weapon. The two men strained for control. Jack's muscles trembled with the effort and he won the contest. The chair leg was in his hands.

Tranville backed away.

At that moment someone pounded at the door.

Jack glared at the older man, who was clutching his sides, trying to catch his breath.

'Enough!' Jack threw away the chair leg. 'Let it be over.'

Jack walked to the door and opened it.

An army officer, wearing the red coat and white lace of the Royal Scots, stood there. 'General Lord Tranville?' he said with surprise.

Jack gestured to where Tranville leaned against the wall, wiping blood from the corner of his mouth. 'What do you want?'

The man still looked mystified. 'Sir. I inquired at your townhouse and was sent to the lodging of Mrs Vernon, who sent me here.'

Tranville waved a hand. 'Yes. Yes. For what?'

The officer stood ramrod stiff. 'I have been sent to inform you that your services for your country are again requested. It is my duty to inform you that the Emperor Napoleon has escaped from Elba and is now in France raising an army.'

Tranville managed to stand upright. 'Napoleon escaped?'

The officer clicked his heels. 'Your presence is requested immediately at the Adjutant General's Office.'

Tranville tried to straighten his clothing. 'I will come with you at once.' When he passed Jack, he growled, 'It is not over, Jack.'

He followed the soldier out to the street and into a waiting carriage.

Jack leaned against the door jamb. Only one thing was decided as a result of their altercation.

Jack was about to go back to war.

Chapter Twenty

Quatre Bras—16 June 1815

Jack rode into the protection of the centre of the square. The East Essex regiment quickly assumed the formation as the French lancers began their attack. The regiment had already endured artillery fire, now the terrifying aspect of charging horses and men with tall plumed helmets and long pointed lancers filled their vision.

'Make ready,' Lieutenant Colonel Hamerton shouted as the lancers' horses pounded through the tall rye grass, racing towards them.

The infantrymen's fingers twitched on the muskets' triggers.

'Wait for it,' Jack cautioned.

Napoleon had marched from Paris faster and sooner than anyone predicted. Blücher's forces were still some distance away in a battle of their own. If the French army was victorious here at Quatre Bras, there might be no stopping Napoleon.

The sight of the soldiers in the square, the smell of men who'd marched since midnight, the pounding of guns and advancing horses' hooves seemed more real to him than his life as an artist. Maybe he'd dreamed Sir Cecil's instruction, the exhibition at Somerset House, Ariana's portrait.

Her lovemaking.

He'd said goodbye to her and refused to encumber her with promises. If *Antony and Cleopatra* was a sensation, who knew where success might lead her? Even Tranville could not stop her then.

'Present!' Hamerton shouted. The lancers were so close Jack could see the hairs of their moustaches.

The men took aim.

'Fire!'

The muskets exploded in the summer air.

'Reload,' Jack called through the smoke, but the men near him didn't need reminding. After reloading, the front line fired and dropped down so that the back line could fire. The men moved in a steady, methodical rhythm, one line firing, the other reloading, while the lancers came at them, shouting, firing, impaling. When the first wave passed, more cavalry came, a never-ending onslaught.

Some of their lances hit their mark and men fell. They were quickly pulled into the centre of the square and others immediately closed ranks. Their firing never ceased. Jack kept moving, encouraging the men, watching for weak points, firing his pistol.

It all seemed so automatic, so familiar.

For one second time froze in Jack's mind and he saw the scene before him as if it were a painting. Blue sky and clouds like cotton wool, tall rye, still green and waving in the wind, verdant, thick woods in the distance. The violence, death and destruction marring its beauty.

A man screamed and blood gushed from his eye. He staggered backwards to join the growing number of dead and wounded. One brazen French lancer took advantage and broke through the square, riding straight for Jack. Jack raised his pistol and fired. The Frenchmen fell and his dazed horse galloped away. They threw his body outside the square.

The cavalry still came, slowed only by the piles of their own dead, until the East Essex were strained to fatigue. The square, becoming smaller and smaller as the numbers of killed and injured grew, could not hold for ever. Despair showed on the tired soldiers' faces.

Hamerton shouted, 'Look, men! The Scots!'

The Royal Scots regiment appeared, quickly forming a square and joining the fight. Jack glimpsed Tranville among them and all his rage at the man came rushing back.

After Tranville had left Jack that day of their altercation he'd sent a missive informing Jack that he had not abandoned his plan to ruin him, his family and Ariana. Their destruction would merely be delayed until he and Jack returned from Belgium.

If they returned.

A pistol shot zinged past Jack's ear, and he raised his hand as if he could ward off another one. He'd be damned if he would allow death to catch up to him now. His family depended upon him to come through.

And he wanted to at least glimpse Ariana one more time.

Ariana feared she had entered a nightmare.

Four days earlier Ariana, Jack's mother, her maid and her manservant, Wilson, boarded a packet at Ramsgate and travelled, first by sea, now by land, bound for Brussels.

Ariana had come in order to see Jack, to spend with him whatever time they might have before the battle.

She was too late. The battle with Napoleon had begun.

The sound of cannon fire had reached them early that afternoon and it boomed louder and louder the closer they came to Brussels.

Ariana had begged to accompany Jack to Belgium, so she could see to his needs or tend his wounds or whatever women do who follow the drum. If the unthinkable happened, she wanted to hold him in her arms one last time.

Jack had refused her.

He insisted she stay to perform in *Antony and Cleopatra*, to become the sensation on stage she had once so desired. Her success was her best protection against Tranville, he'd said. Worse, he refused to bind her to him. When he had said goodbye, he'd freed her.

But Ariana did not wish to be free. In her mind she was already bound to him.

Ariana performed the play and used the second Cleopatra portrait, the near-naked one, to advertise her role in it. The painting was displayed in the foyer of the theatre and its engravings appeared on handbills, in print shops and in magazines. The scandal it created filled the theatre seats.

It was soon forgotten. Napoleon's return drove all else from everyone's minds.

As soon as *Antony and Cleopatra* closed, Ariana turned down all future roles and instead made plans to travel to Brussels. Half of London was travelling there, why not she? At least in Brussels she'd have a chance to spend more time with Jack again, even if only an hour, a day, a week.

Or so she had thought.

Jack's mother had insisted upon coming with her, and Ariana had been unable to refuse her after causing the woman so much misery. The two ladies sat opposite each other now in the crowded carriage bound for Brussels. Above the din of the creaking springs and clopping hooves could be heard the sounds of cannon fire.

The battle had begun and Jack was very likely in it. He'd be enduring the sort of horror Ariana had seen in the battle paintings against his bedchamber wall.

Boom. Boom. Boom.

Mrs Vernon flinched and covered her mouth with her hand.

Major Wylie, an aide-de-camp of Wellington's who was travelling in the carriage with them, patted her arm. 'Do not fear, ma'am. The guns are at least ten to twenty miles distant.'

Ariana glanced out of the carriage window. All day long they had seen throngs of people travelling in the opposite direction, away from Brussels. Now the crowd of travellers was even thicker.

'Major, if there is nothing to fear, why are all these people leaving Brussels?' she asked.

'I questioned some of them at the last posting inn.' He smiled reassuringly. 'They are merely being cautious. There are many who have remained in the city. Why, the Duchess of Richmond was said to have given a ball last night. Wellington attended it. He does not sound worried, does he?'

Ariana was not convinced.

The quaint hamlets and farmland receded and soon they entered the city streets of Brussels.

'No turning back now,' she murmured.

The carriage made its way up a long, winding hill, past large ornamented houses, shops sporting signs written in French, and a majestic cathedral. The summit of the hill was the finest area of the city, where the Parc of Brussels was surrounded by the Palace of the Prince of Orange and extraordinary public buildings.

Major Wylie offered to help them procure rooms at the Hôtel de Flandres adjacent to the Parc. When the coachman stopped at the hotel's entrance and Major Wylie jumped down, more cannon fire sounded. His faced creased in worry, but he escorted them into the hotel and easily arranged rooms for them. The hotel had been full, the clerk explained, but many of their guests had left that morning. Several good rooms were available.

Wylie left them as he was to report to the Place Royale, and Wilson accompanied him, hoping to bring the ladies back some reliable news. Ariana felt too restless to sit and wait for his return.

'Come, Mrs Vernon,' she said. 'Let us take a walk, explore the Parc.'

Mrs Vernon nodded.

The Parc was even more beautiful than Ariana had expected, so huge the squares of London paled in comparison. Its wide expanse of grass was criss-crossed with gravel walkways and dotted with shade trees, fountains and statues. Magnificent ornate buildings surrounded it like a decorative frame. Few people were strolling there, although Ariana could easily picture how it might have looked filled with soldiers and their ladies, walking and lounging in the warm summer weather.

As she and Jack might have done.

'They said that the battle would not happen for weeks,' Mrs Vernon said, more to herself than to Ariana.

Mrs Vernon had proved to be a sad and silent travelling companion, only speaking to Ariana when absolutely necessary. She could not blame the older woman for not wishing to be companionable. Ariana had caused Mrs Vernon's sadness, after all.

'Indeed,' she responded, more to herself than to Jack's mother.

A sudden burst of cannon fire startled them, and Mrs Vernon lost her footing. Ariana steadied her.

She drew away. 'How clumsy of me.'

'You are fatigued.' Ariana withdrew her hands. 'Shall we turn back? See if our rooms are ready? You can rest a little. We can dine and retire early.'

'As you wish,' the older woman said.

Ariana gave an inward sigh.

They retraced their steps, and Ariana distracted herself by trying to see the sight as Jack might have seen it, as he might have painted it.

It was too painful.

She attended instead to the style of architecture. 'Michael would like to see all these buildings, would he not?' she commented to Mrs Vernon.

'I suppose,' the woman answered.

Michael and Nancy had rushed back from Gretna Green when the news of Napoleon's escape reached them. Husband and wife now, they were presently staying in Mrs Vernon's rooms on Adam Street.

'It is lovely here.' Ariana glanced towards Mrs Vernon.

She had tears in her eyes.

Ariana touched her hand. 'Do not be distressed. Jack will come through this.'

'Jack—' Mrs Vernon's voice was almost as soft as the breeze. 'We cannot know what will happen.'

Ariana put an arm around her. 'We shall pray for him.'

The cannons fired again and Ariana whipped her head around as if expecting to see French soldiers charging down the scenic paths.

Instead Wilson approached.

They hurried to meet him. 'What news, Wilson?' Mrs Vernon asked. 'What did you discover?'

'There is a battle not too far distant.' The manservant took a moment to catch his breath. 'Fifteen or twenty miles from here at a place called Quatre Bras.'

'Is Jack in it?' Ariana asked.

Wilson swallowed. 'We must assume he is. His regiment, the East Essex, is in it.'

'And Lord Tranville?' Mrs Vernon's voice rose.

'Lord Tranville!' Ariana could not believe her ears.

Wilson looked at Mrs Vernon with great sympathy. 'He should be in the battle as well. He is assisting General Pack with the 9th Brigade.'

The older woman turned ashen. 'I would like to return to the hotel.' She walked briskly away.

Ariana turned to Wilson. 'I cannot believe this.'

Mrs Vernon had made this journey because of Tranville.

Wilson looked grim. 'The East Essex is in the 9th Brigade, miss. They may encounter each other.'

Adriana nodded.

An encounter with Tranville could not be good for Jack.

Early the next morning Ariana discovered the city was in a panic. Belgian soldiers galloping through had proclaimed the French were on their heels, but other reports declared that was not true. Ariana walked toward the Place Royale in search of someone who could give her reliable information. She ran into Major Wylie, who told her that the previous day's battle had been a draw, at best. The English forces had held their own, but Wellington was readying for another even bigger battle.

While people continued to flee the city in any sort of vehicle they could find, other wagons rolled in full of wounded men, their eyes fatigued with pain, their uniforms stained with blood. Ariana grieved at the sight of them.

'Are they from yesterday's battle?' she asked a man who also watched the grim parade.

'From Quatre Bras,' he said.

Wagon after wagon passed, with more and more soldiers. Ariana was riveted to the sight, fearing the next wagon might carry Jack. Finally one of the wagons was full of soldiers whose uniforms looked like Jack's.

She ran along side. 'Are you from the East Essex?'

'We are,' one man answered wearily.

'Do you know Lieutenant Vernon? Do you know how he fared?' she asked.

'Last I saw he was in one piece,' the man told her.

In one piece. Her heart leapt with joy.

'Do you know about General Lord Tranville?'

They did not know.

She asked every wagon after that one if they were from the 9th Brigade, if they knew anything about Tranville.

She must have asked twelve wagons before a soldier answered. 'I am Royal Scots. We were with the 9th Brigade.'

'Do you know the fate of General Tranville?' she asked.

The man laughed derisively. 'Oh, he is as he ever was.'

She did not know what that meant. 'He is unhurt, then?'

'Unhurt, miss,' the man said. 'And a damned shame it is.'

Ariana hurried back to the hotel to give Mrs Vernon the news. Mrs Vernon, her maid and Wilson were waiting for her in a sitting room.

She approached Mrs Vernon's chair and lowered herself to look directly in the lady's eyes. 'I've learned that Jack and Lord Tranville are unhurt.'

Mrs Vernon closed her eyes. 'Thank God.'

Wilson touched her shoulder. 'I have secured space for us in a carriage, but we must leave now.'

'You three must go.' Ariana stood. 'I am staying.'

'Staying? Why?' Mrs Vernon leaned forwards in her chair.

Ariana gave her a resolute look. 'There is to be another battle. If Jack is hurt in it, he will probably be brought here.' Her throat tightened with emotion. 'And I will be here to take care of him.'

'Then I will stay, too.' Mrs Vernon leaned back.

Wilson bowed to her. 'I must remain with you, ma'am.'

The maid's eyes darted from one to the other. 'Well, I am not going off alone.'

The hotel soon filled with wounded men and they all assisted in their care, waiting for the next battle and what news it would bring.

That evening it rained as if the heavens had opened up. Tranville glanced around the peasant's hut and sniffed in disgust. His billet for the night was no more than one room with a straw mattress for a bed and a table and chairs of rustic wood worn smooth by generations of use. He glanced heavenwards. It was dry, at least, and its fireplace was well stocked with wood.

He had plenty of orders for the officers, most of whom had done well the previous day, he had to admit.

He fixed the men with a glare. 'I'll have no laggardly behaviour, do you hear? You tell your men they are to hop to or they'll answer to me.'

'Yes, sir!' chirped a young lieutenant.

Captain Deane merely assumed a bland expression. Tranville detested that. Never could tell what the man was thinking. Captain Landon merely nodded.

'Landon, I want you to find Picton tonight. See if he has any message for me.'

Landon glanced over to the small window, its wooden shutters clattering from the wind and rain. 'Yes, sir.'

'And stay available to me tomorrow. I may need you during the battle.'

'Yes, sir.'

Landon was a good sort. Knew his duty. Got messages through posthaste. The result of good breeding, no doubt. Landon came from a good family, not a middle-class upstart like Deane, who'd risen to Captain through the ranks. That was a high enough rank in Tranville's mind and he'd seen to it that Deane rose no further. Pity Landon chose to befriend Deane.

It would have been better if Landon had made friends with Edwin. Landon and Edwin deserved their promotions to Captain. Tranville had only wished he could have advanced Edwin even higher in rank, but it had not been all up to him.

He glanced over at his son, who was sitting on a stool near the door sipping some brandy from a flask he'd packed with him. Yes, indeed, Landon would be a good influence on Edwin.

There was a knock on the door, and Tranville signalled for Edwin to open it. With a desultory expression, Edwin complied.

'Oh, Good God,' Edwin drawled, stepping aside.

Jack Vernon stood in the doorway, half a head taller than Tranville's own son.

'Mind your boots, Vernon,' Tranville said. 'This dirt floor is bad enough without you tracking in mud.

Jack kicked the cakes of mud off his boots on the doorjamb.

'Hurry up,' Tranville ordered. 'You are letting in the rain.'

Jack removed his shako and shook off its moisture before he finally stepped through the doorway, his top coat dripping on the floor. Tranville might have rung a peal over Jack's head for it, but he'd been distracted by Captain Deane, who poked Landon and inclined his head towards Jack. What the devil was that was about?

Jack exchanged a glance with the two men before turning back to Tranville, but not quite looking him in the face. He stood at attention. 'A message from Lieutenant Colonel Hamerton, sir.'

Tranville snatched the message from Jack's outstretched hand. Favouring Jack with the nastiest glare he could muster, he took his time opening the folded paper and reading it. He folded it back again. 'You will wait for my reply.'

If the others wondered why he did not order Jack at ease, let them. Jack well knew why. This was a good opportunity to remind Jack that there was unfinished business between them. The ruin of Jack, his family, and his...*actress*.

No one would believe those fool pictures of Jack's. He'd invented them. Edwin might be a coward, but no Tranville would assault a woman and child, even if they were Spanish papists.

Besides, Edwin had proved he was not a coward. At Quatres Bras he'd remained just where he was supposed to remain. At his father's side. It was not quite being in the throes of combat, as Jack had been, but they were inside a square, somewhat exposed to artillery fire and musket balls.

Tranville stretched his arm and wrote as slowly as he could, making a show of pausing between each word, as if he were considering what to write. When he finished he folded the note and gestured for Jack to come closer. 'A word with you, Vernon.'

Jack was forced to lean down to him. Tranville expelled a breath on purpose, directly on his ear. 'You had better hope some Frenchman runs you through, Jack. Otherwise, when we return to England, you and your family will wish you were dead.'

Jack straightened, a muscle flexing in his jaw.

'Leave now.' He pretended to re-read Hamerton's letter.

'With your permission, I'll leave now as well,' Landon said.

'Go.' He waved him away.

Jack executed an about-face and walked out of the door, Landon right behind him.

'Do you have further need of me?' asked Deane.

'Of course not,' snapped Tranville. 'All of you go.'

Deane and the others filed out, the last man not quite latching the door. Edwin was forced to get off his stool to close it.

Tranville pointed a finger at him. 'You had better do yourself credit in battle tomorrow. Show some gumption for a change.'

Edwin's face turned pale and he took a long draught from his flask.

Once outside of Tranville's billet, Landon and Deane pulled Jack aside. 'Do you have time for some tea?'

Jack nodded gratefully. The rain, still falling in sheets, had soaked him through and left a chill.

They led him to a small storage building, which was their shelter for the night. At its entrance they'd made a small fire from bits of wood. A kettle rested in its coals. As they stepped inside, Jack saw another officer wrapped in a blanket and snoring in a corner.

Over tin mugs of tea, Jack told the two men how and why he'd broken his word to them.

'You are safe,' Jack assured them. 'I did not show enough to identify you, not even your uniforms.'

Deane rubbed his face. 'I hope some Frenchman puts a ball through his head.'

'Watch your tongue, Gabe,' Landon cautioned.

Jack rose. 'I had better deliver my message.'

He shook their hands and hoped they both made it through the following day.

Before he walked out he turned to Deane. 'Did you find safety for the woman and her son?'

'I did,' Deane answered. 'In fact, I saw her in Brussels. She lives here.'

Landon sat up straight. 'You did not tell me that.'

Deane shrugged.

'And the boy?' Jack asked.

Deane looked from one to the other. 'In the army.'

Jack shook his head. The boy could be no more than sixteen, too young for battle. Some of the Belgian forces had cut and run from Quatre Bras. Perhaps the boy had been with them and would be safe from combat tomorrow.

Would that they all could be safe.

The next day it was almost noon before the cannonade began again, louder and closer.

Ariana and Mrs Vernon continued to help to tend the wounded men, bringing water and clean bandages, trying to comfort them as best they could. A few of the soldiers had come from Jack's regiment and she'd asked each of them if they knew how he fared. Last they'd seen he was still standing.

All the while, the distant sounds of battle continued. Ariana thought of Jack with each boom of artillery fire. She went out as often as she could, in search of news of the battle.

More wounded men rolled into the city, some reporting that all was lost, others saying, 'Boney is licked.' No one really knew which it was.

It was late that night when word finally reached them that the French were in retreat. The Allies had won the battle, but at great cost. It was said the battlefield was littered with the dead and dying. Ariana prayed Jack was not among them. Surely she would know if he were wounded. She would feel it in her own heart.

By morning the wounded were still arriving in droves. Hospitals, homes and hotels were full and the wounded poured out into the street.

Mrs Vernon insisted upon going to the Place Royale personally to find word of Lord Tranville. Because he was a general, she was convinced someone would know if he was alive, wounded or dead. Ariana only hoped they also would have word of Jack.

The officials at the Place Royale were too busy to spare them even a word. As they were ushered out, a young officer approached the building.

Edwin Tranville.

'It is Edwin!' Mrs Vernon ran up to him.

'Good God,' he said, his voice dripping with disdain. 'It is you.'

She ignored his rudeness. 'Your father. Do you know of him? Is…is he—?'

Edwin rubbed the scar on his face. 'He was struck down!' he wailed. 'Struck down in the battle. In the hedges near the sunken lane. Our men saw him fall. I—I could not be in the battle, you must understand. My horse went lame. I was forced to stay behind.' He dropped his hands and gazed heavenwards. 'If only I had been there.'

Mrs Vernon turned white. 'Edwin. Do not say he was killed. Do not say it.'

He lifted a shoulder in a casual gesture. 'He did not come back from the battlefield. That means he is dead or will be shortly.'

She rushed at him, clutching the front of his coat. 'He might still be alive and you left him there?'

He pried her fingers away. 'Madam. The battlefield after the battle is a very dangerous place. Looters do not care who they kill.'

She seized his coat again. 'You tell me exactly where the men saw him fall. Exactly where.'

He gave her the direction, although his description meant little to Ariana. Mrs Vernon released him, and Edwin brushed himself off and started to walk away.

Ariana stopped him, fear of his answer nearly keeping her from speaking. 'What of Jack?'

He snorted in disgust. 'Last I saw he was standing, but one can always hope.'

She struck him across the face.

He raised his arm and she expected him to hit her back but a general hurried by and he gave it up, leaving her only with a scathing look.

Mrs Vernon came to Ariana's side. 'I am going to go and find Lionel, Ariana.' Her chin was set in resolve.

'You will do no such thing!' Ariana exclaimed. 'It is ten miles away.'

'I do not care.' She started for the hotel. 'I will never forgive myself if I do not try.' After the rigours of travel and exhaustive work helping care for the wounded, Mrs Vernon already looked ready to drop.

'You cannot do this,' Ariana cried.

'I must. I cannot bear to think he will die in some field.' Her whole body trembled.

Ariana held her by the shoulders and took a deep breath. 'I will go. I will find him.' And as she searched for Tranville, she would look for Jack and hope not to find him among the dead.

Chapter Twenty-One

Jack shifted the burden on his shoulder and told himself to take one more step, then another, and another. The sun was hot and he was thirsty, but he dared not stop. Furrows from wagons that had travelled the road after the rains made walking even more difficult.

His burden groaned.

'Stay still, Tranville.' Jack almost lost his footing.

'Ought to walk.' Tranville's voice cracked with pain.

'Faster this way,' Jack managed.

Tranville couldn't walk. His leg was broken and the wound in his side would start bleeding again if he tried to hobble on one foot. There was nothing for it but for Jack to carry him.

During the fierce fighting of the first infantry attack, Jack had glimpsed Tranville fall. After the battle, he heard that Tranville had been left on the field. No one could verify he'd been killed, and because it was getting dark, no one was inclined to go and search for him.

The end of Tranville and his threats. Jack ought to have felt…something. Triumph? Relief? He did not know.

All he could feel was hunger and thirst. Jack ate and drank and his mind cleared.

What he felt was grief—on his mother's behalf. Tranville's death would break her heart.

No matter how Jack felt about the man, his mother had loved him for more than twenty years. How could Jack look her in the eye if he did not at least try to find him?

Covering his mouth and nose with a cloth, Jack had returned to the battlefield and picked his way back through the dead to where he'd seen Tranville struck down. He found him.

Alive.

After a hellish night listening to the wails of the dying and fending off looters who were combing the fields and stripping the dead, Jack carried Tranville out and joined throngs of wounded soldiers walking on the Brussels road.

He shifted Tranville on his shoulder and staggered on, wishing they'd not missed the wagons carrying the most seriously wounded. He tried to keep his mind blank, but the sights, sounds and smells of the battle forced their way back in. He again saw flashes of the artillery canister that had struck down his horse, and the shock on the Imperial Guard's faces when the British squares refused to break. He again saw his men cut down, heard their screams and smelled blood, excrement, gunpowder and sweat.

Jack shook his head. His back ached and he faltered under Tranville's weight. Pausing to balance himself again, he was relieved when Tranville lost consciousness. It made it easier to pretend he carried a sack of potatoes instead of the man he'd detested almost his whole life.

Jack pretended he would see Ariana again if he only kept moving. One step, then another. The ploy worked; his pace picked up. He wished he'd painted a miniature of her. The days of battle had blurred her image in his mind. After Quatres Bras he tried to draw her, but the rains soaked his paper and her image washed away.

It might take months or a year before he'd be able to leave

his regiment, and by then who knew what changes might have occurred in her life.

In the distance, coming in the opposite direction, Jack caught sight of a horse led by a man and woman. His mind immediately became riveted to that horse. He'd give anything for it…

He kept his eyes on the animal as best he could, but it was often out of view in the thick crowd on the road. He wondered if Tranville had enough money in his pockets to buy the horse.

Suddenly it seemed as if the men in front of him parted like the waters of the Red Sea, giving him a clear view of the horse and the woman who led it. He could not see her face, but something about her made it hard for him to breathe. She stopped and seemed to stare at him.

He did not dare believe.

'Jack!' She ran towards him.

His voice came out no more than a whisper. 'Ariana.'

She reached him and gaped at the burden he carried. 'Oh, my,' she cried. 'Oh, my.' She reached for him tentatively. Because he was so laden, she merely touched his face.

Her hands felt too gentle, too real.

The men surrounding them called out in approval, and her companion led the horse over to where they stood. Jack had to blink. His mother's manservant, Wilson, held the horse.

'Master Jack.' The man's voice cracked. 'I'll help you.'

Ariana quickly took hold of the horse's head while Wilson relieved Jack of Tranville, who groaned with the shift in position and roused momentarily while Wilson lay him over the horse's back.

Ariana wrapped her arms around Jack. They stood still, simply holding each other. He inhaled the scent of her hair, savoured her familiar curves, felt as if he were where he most belonged. Holding Ariana. His throat was so tight with emotion he could not speak.

'I told you I would not say goodbye to you,' she rasped. 'I never will.' She clung to him, then suddenly moved out of his embrace, putting her hands on his face, his arms, his chest. 'Are you injured?'

He shook his head, but, truly, he could not remember.

'Come.' She draped his arm around her shoulder to bear some of his weight. 'I will tell you of Brussels.'

She asked nothing of him, instead filled the long walk with details of their journey, descriptions of their time in Brussels. When they finally reached the hotel, she took him straight to her room. Jack collapsed on her bed and fell into a deep, dreamless sleep.

Jack woke to bright sunlight pouring into the room and to the scent of hot tea and porridge.

Ariana stood nearby with folded clothing in her hands. 'You are awake at last.'

He sat up. 'How long did I sleep?'

She smiled. 'About fifteen or sixteen hours. It is Tuesday morning.'

He looked around for his clothes. 'I must report to my regiment.'

She handed them to him. 'Wilson has performed some magic and found you a fresh laundered shirt and stockings. He has cleaned and mended your uniform so it looks almost new, and he polished your boots.'

Jack grasped her hand and pulled her down next to him, placing his lips upon hers. 'I fear this is all a vision. I fear that you, the food, those clothes will disappear—' He stopped himself and shook the thought from his mind. 'How is Tranville?'

'He is much better. Wilson found a surgeon to set his leg. Your mother is taking care of him.' She melted against him and kissed him in return. 'You need not worry about reporting to your regiment,' she murmured. 'Wilson got word to someone that you saved Lord Tranville. You do not have to hurry back.'

He released a deep breath, too grateful for words. 'Wilson has been a busy man.'

She stood. 'Eat your breakfast and get dressed. All the hotel could provide today was porridge.'

Porridge smelled like ambrosia.

She moved a table near to the bed and placed the breakfast tray on top of it. 'I will be right back.'

He looked at her in alarm. 'Do not leave.'

She smiled. 'I will not be long.'

He hated to have her out of his sight, even for a second, but hunger took over and he devoured the porridge and drank all the tea. By the time he was buttoning his coat, she had returned as promised, carrying something else wrapped in brown paper and tied with string.

'This is for you.' She placed it on the table and took away the breakfast dishes.

He untied the string and removed the brown paper.

And gazed in wonder at the contents.

She had brought him a box of charcoal and one of pastels, as well as a stack of fine drawing paper protected between two thick sheets of pasteboard.

He glanced up at her, unable to believe his eyes. 'How? Where?'

Her expression turned so loving it was almost painful for him to look on her. 'A shop in Brussels. I knew you must draw.'

He felt as if he'd been imprisoned in a dark dungeon and someone had given him a key back into the light. He could not speak. He only knew one thing for certain—he would never say goodbye to her again.

She started for the door. 'You need time to draw. I will return later.'

'No! Wait.' He lifted his head. 'Stay for a moment. I first must draw you.'

She returned to him and brushed her fingers through his

hair. 'Very well, but there is no hurry, Jack. You will have many chances to draw me.' Again her face wore the loving expression his fingers itched to capture on paper. 'Because I intend to love you for ever.'

'As my wife?' he asked.

'As your wife,' she replied in a breathless voice.

He laughed with joy, catching her in a quick embrace that made them tumble on to the bed. 'No hurry, wife? Then there is something I must do before filling this paper with drawing.'

She laughed along with him. 'You place loving me before drawing?'

He looked deeply into her eyes. 'I place loving you before everything.'

Epilogue

The walls of the exhibition room at Somerset House were again filled with paintings of every sort covering every inch of wall space, but this year, with Canova's visit and the excitement around Elgin's marbles, sculpture was all the rage.

Jack, virtually alone in the room, gazed up at his painting. It hung in a slightly more advantageous position than his paintings of three years before.

'Progress,' he chuckled to himself.

He'd become successful since returning from the army. His painting of Cleopatra, unbeknownst to him at the time, had made his reputation. He'd come a long way from the artist who had stood in this very room, fighting for his sanity.

He stared at his painting and remembered that day.

'Which painting pleases you so?' a low, musical—and amused—voice asked.

He turned and beheld a breathtakingly lovely woman, looking precisely as if she had emerged from one of the canvases.

She had: *his* canvas.

He greeted her with a kiss upon her alluring pink lips, a liberty the nearly empty room afforded him.

She smiled. 'Do say it is the portrait of the mother and child.' She pointed to his painting.

'Do you like that one?' he asked.

'I do, indeed.' She stood on tiptoe and repaid his kiss with one of her own. 'It is most lovingly painted.'

'Lovingly painted?' Jack tore his gaze away from her face and back to the painting. 'I agree. Most lovingly painted.'

'Yes,' she murmured.

The painting showed Ariana seated in a garden, smiling down at an infant with curly auburn hair and green eyes. Their daughter, Juliet, the very image of her mother.

Members of the Royal Academy hailed the painting as a modern Madonna. It brimmed with emotion, the members said, perfectly capturing maternal love.

He and his wife remained arm in arm, gazing up at it.

It was a long time before Jack spoke. 'Where are my mother and Nancy?'

'They are all with everyone else looking at the sculptures. Nancy said to bid you adieu, though. She was feeling a little fatigued. That happens, you know, in those first months. Michael took her home.'

Nancy was expecting her second child. Her first had been born over a year ago, a boy who delighted in stacking blocks. You'd have thought the sun rose and set with him the way Nancy and Michael doted on him.

Jack understood perfectly. All little Juliet had to do was break into a smile and his insides melted like candle wax.

'And Mother? Is she fatigued as well?' he asked.

'She very well may be, but you know she will not say a word about leaving if she thinks Tranville wishes to stay.'

Tranville.

Jack had certainly failed to separate them from Tranville.

Jack's mother had married him. Tranville proposed after Jack's mother had nursed him through the fevers that came after his injuries. He recovered eventually and his broken leg healed, thanks to her care. During those months Tranville became rather dependent upon her. She, predictably, forgave him everything.

Jack had hired solicitors to make certain she had an excellent marriage settlement and generous pin money, both of which Tranville could not alter under any conditions.

Tranville acted as if the whole episode with Jack's family and Ariana, even his rescue, had never happened. Jack was not quite so forgetful. He tolerated Tranville out of love for his mother. As it had always been.

Jack and Ariana did not see them often. The *ton* apparently had forgiven Jack's mother her fall from grace as soon as she became Lady Tranville and their lives ran in a different social circle.

At least Jack did not have to endure Edwin's company. Edwin was unwelcome at his father's house and there was nowhere else Jack might encounter him. Tranville paid Edwin's allowance, but rarely spoke of him. It seemed Tranville could forget a son as easily as forgetting the havoc he'd created in so many lives.

'You are looking serious,' Ariana told him.

He smiled at her. 'Well, you mentioned Tranville.'

She made an annoyed face. 'Do not let him spoil our enjoyment of your success.' She gazed back at the portrait and sighed. 'Is our daughter really so perfect?'

'She is like her mother.'

She held him tighter. 'More talk like that and I might allow you to paint me as Katharine.'

Ariana was rehearsing for an August production of David Garrick's *Katharine and Petruchio*.

'I would be delighted.' Jack glanced around the exhibition

hall and saw they were alone. 'This room will always signify a moment when my life was altered for ever.'

'When your first paintings were selected for the exhibition?' She smiled.

He shook his head. 'When I first saw you.' Jack placed one hand against her cheek and gazed into her eyes. 'There is something I wanted to do then, but could not.'

'What?' Her voice was breathless.

'This.' He took her in his arms and placed a kiss upon her lips more scandalous than the portrait of Cleopatra.

Author Note

My apologies to Miss O'Neill, the actress who really did play Juliet to Edmund Kean's Romeo at Drury Lane Theatre, January 1815, and Katharine in *Katharine and Petruchio*, August 1817. There was no performance of *Antony and Cleopatra* at Drury Lane Theatre in April of 1815, but Kean, who played many Shakespearean roles, might have performed the play. My story is peppered with other real people and places. Mr Arnold, the theatre manager, was hired when Sheridan's newly rebuilt Drury Lane Theatre almost fell into financial ruin. A committee similar to the one to which Lord Tranville is appointed really did exist and included Lord Byron for a brief time. The places my characters visit in London were all real, the Egyptian Hall, Somerset House and its Royal Exhibition, the perfume and colourist shops.

The Royal Scots and East Essex regiments were part of the same brigade and fought together at Quatre Bras and Waterloo. Lieutenant-Colonel Hamerton, Major-General Pack, and Lieutenant-General Sir Thomas Picton really were in the battles of Quatre Bras and Waterloo. The depiction of those battles is as accurate as I could make it.

The glimpse of Brussels in June 1815 is from a memoir,

Waterloo Days; The Narrative of an Englishwoman Resident at Brussels in June 1815, written by Charlotte A. Eaton, who travelled to Brussels with her brother and sister, arriving on 15 June one day before Ariana, the day of the Duchess of Richmond's ball. Accompanying Miss Eaton was Aide-de-Camp, Major Wylie, although I made him travel with Ariana one day later. It is Miss Eaton's account of Brussels that showed me what Ariana witnessed there.

Miss Eaton visited the Waterloo battlefield after all the dead had been buried. She wrote:

> …but it was impossible to stand on the field where thousands of my gallant countrymen had fought and conquered, and bled and died—and where their heroic valour had won for England her latest, proudest wreath of glory—without mingled feelings of triumph, pity, enthusiasm, and admiration, which language is utterly unable to express.

* * *

'THIS EVENING I'm flying to New York for two weeks,' Jasim imparted with a casualness that made her heart sink like a stone. 'That's why I had you brought here. I own this apartment and you'll be comfortable here while I'm abroad.'

'I can afford my own accommodation although I may not need it for long. I'll have another job by the time you get back—'

Jasim released a slightly harsh laugh. 'There's no need for you to look for another position. How would I ever see you? Don't you understand what I'm offering you?'

Elinor stood very still. 'No, I must be incredibly thick because I haven't quite worked out yet what you're offering me.…'

His charismatic smile slashed his lean dark visage. 'Naturally, I want to take care of you.…'

'No, thanks.' Elinor forced a smile and mentally willed him not to demean her with some sordid proposition. 'The only man who will ever take *care* of me with my agreement will be my husband. I'm willing to wait for you to come back but I'm not willing to be kept by you. I'm a very independent woman and what I give, I give freely.'

Jasim frowned. 'You make it all sound so serious.'

'What happened between us last night left pure chaos in its wake. Right now, I don't know whether I'm on my head or my heels. I'll stay for a while because I have nowhere else to go in the short term. So maybe it's good that you'll be away for a while.'

Jasim pulled out his wallet to extract a card. 'My private number,' he told her, presenting her with it as though it was a precious gift, which indeed it was. Many women would have done just about anything to gain access to that direct hotline to him, but his staff guarded his privacy with scrupulous care.

Before he could close the wallet, his blood ran cold in his veins. How could he have made such a serious oversight? What if he had got her pregnant? He knew that an unplanned pregnancy would engulf his life like an avalanche, crush his freedom and suffocate him. He barely stilled a shudder at the threat of such an outcome and thought how ironic it was that what his older brother had longed and prayed for to secure the line to the throne should strike Jasim as an absolute disaster....

* * *

What will proud Prince Jasim do if Elinor is expecting his royal baby? Perhaps an arranged marriage is the only solution! But will Elinor agree? Find out in DESERT PRINCE, BRIDE OF INNOCENCE by Lynne Graham [#2884], available from Harlequin Presents® in January 2010.

HPEX0110B

HARLEQUIN® *Blaze*™

New Year, New Man!

*For the perfect New Year's punch,
blend the following:*

- *One woman determined to find her inner vixen*
- *A notorious—and notoriously hot!—playboy*
- *A provocative New Year's Eve bash*
- *An impulsive kiss that leads to a night of explosive passion!*

When the clock hits midnight Claire Daniels
kisses the guy standing closest to her, but
the kiss doesn't end after the bells stop ringing....

Look for

Moonstruck

by *USA TODAY* bestselling author

JULIE KENNER

Available January

red-hot reads

www.eHarlequin.com

HB79518

Welcome to Montana—the home of bold men and daring women, where tales of passion, adventure and intrigue unfold beneath the Big Sky.

Rogue Stallion by DIANA PALMER

Undaunted by rogue cop Sterling McCallum's heart of stone and his warnings to back off, Jessica Larson stands her ground, braving the rising emotions between them until the mystery of his past comes to the surface.

Montana ★ MAVERICKS™

RETURN TO BIG SKY COUNTRY

Available in January 2010 wherever you buy books.

REQUEST YOUR FREE BOOKS!

Harlequin® Historical
Historical Romantic Adventure!

2 FREE NOVELS PLUS 2 FREE GIFTS!

YES! Please send me 2 FREE Harlequin® Historical novels and my 2 FREE gifts (gifts are worth about $10). After receiving them, if I don't wish to receive any more books, I can return the shipping statement marked "cancel". If I don't cancel, I will receive 6 brand-new novels every month and be billed just $4.94 per book in the U.S. or $5.49 per book in Canada. That's a savings of 20% off the cover price! It's quite a bargain! Shipping and handling is just 50¢ per book.* I understand that accepting the 2 free books and gifts places me under no obligation to buy anything. I can always return a shipment and cancel at any time. Even if I never buy another book, the two free books and gifts are mine to keep forever.

246 HDN EYS3 349 HDN EYTF

Name _____ (PLEASE PRINT) _____

Address _____ Apt. # _____

City _____ State/Prov. _____ Zip/Postal Code _____

Signature (if under 18, a parent or guardian must sign) _____

Mail to the **Harlequin Reader Service:**
IN U.S.A.: P.O. Box 1867, Buffalo, NY 14240-1867
IN CANADA: P.O. Box 609, Fort Erie, Ontario L2A 5X3

Not valid to current subscribers of Harlequin Historical books.

Want to try two free books from another line?
Call 1-800-873-8635 or visit www.morefreebooks.com.

* Terms and prices subject to change without notice. Prices do not include applicable taxes. Sales tax applicable in N.Y. Canadian residents will be charged applicable provincial taxes and GST. Offer not valid in Quebec. This offer is limited to one order per household. All orders subject to approval. Credit or debit balances in a customer's account(s) may be offset by any other outstanding balance owed by or to the customer. Please allow 4 to 6 weeks for delivery. Offer available while quantities last.

Your Privacy: Harlequin Books is committed to protecting your privacy. Our Privacy Policy is available online at www.eHarlequin.com or upon request from the Reader Service. From time to time we make our lists of customers available to reputable third parties who may have a product or service of interest to you. If you would prefer we not share your name and address, please check here. ☐

HH09R

COMING NEXT MONTH FROM

HARLEQUIN®
HISTORICAL

Available December 29, 2009

- **THE ROGUE'S DISGRACED LADY**
  by **Carole Mortimer**
  (Regency)
  Society gossip has kept Lady Juliet Boyd out of the public eye: all
  she really wants is a quiet life. Finally persuaded to accept a summer
  house-party invitation, she meets the scandalous Sebastian St. Claire,
  a man who makes her feel things, want things, *need* things she's never
  experienced before…. But does Sebastian really want Juliet—or just the
  truth behind her disgrace?

- **THE KANSAS LAWMAN'S PROPOSAL**
  by **Carol Finch**
  (Western)
  Falling in love with dashing lawman Nathan Montgomery was not the
  outcome Rachel expected when she joined a Kansas medicine show
  wagon! But Dodge City is no place for a single young seamstress, and
  despite the secrets that Nate and Rachel hide, they soon begin to need
  each other's comfort and protection far more than they anticipated….

- **THE EARL AND THE GOVERNESS**
  by **Sarah Elliott**
  (Regency)
  Impoverished, alone and on the run, Isabelle Thomas desperately needs
  the governess position William Stanton, Earl of Lennox, offers her. But
  when their passion explodes in a bone-melting kiss, Isabelle knows she
  must leave—only the earl has other plans for his innocent governess….

- **PREGNANT BY THE WARRIOR**
  by **Denise Lynn**
  (Medieval)
  Lea of Montreau must marry and produce an heir, or lose her lands. The
  headstrong and beautiful lady plots to seduce a particular stranger to
  produce an heir—but the stranger is none other than ruggedly handsome
  Jared of Warehaven—her onetime betrothed childhood sweetheart! Lea
  previously rejected Jared, and now he wants his revenge—by marriage!